P9-CSH-842
3 2487 00011 5189
WITHDRAWN
481474
Michaels, Barbara
The dark on the other sid
DUE I
14 DAY
LOAN
Newark Public Library
BOOKMOBILE

The Dark on the Other Side

Also Available in Large Print by Barbara Michaels:

Someone in the House
The Walker in Shadows
Wings of the Falcon
The Wizard's Daughter

The Dark on the Other Side

Barbara Michaels

G.K.HALL &CO.
Boston, Massachusetts
1983

Library of Congress Cataloging in Publication Data

Michaels, Barbara, 1907-
The dark on the other side.

1. Large type books. I. Title.
[PS3563.E747D3 1983] 813'.54 82-21364
ISBN 0-8161-3414-6

All the characters in this book are fictitious, and any resemblance to actual persons, living or dead, is purely coincidental.

Published in Large Print by arrangement with Dodd Mead & Company.

British Commonwealth rights courtesy of Souvenir Press

Set in 18 pt English Times

To *LAURIE,*
who likes to read about adventures;

and *AMY*,
who likes to have them;

and *MIKE,*
because he let me use his name;

and *DOUGLASS,*
because he is Douglass

With love

One

The house talked.

The objects in it talked, too—chairs, tables, couches, a big, squashy hassock that squatted obscenely in a corner of the bedroom. But the voice of the house was loudest. It was a thin, high voice, like that of an old woman. Hunched on its hill, like a fat old woman crouching on her haunches, its wings spread out like the folds of a ragged skirt, its wide terrace apronlike, its tower a thin neck, wattled and scaled with lichen, the house talked. Sometimes it said, *Run away . . . leave him . . . if you can.* Sometimes it wailed, *I wish he'd die. . . .*

Sometimes its suggestion was more direct.

II

Gordon didn't tell her that there would be a guest until just before dinner. Linda was sitting at her dressing table, elbows carelessly asprawl on the polished glass top. In the tall triple mirrors, her bedroom looked strange—not like a reflection of reality, but like another room, all the more disturbing because it contained the same furniture as her room, in the same positions, and yet looked subtly wrong. Like hers, it was decorated in shades of blue and white—cool, virginal colors, restful and remote. The drapes framing the tall windows were the deep, rich blue of the sky at late evening; their heavy velvet did not reflect light, but drank it in and absorbed it, so that the hoarded gold gave the blue a glowing luster. Because she had expressed a dislike for wall-to-wall carpeting, Gordon had the floors redone; they were stained dark, unvarnished but shining like black glass with repeated applications of wax. Glass, or black water. . . . The scattered rugs lay like little icebergs on a dark sea. Now, reflected, the ragged white islands seemed to move, rocking slightly as if shifted by the dark, shimmery surface on which they lay.

When Gordon came in, she didn't look up. Behind her mirrored image his face floated into view like something conjured up into a crystal ball—but familiar, wearing its old look of fond anxiety.

He was a very handsome man, Gordon. He'd be forty on his next birthday; and he was as alarmed, and as amused at his own alarm, as any pretty woman would be at the onset of that ominous day. The years had only added to his good looks—a brush of white at the temples, stark and distinctive against his thick black hair, a deepening of the lines of laughter that fanned out from the corners of his eyes. A man with eyes like that oughtn't to look so masculine; they were big and dark and luminous, fringed with lashes so long and thick they looked artificial. But there was nothing in the least effeminate about Gordon's face—or mind, or body.

Next to his, her own face was wraith-like. Too pale, too thin, with suggestive dark circles under the eyes and an undue prominence of certain muscles. Those long tendons in the throat especially—the throat he had admired, had compared with that of the lovely statue of Nefertiti . . .

She turned her head, watching the effect, and her pale mouth, as yet unpainted for public appearance, writhed distastefully as the lines tightened and drew. Gordon's mouth moved. She raised her eyes to meet his mirrored eyes, and felt herself frowning.

"What?"

"I said," he repeated patiently, "that we have a guest for dinner, and the weekend. So look your loveliest, won't you? If you are to be immortalized, I want it to be as you really are."

He was always so patient. It was almost the most maddening thing about him.

Then the meaning of what he had said finally penetrated, and she turned her head to stare at him.

He had retreated to the hassock, the one she particularly loathed, and was sitting with a grace a twenty-year-old might have envied, one knee bent, his long brown hands curled around it.

"Immortalized?" she repeated, articulating carefully.

"But, darling, I told you last week. . . ." He stopped. That was one of the things he must never do, remind her that she kept forgetting things. He started all over again, as if she had never heard the subject mentioned; only the straight vertical line between his brows showed his perturbation.

"Our guest's name is Michael Collins. He's the young man *Manhattan* magazine has commissioned to do a series of profiles on me. I'm very flattered, you know; usually they select important people as subjects."

"You're important," she said. It was not a compliment. It was simply a statement.

"Maybe I was, once. But you know I don't give a damn about being what the idiot world calls important."

Linda shrugged and turned back to the mirror. The top of her dressing table was covered with bottles and jars, with creams and lotions and cosmetics, all the expensive playthings of a woman of wealth and fashion. They were in perfect order, their shining caps free of the slightest speck of dust. Anna, her maid, straightened them every day.

She reached out at random and took a lipstick out of a jeweled holder that held a dozen of them. Applying it to her mouth, she said, "I suppose you want me to get dressed up."

"What about that robe I got you last week? The one with the gold threads?"

"It's too big." She tipped her head, studying her mouth. "My lipstick's on crooked."

"As a mere male it's not up to me to comment," said Gordon drily. "But if you will insist on talking while you apply the stuff—"

He broke off at the sound of a knock on the door. In some big houses servants weren't supposed to knock; so Linda had read. But Gordon insisted on his privacy. She watched, in the mirror, as the door of that other room opened, and the reflected image of her maid, Anna, sidled in. The girl looked even sillier in the glass. She was a silly-looking creature at best, with her teased blond wig and adenoidal, half-witted gape; and the mirror distorted her face as it warped every other object it reflected. The sidelong glance she gave Gordon had a sly, conspiratorial gleam. Of course, she had a crush on him; all the women in the house had, from the fat Bavarian cook to the gardener's ten-year-old daughter.

Even in the foul mirror Gordon's face

remained unchanged. She couldn't accuse him of leering at the maids. But he had better taste than that. Anna's figure was good, and was adequately displayed; Gordon insisted on uniforms, but he went along, good-humoredly, with the shorter skirts, and Anna's black dress verged on a musical-comedy maid's outfit. She had good legs. But that staring, vacant face . . .

Linda whirled around.

"I don't want you," she said. "Get out."

"Now, honey." Gordon rose; coming up behind her, he lifted the heavy masses of her black hair between his hands. "Let the poor girl fix your hair, at any rate. I told you, I want you to look beautiful. Anna, Mrs. Randolph will wear that gold thing—I don't know what you women call it—"

"The Persian brocade hostess gown," Anna said promptly. "If you mean the dress you bought last week, Mr. Randolph."

"That's the one. Hostess gown? You're right; that's what the salesgirl called it." He grinned at Anna, who, without moving a muscle, managed to suggest a puppy wriggling happily at a caress. "Well, I'll get out of the way and leave you to it."

Linda wiped off the crooked outline on her upper lip and sat with lipstick poised, watching Anna trot over to the long closet and take out the dress. As the girl laid it carefully across the bed her hands lingered, smoothing the heavy fabric. It was a beautiful thing; heaven only knew what treasured antique the dressmaker had cut up in order to make it. It didn't look like modern fabric; the muted blues and pinks and golds might have formed part of a sultan's regalia a century before. Linda reapplied her lipstick. It was a bright orange-red. The color would clash horribly with the dress. She ought to use another shade.

She dropped the carved gold case on the table top and reached down into the lowest drawer of the dressing table.

"Get me a glass," she ordered, taking the top off the bottle. The contents, half gone, swam amber gold with the movement of her hands.

Anna hesitated, her eyes bulging as they focused on the bottle.

"Didn't you hear me?" Linda asked gently. "Hurry up. You lazy little fool."

Anna jumped, and then ran into the bathroom. Linda took the glass without looking at it or the girl who held it. She poured it half full. Her elbows on the table, she sipped, and watched Anna in the mirror; and Anna stared back with her big, bulging, watery-blue eyes.

Cocktails in the den before dinner. Very classy, Linda thought, for a cop's daughter from Cleveland. She came down the stairs carefully, holding up her heavy skirts with one hand. The other hand, beringed and graceful, trailed nonchalantly along the curved mahogany rail. She didn't need to hold on. A couple of drinks—or even three or four—didn't affect her at all, physically, except to dull the sharpness of her hearing. With a couple of drinks—or maybe three or four—she could hardly hear the voice of the house.

There was no one in the marble-floored foyer to appreciate her entrance, so she turned to the right and went along the hall, past the drawing room, past the morning room, past the dining room; her skirts rustling stiffly, her head high. Why not the drawing room for cocktails? she wondered. Why the study? That was Gordon's room, as the dainty-chintz morning room was supposed to be hers. Usually he didn't allow casual visitors into his sanctum. Oh, but this man was not a casual visitor. He was . . . something about a biography. That explained the study. Michael What's-'is-name was going to get the full effect—the rows on rows of learned volumes, the windows opening onto the beauty of the countryside. And in the midst of it all, Gordon himself, the sage, the scholar, who had abandoned the hollow sham of the world for a life of contemplation.

The door was open. She could hear their voices as she approached: Gordon's mellow baritone, the softer, higher voice of Jack Briggs, Gordon's secretary, and another voice . . . deeper even than Gordon's, slower, drawling. For no reason at all, a shiver ran through her and she stopped, knees waxy-soft, and put one hand out blindly for support against the satiny surface of the paneled wall.

The spasm lasted only a second. She shook herself and went on, wondering. Something was going to happen. Good or bad? Were there such categories, or were things—happenings, people—amoral, to be judged only by their effects on others? "There is nothing either good or bad, but thinking makes it so. . . .''

She came to the door and stood there, looking at them.

Amid the bustle of their rising, she caught two swift impressions. One was the barely perceptible relief in Gordon's face as he took in her appearance: exquisitely gowned, coiffed, and made up, poised and calm. The other impression was simply that of a man, a stranger, and never, afterward, could she reduce it to details. He was there; his presence was enough.

Yet he was not, on second glance, a particularly good-looking man. A few inches taller even than Gordon's respectable height, he seemed to be strung together with old elastic, so that his movements looked gawky and abrupt beside Gordon's disciplined grace. His hair was mousy brown, combed carelessly back from a side parting; his mouth was too wide and his face had a lopsided look, as if one jaw were longer than the other. The only feature that might be called handsome were his eyes, and their beauty lay in their expression rather than their color, which was a brown slightly darker than his hair.

''How do you do,'' she said, and gave

her hand. With the touch of his hard, square fingers, the flash of empathy faded. He was just another man, and this was just another normal social occasion.

She sat down in one of the big soft leather chairs and watched with amusement as Collins tried to get his long arms and legs folded back into a sitting position. Gordon was hovering. He looked pathetically pleased, and it was significant, she knew, that he nodded at Briggs without making her ask for a drink.

Briggs bustled over to the bar and began fussing with ice cubes, bottles, and glasses. Linda's nerves tightened as she watched him. She detested him even more than she did the other servants—although, as Gordon's secretary, he was not to be regarded, or treated, as a servant. He was a pale, puffy man; the texture of his skin suggested clay or bread dough, some substance that would not rebound elastically from the prod of a finger, but would retain the impression. Gordon claimed that he was a very efficient secretary. She found that hard to believe. His movements, when away from the typewriter, were fussy, slow, and inept. Finally he came back with her drink, and she tried not to touch his hand as she took it. His fingers were always damp.

"We were just discussing Michael's last book, Linda," Gordon said. "I think you read it; I know I recommended it to you."

So they were on first name terms already.

"Oh, yes," she said, and sipped her drink. "I read it. It was very good."

She saw Michael flush a little at the coldness of the compliment, and added smoothly, "I particularly liked the chapter on the relationship between Emily and Bramwell. You caught something there which no other biographer has understood."

His wide mouth curved up, bringing out a line in one cheek, a line too long to be called a dimple.

"What was that?"

Linda looked at him in surprise. So Michael Collins wasn't quite the gauche young fool he looked. A compliment was meaningless to him unless it was genuine.

"The fact that, though he loved her desperately, he resented her talent. Oh, I know the point's been made; but you seemed to comprehend so fully the effect on the frustrated male ego, and the conflict between her feeling of feminine inferiority and the inevitable awareness of her own genius. Very few men can look at that problem dispassionately, with sympathy for both points of view."

He settled back in his chair, nursing his glass between his hands and smiling. His eyes were remarkable, Linda thought; they mirrored his feelings candidly, without evasion or concealment.

"And," she added, "you did it without resorting to the psychological jargon that's so popular today."

"It's hard to avoid," Michael said. "It has become part of our unconscious thinking."

Gordon said interestedly, "A person untrained in psychology—which includes most of us, I suppose—doesn't even use the jargon accurately. If a psychiatrist speaks of paranoia, he is trying to pinpoint a specific syndrome. Whereas a writer, and the majority of his readers, get a much more generalized, and probably wildly inaccurate, picture of behavior."

"That's true," Michael agreed. "But I was thinking more in terms of the way vocabulary reflects changing cultural patterns. Words don't convey a single specific image; they suggest a vast complex of ideas, emotions, and states of knowledge. When we speak of 'guilt,' for instance, we're using the same word that occurs in—oh, St. Augustine, let's say, and Sophocles. But for each of them the word had implications which a modern jurist no longer considers."

"A better example might be the word 'mad.' "

The voice was soft and gentle. There was no reason why it should have startled Linda so badly that the glass almost fell from her hand. She drained its contents. Briggs, rising to refill it, continued in the same mellifluous voice.

"The medieval world, assured of the reality of God and the devil, regarded madness as possession by an evil spirit. We have murdered God by reason; we try to deny the powers of evil by inventing new terms to explain the aberrant behavior that men of the Middle Ages attributed to demons."

"Yes, that's exactly what I meant," Michael said. "Vocabulary reflects the accepted world view of the period. Psychological terminology, however badly used, indicates our rejection of the cruder superstitions of the past."

There was silence when he stopped speaking. Linda sat upright in her chair, feeling, but not responding to, the intense anxiety of Gordon's regard. Belatedly, Michael seemed to sense the change in the atmosphere.

"I try to avoid jargon of all kinds in my writing," he said awkwardly. "Just as I try to avoid strained interpretations of human relationships based on the standard perversions."

"Well, I'm glad to hear that," Gordon said heartily, and Michael laughed. Linda's hand clenched around the glass Briggs handed her. The secretary went to refill the other glasses.

"Gordon's dying to know what you'll say about him," Linda said. "But of course he's too smart to ask outright."

Gordon started to speak, but Michael anticipated him, so smoothly that perhaps no one except Linda noticed how he used the words like a barrier, to shield Gordon from the malice of the speech.

"I don't know myself, yet. What I'm doing now is soaking up atmosphere, if you'll pardon the expression. And very pleasant it is—thank you."

He lifted his glass with a slight bow that was aimed, impartially, at a spot midway between his host and hostess.

"We're trying to prejudice you," Gordon said, smiling.

"I'm always prejudiced right from the first. I'm in favor of people."

"How nice of you," Linda murmured.

This time it was Gordon who came to the aid of his guest. The two of them, Linda thought irritably, worked together as smoothly as Laurel and Hardy. The flush on Michael's face subsided as Gordon talked, blandly and inconsequentially, of words and their meanings, of books and authors and libraries.

"I covet your library," Michael said, looking appreciatively around the room. "When I was an impractical college student I dreamed of having a place like this."

"It's copied from a library in an English country house," Linda said. She smiled sweetly at Gordon. "Volume for volume."

She finished her drink, and Briggs waddled over to take the empty glass.

"I don't think we have time for another, do we?"

The pause, before Gordon spoke, was just long enough to underline the fact that the mistress of the house should have made this comment. "Didn't you order dinner at eight, darling? Ah, yes—here's Haworth."

The butler's quiet "Dinner is served" brought the men to their feet. Linda rose more slowly.

"I'll take my drink with me—darling," she said.

Taking the glass Briggs handed her, she led the way to the dining room.

III

It was a good many years before Michael could think of his first dinner with the Randolphs without a reminiscent shudder. His host was too nervous to eat, his hostess steadily drank herself, not into a coma but into sharp-tongued virulence, and the pallid secretary stealthily gobbled enormous quantities of food.

When Linda Randolph first entered the library, he realized that she had been drinking; but that fact seemed irrelevant in the presence of such unusual beauty. Her hair was the rare, true black, with a sheen like that of silk; its heavy masses framed a face modeled with a precise delicacy that he had, up till now, seen only in a few masterpieces of sculpture. It was not a conventional type of beauty; many people would think it flawed by the character which gave the features their final definition—a character too strong, too individual for a woman's face. She would never get past the semi-finals in a Miss Wheat Cereal contest. But the Wheat Cereal queens didn't have the kind of face that launched ships or burned towers. Linda Randolph did. Helen and Cleopatra probably hadn't been conventional beauties either.

He knew why he had thought of Cleopatra. Linda . . . what an insipid name for that dark, exotic girl. The heavy, gold-trimmed dress emphasized the Egyptian look, but it didn't suit her; stiff with embroidery and gold thread, it stood away from her body and made her look like a well-dressed doll. Her shoulders seemed bowed under the weight of it. She was too thin.

How thin he didn't realize until she came nearer and sat down in a chair only a few feet away. The contrast between the splendid, remote figure in the doorway and the same woman at close range was a little shocking. Michael assumed she was painted and powdered, as all women were, but the best cosmetics in the world could not conceal the underlying pallor and tension of her face. Her hands, dwarfed by the wide sleeves of the robe, looked like little white claws.

He had known a lot of people who drank too much, and some who were genuine alcoholics. Linda Randolph wasn't an alcoholic yet. Not quite.

She held her liquor well, he had to admit that. She'd probably had a few before she came down, but her conversation in the library had been reasonably coherent, even bright. Those digs at her husband . . . Well, married couples did that, especially after a few drinks. *In vino veritas*—and, apparently, the closer the relationship, the nastier the truth. Parents and children, husbands and wives . . . Maybe that was why he'd chosen to remain a bachelor.

During the meal she finished her drink and then started on the wine—a superb Montrachet, too good to be swallowed down like water. The silent butler kept her glass filled. Well, Michael thought, what else can he do? She spoke to the man sharply once, when he was a little slow. Gordon, who would probably behave like a gentleman on his way to be hanged, couldn't object without risking a scene. But his conversational abilities declined noticeably. Finally, in desperation, Michael broke the rule he had made, about discussing business during social hours, and started asking questions.

"Athletic career?" Gordon smiled, and shrugged. "I quit while I was ahead. Never had the necessary motivation to become a professional. That takes concentration. I was interested in too many other things."

He broke off, to sample the wine that was being served with the next course, and Michael brooded. Motivation? Lack of interest? That was the obvious answer to the enigma of Gordon Randolph—athlete, writer, politician, teacher—who had abandoned, of his own choice, each of the professions in which he was expected to excel. The man who had everything—and who wanted nothing. But lack of ambition was too facile an answer.

"Anyhow," Randolph went on, with a nod at the butler, "I was never an all-round athletic type."

"Tennis and swimming," Michael said. "You know, I'd have thought you'd be a good quarterback. You have the build for it, and the coordination."

Gordon grinned.

"I'm a coward," he said amiably. "Didn't care for the prospect of being jumped on by all those big, booted feet."

"No contact sports," Michael said thoughtfully. "And no team sports."

"That's rather perceptive. Even if it does make me sound like a cowardly snob. Or a snobbish coward."

"Maybe just a man of sense," Michael said, smiling. "I can see why those activities might have bored you eventually. What a lot of people hold against you is your failure to write another book."

"Again, I stopped while I was ahead. They say, don't they, that everyone has one good book in him? But how many people have two?"

"Most people don't even have one. And very few have a book as good as *The Smoke of Her Burning*. It's a good title."

"Rather unsubtle, I'm afraid."

"The allusion is to Revelations?"

"Yes. The destruction of the whore of Babylon. Very theatrical."

The conversation had degenerated into a dialogue. Michael preferred it that way. Briggs never had his mouth empty long enough to frame an intelligible comment, and Linda had relapsed into a silence so profound that she might not have been there at all. Only the dress, holding its own shape, sitting empty at the foot of the table . . . It was a gruesomely vivid image, and when his hostess spoke, Michael flinched.

"You haven't read Gordon's masterpiece?"

"Not yet."

"Dear, dear. How inefficient of you." Her voice wasn't slurred; only the extra precision of her enunciation betrayed her condition.

"Well, you see, I have a theory. This is the first time I've tried a biography of a living person. I thought I'd get a personal, over-all impression first, like a quick outline sketch. Then I'll start filling in details."

"But you already knew some of the details. Like the tennis."

"Unfortunately, I can't start with a clean slate in the case of a man like Gordon. I knew most of the basic facts; a lot of people know them. He is a well-known figure."

"Was," Gordon corrected.

At the same moment, his wife said, "The famous, brilliant Gordon Randolph."

Most wives could have said that, in the right tone and with the right kind of smile, and made it sound like an affectionate little joke. Michael thought he had never heard an obscenity that sounded quite as vicious. He said quickly, "That's quite true. Of course I have a certain personal interest. You were one of my father's students in college, weren't you, Gordon?"

"Yes. And going back to that word 'brilliant,' which we use so freely these days, your father was one of the few teachers who really merited the adjective."

"Thank you. I was an uncouth high school brat at that time, but I seem to recall his speaking of you."

"Then you can't claim to have approached me without prejudice," Gordon said pleasantly.

"Yes, I can. I was only interested in

two things then—one of them was basketball—and I'm afraid I didn't pay much attention to the conversation of the over-thirty crowd."

"Over thirty or under thirty, they were all the same," Linda said. Her voice had become a little thick. "Members of the fan club. The St. Gordon fan club."

Gordon gave his wife an anguished look, and Michael burst into speech.

"Speaking of my father reminds me of something I've been wondering about. Call it idle curiosity. But I know you haven't permitted an interview for many years. What I wondered was—why me? Sam Cohen, my agent, said you'd specifically mentioned my name. I'm not the most modest member of the Author's Guild, but neither am I the most famous. Was it because of Dad?"

He had meant to insinuate that question at some point, but it came out sounding a good deal more gauche than it might have under other circumstances. He could feel his face getting red as Gordon's quizzical eyes studied him, and he was painfully aware of Linda's unconcealed amusement. She wasn't too drunk to be unaware of his embarrassment.

"What are you doing, fishing for an insult?" Gordon asked with a smile. "Naturally I followed your career with more interest than I would have done, because of your father. But that career itself impressed me with your ability. I like the way you approach your subjects; Linda summed up my feelings exactly. There's warmth and sympathy in your interpretations, and you always see both sides. And, lest your vanity get too swollen, I might add that I mentioned several names. Yours was one."

Michael hadn't gotten that impression; but then, he thought, a good agent—and Sam was one of the best—automatically administered periodic doses of ego booster. Writers need compliments. The ones who said they welcomed criticism were liars; what they wanted was praise—the more effusive, the better. But then, he thought, who didn't? Probe deeply enough under the slickest façade of confidence, and you tapped a vein of self-doubt or a hidden fear. Irrational fears and baseless doubts, many of them, but that was precisely why constant reassurance was necessary to the human animal. Maybe, if you reduced the thing to its simplest terms, that was the secret of his success as a biographer. Find the Hidden Fear. Well, at least he didn't sneer at other people's weaknesses, even if they were not his own.

With an effort Michael brought his mind from one of the peripheral, fascinating side tracks in which it was only too prone to get lost. He was neglecting his duties as guest. With his withdrawal from the conversation, a heavy silence had fallen. Gordon had turned to look at his wife, and the expression on his face, momentarily unguarded, was a graphic and pitiful example of what Michael had been thinking about. He knew what Gordon Randolph's hidden weakness was. Linda was as unresponsive as a Sphinx. (That Egyptian motif again!) She had withdrawn into her own thoughts (and what a hell that world must be), and again Michael had the grisly impression that the far end of the table was occupied by an empty gold-trimmed dress.

He stared blankly down at his empty plate. What the hell had he been eating? The others were finished, except for Briggs, who was methodically chasing down a last fragment of meat. What a pig the man was. Not a fat, healthy, pink pig; a dead pig, already soft with incipient corruption . . .

Michael made a voiceless movement of disgust and protest; and Briggs, having captured and subdued the last bite, looked up.

"Dear me," he said mildly. "I'm afraid I'm keeping you. Gordon's cook is marvelous. And gluttony is, I fear, my abiding sin."

He passed the tip of his tongue over his pale lips, and Michael forced a stiff smile. Taking his secretary's words as a sign that he had finished, Gordon pushed back his chair. Michael understood his need for haste. The man wanted to get his wife into the drawing room, and some coffee into his wife, while she could still walk. His eyes on his hostess's blank, perspiring face, Michael suspected that Gordon had waited too long.

Briggs was closer; he reached Linda first, moving with a scuttling speed that brought another unpleasant zoological comparison to Michael's mind. There was a sly violence in the way he jerked at her chair; and the readiness with which his pudgy hands caught at her, as she staggered, filled Michael with distaste. She turned on him like a cat, her lips drawn back in a snarl, and struck at his hands. Briggs retreated; and Gordon, reaching the foot of the table in two long strides, caught his wife just as she toppled ungracefully forward toward the plates and silverware. His face was a mask of controlled tragedy; but even in that moment of supreme humiliation he had grace enough left to throw a mechanical apology in Michael's direction:

". . . not feeling well."

He carried his wife out; and Michael closed his hanging jaw and looked at Briggs. The little man spread his hands and gave Michael a wistful smile.

"She doesn't like me. It hurts me so much. I have such enormous admiration for the dear lady. And I do try to spare Mr. Randolph all I can."

"I'm sure you do," Michael said.

"You can find your way to the drawing room, can't you? I'll just run along and see if I can be of any help."

Making his way down the interminable corridor, Michael wondered whether Randolph really meant to reappear that evening, much less sit and talk calmly about the projected story of his life! What a life! Didn't the poor devil have any friends, any associates who were comparatively decent and normal? Michael found himself, on that first evening of his visit, filled with a profound pity for the man who had everything.

Two

Michael came down late the next morning to find the breakfast room unoccupied. Gordon had explained that they followed English country-house habits in the morning; he considered it a tyranny to demand that his guests appear at a specified hour for a meal as trying as breakfast.

One of the servants, a well-stacked blonde with skirts so short they took Michael's mind off coffee for several minutes, had shown him the way to the "small dining room." It was a sunny, pleasant room with a table in a circular bay window and silver chafing dishes set out along a sideboard. Michael surveyed the effect approvingly. He wished he knew more about furniture, and all that sort of thing. This stuff was what they called Provincial, he supposed—light in design and color, with flowered drapes and blue-and white delft pots filled with blooming branches standing around. It was very different from the somber large dining room, with its heavy dark furniture and velvet hangings and family portraits. He wondered how much Linda had had to do with the decoration of the house, and which, if either, of the two styles represented her taste.

He forgot Linda as he foraged happily among the chafing dishes. The butler, bringing fresh coffee and toast, informed him that Mr. Randolph and his secretary had already breakfasted and gone to work; Randolph had said that they would meet for lunch, and suggested that in the meantime Michael explore the grounds. Mrs. Randolph? The butler's face was impassive. Mrs. Randolph always breakfasted in her room.

Along with one hell of a hangover, Michael thought. He finished his coffee and decided he might as well follow Gordon's suggestion of a walk. The view from the window was beautiful; it reminded him of Devon, where he had spent a memorable month slogging through the mud and declaiming the inevitable lines of Browning with the ardor of an eighteen-year-old. Illumined by sunshine, the spring colors of flowers and new leaves were as bright as if they had been freshly painted.

He had to ask directions again to get out of the house. Finally he found his way onto the terrace, an immense flag-stoned expanse with half a dozen low steps leading down to a lawn like apple-green velvet. Tulips, one of the few flowers Michael knew by name, made swatches of crimson and yellow along a graveled path. There were other flowers: pink ones and blue ones and spotted ones. The air effervesced like champagne when he breathed it in; he felt dizzy with it. Something smelled good. Must be the pink and blue flowers. As an expert on tulips, he recalled that they didn't smell.

Breathing in and out with self-conscious virtue, he went down the steps, heading for a copse of trees that looked like a pale-pink, low-hanging cloud. Cherry trees, maybe. Or apple. There had been apple trees on his grandmother's farm . . . how many years ago? He was just old enough to revel in nostalgia, instead of finding it hurtful, and his mood was pleasantly self-reproachful as he wandered along the path. Something wrong with people who gave up this kind of life for a foul den in a smoggy hive of sterile buildings and packed humanity. Maybe he would buy himself a cottage someplace. If this book was a success . . .

Midway along the path he turned for a backward look, and stopped short. The night before, he had got only the vaguest impression of the house, which was approached by a long drive through a grove of pines. It had been twilight when he arrived; he had seen a vast, dark bulk, which in the tricky dusk had loomed larger than it was. Or so he had thought. The place *was* big. Built of gray stone, it had three stories and a roof with dormers that might conceal attics or servants' quarters. The wings stretched out on either side of the terrace and the garden. The tower . . . Something wrong with the tower. Michael studied it, frowning. The same gray stone, a handsome slate roof . . . The shape, that was what was wrong. It was too tall, too thin to harmonize with the bulk of the house. And the stairway that wound up, around the exterior, didn't harmonize either. It looked like an afterthought.

Still, the overall effect was impressive. It was a good-looking house. But the impression foremost in his mind was not so much aesthetic as financial. Money. What a hunk of dough this place must have cost, even in the laissez-faire days of Randolph's grandfather. And what it must cost, now, to maintain.

He wandered on, while another long-forgotten memory worked its way to the surface. His mother, in an enormous floppy straw hat and a shapeless skirt—women didn't wear slacks in those days, at least his mother didn't—kneeling on the ground, wielding a busy trowel. She had been an enthusiastic gardener. Maybe, if she had lived longer, she might have been able to impart knowledge about some other plants than tulips. He had been eight when she died. He had hated her for dying. But still there was that undefined feeling of pleasure and content when he saw flowers pink and blue and sweet-smelling. . . .

Rounding the end of the left wing, he saw a bank of flowering bushes and struck off at a tangent to investigate them. With the sunlight full upon them they blazed like fire—orange and purplish red and pink—a brighter shade of pink than the fat flowers in the beds. It was not until he got close that he saw the kneeling figure; and because of his odd mood of reminiscence and receptivity he was struck suddenly breathless. A familiar figure, in a big floppy straw hat, kneeling, the bright flash of a trowel twinkling in its gloved hands . . .

But the straw hat was circled by a strip of figured chiffon, and he had seen its like in shop windows along Fifth Avenue. The kneeling figure wore tight slacks, not a shapeless cotton skirt; and the face that looked up at him, shaded by the brim, had the wide tilted eyes of an Egyptian court lady.

It was reassuring to know that he was not facing a revenant, however fragrant her memory; but the girl who was digging in the dirt was almost as much unlike his hostess of the previous night as she was unlike his mother. If she had a hangover, it didn't show. The lock of hair hanging down over one cheek shone in the sunlight like a blackbird's wing; she brushed it back with a gloved hand and left a smudge of dirt along the exquisite cheekbone.

"Good morning," she said coolly. "I hope Haworth gave you something decent for breakfast."

"More than decent. How was yours?"

She dismissed the inanity with the shrug it deserved.

"Are you soaking up atmosphere or just taking a walk?"

"The latter," Michael said shortly.

"Then allow me to be the perfect hostess. I'll give you the guided tour."

"Don't let me interrupt you."

"This is therapy, not productive labor. There are four gardeners, and they regard me as a necessary nuisance."

She got to her feet, in a movement so smooth that Michael's incipient offer of a helping hand was left dangling. In her flat shoes she came up to his chin. The brim of the hat brushed his nose, and she swept it off, tilting her head back and laughing.

She wore a yellow sweater over her white blouse, with dark-brown slacks. He had thought of her as thin, the night before; now he searched for other adjectives. Slim; wiry; slender . . . No, not slender, that suggested a delicacy, a yielding grace; and the alert tension of her pose was the reverse of graceful. Michael damned his incurable writer's tendency to wallow in words, and smiled back at her.

"The place is beautiful. Are you the genius who planned all this?"

"Heavens, no. It's been like this for a hundred years. Roughly."

"But surely plants and flowers, even trees, need replacing from time to time."

"Gordon does that." There was a slight pause; he had a feeling that she was considering not what she should say, but how to say it. "His taste is impeccable," she went on. "In everything."

Hm, Michael thought. Probably true. And spoken, if not with enthusiasm, at least with a courteous approval.

"I wish I knew more about these things," he said, indicating the bank of flowering bushes by which they stood. Descriptions of inanimate objects—which, to him, included landscape—were his weak point; he always had to labor over background. But now he found himself searching for color words: Salmon? Fuchsia? (What color was fuchsia, anyhow?) White, of course. That pink wasn't just pink, it was sort of rose-colored and sort of—

"They're azaleas," said his guide, with amusement. "Very common plants."

"Oh." Michael stared blankly at the bushes. "Azaleas. It does sound familiar. I've never seen so many colors."

"Some of the varieties are rare. That group over there is rhododendron."

"Oh."

"You don't have to pretend to be interested." She was laughing, openly; the expression changed her face, robbed it of its oriental elusiveness.

"I am, I am. Keep it up. I'll work it into some book or other and get gushing comments from lady reviewers."

"More likely they'll think you're a woman in disguise—or a bit odd. Men aren't supposed to be interested in flowers."

"Or cats," Michael agreed. "Or birds?"

"Definitely not. You know the stereotype of the male bird watcher."

"Skinny, bespectacled, lisping . . . Interior decoration?"

"Effete," she agreed gravely. "Fashions?"

"Times have changed. I've seen men's boutiques."

The tone of disgust made her laugh again, and after a moment he joined in.

"Sorry, I guess I'm more conventional than I thought. This last century is one of the few eras in history when men weren't concerned with looking like butterflies, when you come to think of it."

"That's right. And you can't think that dandies like Charles the Second and Francis the First weren't one hundred percent male."

"Not if the historical novelists are accurate. Okay. When I get back to town, I'll buy myself a flowered tie and a velvet jacket."

"And flaunt them publicly?"

"Certainly. When I take up a cause, I go all the way."

She looked up at him, with the laughter fading from her face.

"I think you would," she said slowly.

Michael found himself looking, not at her mouth or her chin or her nose, as people ordinarily do when they look at someone, but directly into her eyes. They were extraordinary eyes—so dark that they looked permanently dilated, with the pupils drowned and lost, luminous, shining. . . .

"But," she added, "you wouldn't be easy to convince."

Michael knew he ought to say something, but he couldn't think what. He couldn't even remember what they had been talking about.

Linda broke the spell by turning away.

"You get a good view of the house from here," she said.

Michael shook himself, like a dog coming out of the water, and turned. The view was impressive—and relaxing, after what he had just been looking at. The gray stone of the house was mellowed by sunlight, which sparkled off innumerable windows. Surrounded by a haze of newly leafed trees, with a backdrop of darker green firs, the lovely lines of the house had the appeal of a Constable painting. Except for that damned tower . . .

"It's beautiful," he said.

Linda consulted her watch.

"We can walk down to the grove, and then we'd better turn back. I think Gordon planned to work with you this afternoon, didn't he?"

"He said something about meeting at lunch."

"We'll make it a quick walk, then. You must see the meadow. Gordon's latest scheme, that is; he had it grass planted with daffodils and narcissi, like the meadow at Hampton Court; it's really gorgeous. And the grove is all flowering trees—cherry and apple and plum and almond."

"Oh."

"You'd better take notes," she advised. "Or the lady reviewers will scold you for your errors instead of gushing."

"I have an excellent memory. What are those stout pink and blue things?"

"Hyacinths."

She went on chatting lightly about flowers, pointing out different varieties, explaining that Gordon's rose garden was one of the sights of the neighborhood, and inviting him to come back in June, when it was at its best. The initial mood of their meeting, which had been shaken briefly by that odd exchange of words and glances, was back in full force. Making light conversation, Michael felt bewildered. It was impossible to reconcile this girl, composed and gracious, with the bitter-tongued drunk of the night before. He began to wonder whether he had misinterpreted the incident. Maybe something had happened the day before, something that set her off into a behavior that was not a pattern, but an isolated outburst. Maybe he was starting to read too much into looks and expressions. Maybe . . .

"There's one thing I miss," he said casually, as they passed under the hanging boughs of white blossom.

"What's that?"

"The dogs."

He had gone several steps before he realized she was no longer beside him. Turning, in surprise, he saw her framed in apple blossoms, with a shaft of sunlight polishing the petals.

"What's the matter? Are you ill?"

"Dogs," she said, in a breathy whisper. "What . . . dogs?" Michael was so shocked by her sudden pallor that it took him a second or two to remember what she was talking about.

"Why—animals in general. Pets. I guess I mentioned dogs because they're always there in my mental picture of country estates. Those brown-and-white hunting dogs . . . You look terrible. Sit down for a minute."

He put his arm around her rigid shoulders. For a moment they resisted, like rock; then her whole body sagged, so suddenly that he fell back a step under the weight of it, and put his other arm around her to steady her.

Over her bowed head he saw her husband come into sight, at the end of the avenue of cherry trees.

Michael was too concerned for his hostess and too confident of his host to feel any embarrassment at his farcical position. Randolph's smiling face changed and he began to run; but his first words made it clear that he had not misinterpreted the situation.

"Darling, what's wrong? She gets these dizzy spells," he explained distractedly. "Too much sun, or not enough vitamins, or something . . . Linda . . ."

He put his arms around his wife, and Michael hastily removed his. Linda straightened.

"I'm all right. Sorry, Mr. Collins."

"You scared the hell out of him," Gordon said, sharp in his relief. "Damn it, honey, this time I'm not kidding. You've got to see a doctor."

Linda started back toward the house.

"I don't need a doctor."

Her footsteps were a little unsteady, but Gordon made no move toward her. As if by mutual consent, the two men fell into step together, following Linda's slight figure.

"What did you say that set her off?" Randolph asked, under his breath.

Michael stiffened.

"I hope you don't think—"

"Oh, for God's sake. Don't talk like a fool. I meant, what were you talking about when she came over queer?"

Gordon's candid gaze was one of his most attractive features. It was not in evidence now; he scuffed his feet and stared at the ground like a delinquent caught in the act. Michael saw the truth then, and cursed himself for his stupidity. Alcoholism was a symptom, not a disease. Naturally Gordon couldn't come right out with it, not to a stranger. . . .

"I don't remember exactly," he said truthfully. "But it certainly wasn't anything that might frighten or distress her. Something about the grounds—flowers, animals, damned if I can recall."

They had been muttering, like stage conspirators. Linda was about ten feet ahead of them. She stopped and turned, and Gordon's reply was never uttered.

"Wait up," he said easily. "What's the hurry?"

"I thought you wanted to get to work. Didn't you come in hot pursuit of your biographer?"

The color had come back to her face, and it was perfectly composed. Too composed; the animation that had given it life was gone, and she looked like a tinted statue.

"No, I finished the letters and thought I'd like a walk." Gordon came up beside her, but he did not touch her or take her arm. "It's a beautiful day," he added.

"Yes, isn't it."

They walked on together—a perfect picture, Michael thought sardonically, of a happy threesome spending a morning in the country. Diffused sunlight trickled through the overhanging boughs, waking highlights in Linda's satiny black hair, turning the tan on Gordon's bare forearms to a golden brown. They made a handsome couple.

"By the way," Linda said casually, "Andrea is back. I've asked her to dinner tonight."

"Oh, for God's sake!" The words were explosive, but there was more amusement than annoyance in Gordon's voice. "Not Andrea!"

"I thought I'd better warn you well in advance," Linda said, smiling up at her tall husband from under the brim of her hat. It was a charming, provocative look; no doubt, Michael thought, it was the oblique slant of those oriental eyes that made him think of something sly and malicious peering out between dark leaves.

"Oh, I don't mind," Gordon said resignedly. "I find the old witch amusing, even if she does hate my guts. But I don't think you're being fair to Mike."

"I thought he might find her amusing too," Linda murmured.

"Who is she?" Michael asked.

"Just what I said." Gordon was smiling. "The local witch."

"What?"

"She lives in a stone cottage that's over two hundred years old," Linda said dreamily. "She keeps cats. One whole wall of the kitchen is fireplace—brick, darkened by centuries of smoke. There's a black pot hanging over the flames, and oak settles on either side of the hearth. The roof is raftered; things hang from hooks in the beams. Bundles of herbs—vervain and mandragora, and Saint-John's-wort. And a stuffed cockatrice."

"And hams and strings of onions," Gordon said drily.

"You're putting me on," Michael said, looking from one smiling face to the other.

"Her mother was a witch, too," Linda murmured. "And her grandmother. It goes back for generations, like the house."

"Cut it out, honey," Gordon smiled. "The old lady is a little touched in the head, that's all. She calls herself a white witch and denies all traffic with the powers of darkness. I think she really believes it herself, which makes her an entertaining conversationalist."

"I'm looking forward to meeting her," Michael said. "One forgets that people really do believe these things, even in this day and age."

" 'There are more things in heaven and earth . . .' "

"That, of course." Michael studied his host with new interest; none of his perfunctory research had exposed a mystical streak in Gordon Randolph. "The limitation of human knowledge, at any given point, must be admitted by any rational person. What I meant was that some people believe, literally, in those old superstitions. I read some books once by a man named Summers—a twentieth-century priest, Anglican or Catholic, I forget which, but a trained scholar—who believed in witchcraft. Not as a historical phenomenon, but as a living force. He thought—"

"I remember old Montague," Gordon interrupted. "Amazing mind."

"But it follows logically, doesn't it," Linda said, in a high voice. They had reached the terrace; she stopped, outside the French doors. "Especially for a priest. If you believe in God, you must admit the existence of His adversary."

"Certainly; but orthodoxy in these matters is a narrow tightrope to walk. You can't deny Satan; but you can't attribute too much power to him without risking the heresy of Manichaeism. Good and evil—two equal, opposing powers—that doctrine was condemned at some church synod or other centuries ago."

He would have gone on, for the subject was one that had interested him once upon a time, if he had not realized, tardily, that his audience wasn't listening. Linda's face was as blank as a doll's, and her husband was watching her with that familiar look of concern.

"I'd better go and change for lunch," Linda said.

Michael watched her disappear through the doors. He half expected Gordon to speak to him, but Gordon went after his wife, like a faithful dog. Dog . . . What the hell, Michael wondered, making up the end of the procession—what the *hell* is going on in this house?

II

That afternoon Linda searched her husband's room.

Though their bedrooms were connected through the twin-mirrored dressing rooms, she had not been in Gordon's room for almost a year. Not since that night . . . Her memory shook, and went dark, as it always did when she thought about that night. But surely, today, it would be safe. Gordon and his repulsive secretary were with Michael, and would be until dinner-time. The maids cleaned the bedrooms in the morning. No one else had any business upstairs, except possibly Haworth, the butler, who doubled as Gordon's valet, and she had set him to polishing the silver. It was a week before the silver was supposed to be polished, but . . . so what?

That was what she had said to Haworth when he courteously pointed out the discrepancy. So what?

She repeated it now, taking an infantile pleasure in the cheap defiance of the phrase. She giggled softly, remembering Haworth's face when she said it. Then she stopped the giggle with a quick hand that covered her lips. None of that. She had done well, so far today—except for that one slip. If he hadn't sprung it on her unexpectedly, just when she was beginning to relax, to feel confident of her power to charm and convince . . . That had been a bad one. It was all the more necessary now that she be calm. Calm, and charming, and gracious and . . . sane.

Yet, when the heavy door moved under the pressure of her hand, she caught her breath with a sharp sound, and stepped back, jerking her hand away as if the door had been red hot. Fine courage, she jeered silently. You really hoped, deep down inside, that the door would be locked on the other side. It had been locked on her side; surely Gordon had an even stronger reason to keep his door bolted and barred. But he had not done so.

There had not been bolts on either side of the door at first. She had put hers on herself, after that night, on an afternoon when Gordon was out of the house. The whole thing had come in a neat package, enclosed in plastic—the bolt and the screws with which to affix it. She hadn't remembered the need—the so obvious need—for hammer and screwdriver until she stripped off the stiff plastic, kneeling with pounding heart by the closed door. Even now she could recall the wave of terror that had gripped her when she realized she couldn't do the job without tools. It had taken cunning as well as courage to get rid of *them* long enough to sneak into the hardware store in the village. She could never do it again. The thought of boldly entering the tool shed, where the gardener kept his tools, made her stomach turn over. What if he came in and caught her, standing there, with the hammer in her hand?

In the end, with a resource she had thought long forgotten, she had used the heel of a shoe and a nail file.

The whole performance had been ridiculous, of course. She could see that now. Gordon must have known about the bolt.

If he had not wanted her to have it, he could have had it removed. But he had never said a word about it. Yet someone must have oiled it, because its surface shone as brightly as it had when she took it out of its plastic cover, and it had slid back without a sound.

Gradually her pounding heart slowed, as no noise came from the next room. She pushed the door open wider and looked in.

His room was the twin of hers in size and shape, except that the high windows on the south wall were French doors, leading out onto a stone-balustraded balcony. They had breakfasted there, on summer mornings, in the first year of their marriage. . . . The furnishings, of course, were quite different. Gordon had had her room redone. His still contained the furniture his grandfather had selected —heavy, dark mahogany, with the unique sheen produced by decades of well-trained housemaids. It was a somber room on dark days with its dark maroon hangings and heavy carpeting of the same shade. Now the afternoon sun flooded the room, making the deep pile of the carpet glow like aged Burgundy, reflecting blindingly from the tall pier mirrors in their gilt frames. Another of Grandpa's vanities, those mirrors. Gordon looked a lot like him, according to the family pictures.

Tiptoeing, in stockinged feet, she ventured cautiously into the room, casting a frustrated glance at the door that opened into the hall. She wished there were some way of locking it, so she would have warning if anyone came. But the smooth dark surface of the door was unmarred by bolt or chain. She turned to look at the back of the door by which she had entered the room. No—no bolt there either. So, he had never had one put on.

Why had she supposed that he would? Because she had done so. That was illogical. She knew what he would say if anyone asked him—any one of those few who knew what had happened on That Night. Barring his door to her would have been a symbolic thrusting away, a rejection of need and a denial of trust.

She crossed the room. Carefully, touching only the ornate brass knobs so that no smudge would mar the gleaming wood, she pulled open the top drawer of the dresser. Handkerchiefs, neat, plain, pure white, without even a monogram. She put out her hand and then drew it back, biting her lip. Damn Haworth and his neatness. It would be impossible to touch anything without leaving a sign of disturbance. The corners of the folded handkerchiefs might have been aligned with a ruler. And damn Gordon, too. He was a fanatic about neatness, he had trained Haworth, and he would be the first to notice the slightest irregularity.

More drawers. Pajamas, neatly folded. Coiled belts, looking like flat, curled snakes. Leather boxes, containing studs, cuff links, and his grandfather's ornate rings—one of the old gentleman's habits that Gordon had not emulated. More underwear. Nothing else. Nothing else visible.

She would have to risk it. Her lower lip caught between her teeth, she turned back to the top drawer and delicately lifted a pile of handkerchiefs. There was nothing underneath except the immaculate lining of the drawer. Her hands began to shake as she returned the handkerchiefs to their place and went to the next pile.

Still nothing.

It was hard to control her hands, they shook so. The silence of the room was unnatural; her ears rang with it. No—it wasn't her ears, it was a fly, trapped against one of the windows. Stupid insect. There was an open window within a few inches of its frantic lunges against the glass. For a long moment Linda stood perfectly still, staring at the small, frantic black dot. The buzzing droned in her ears. She turned back to her self-appointed chore with an abruptness that swept a pajama jacket out of alignment. What was under it?

Nothing. Nothing except the lining of the drawer.

Gradually her movements became quicker, jerkier. She shoved at the last drawer of the dresser, turned, before it had stopped moving, toward the tall bureau.

Sweaters. Folded neatly, encased in plastic bags. Nothing under the sweaters. Scarves. Nothing . . .

Slowly, like a creeping stain, the yellow path of sunlight from the window moved across the rug. As its warmth brushed her arm, Linda flinched and jerked around. It was late, dangerously late. How much longer before the conference ended, before Gordon came up to dress for dinner?

It didn't matter. She had finished the

search. There was nothing here, and she ought to have known there would be nothing. Only her desperate desire for something concrete, some proof that might affect an unprejudiced mind, had driven her to what she knew would be a wasted search. It was his study she ought to investigate. His study, or . . .

The sunlight seemed brighter; it hurt her eyes. Her breathing was so uneven, it caught at her throat in sharp gasps. Nerves. She was getting upset. And that was bad, because tonight she had to be perfect. Calm, and composed, and . . . She needed something to calm her nerves.

Gordon's study, or—the other place. The most likely place, and the one room that she could not risk searching. Because the secretary had arranged with the servants to clean it himself, and there was no conceivable reason why she should need to enter Jack Briggs's private quarters. If anyone found her there—if *he* found her . . .

A long shiver ran through her body. Dropping the last scarf back into the drawer, she turned and ran across the room, on soft stockinged feet. The bottle, the comforting, reliable bottle in the bottom drawer of her dressing table . . .

She closed the door and shot the bolt into place—leaving behind the marks of her feet imprinted as clearly in velvety pile as in snow, and two drawers standing open, spilling out their contents onto the floor.

Three

When Linda woke, it was getting dark outside. The high windows were gray oblongs; the dim light within the room reduced furniture and hangings to unfamiliar menaces.

She sat up, brushing the strands of hair back from her face. Her mouth was horribly dry. She reached for the glass of water on the bedside table and swallowed it down, so grateful for the relief to parched membranes that she hardly noticed its stale taste. Still fuzzy with sleep, she didn't think about the time until her half-closed eyes lit on the illumined dial of the clock.

She jumped up from the bed and stood swaying dizzily as the sluggish blood moved down from her head. Late. It was very late. She had meant to take extra time over her dressing, to apply makeup with extra care. She had hoped to speak privately with Andrea before the others joined them.

Where the hell is that stupid maid?

She groped for the buzzer and jabbed it impatiently. She had just found the light switch when the door burst open. Dazzled, Linda blinked at her maid.

"You're supposed to knock," she said angrily. "And why did you let me sleep so long? You know I'm late."

Anna's mouth drooped open another inch. She was silent for a moment, as if trying to decide which criticism to answer first.

"But madam, you've told me time and again not to bother you unless you ring. And this time, the bell—it sounded sort of frantic, and I thought maybe you'd hurt yourself or something—"

"Oh, shut up," Linda said. The very reasonableness of the girl's defense infuriated her. "Straighten up this mess. Find me something to wear."

With a murmured "Yes, madam," Anna picked up the shoes Linda had left in the middle of the floor and carried them to the dressing room.

From where she stood, Linda could see the far wall of the dressing room, which was one huge mirror, polished to shining perfection. Out of its depths, another Anna advanced briskly to meet the one who was entering the room. The identical twin figures were an uncanny sight, but Linda paid no attention to that, or to the expression on the mirrored face, which relaxed when Anna thought herself no longer under observation. Part of the bedroom was reflected in the mirror, and it was, as she had said, a mess. She had thrown herself down on the bed without turning back the spread; the satin surface was wrinkled and ugly, with a dark spot near the pillow where her mouth had rested. Her gardening clothes, which she had changed before lunch, lay in crumpled heaps on the floor. Beside the bed, as if fallen from a nerveless hand, was an empty bottle.

Linda gaped at it in vague surprise. Had she really finished the whole bottle? Surely this one had been almost full when she took it out of the drawer.

She shoved it aside with her foot, wrinkling her nose at the sour reek of spilled liquor. Her tweed skirt was twisted and her right stocking marred by a run. There were stains on the front of her blouse.

"Run my bath," she called, tugging at the zipper of the skirt.

Anna appeared in the doorway.

"But, madam, it's late—"

"Whose fault is that?" Linda asked pettishly. "Oh, for God's sake, I'll make it a shower then. Get my clothes out. The black culotte thing, stockings, the gold sandals—and hurry up, damn you."

She moved toward the bathroom, shedding clothes as she went, watching with malicious satisfaction as Anna stooped to pick up each item. Anna grunted when she bent over. She was too fat, that was her trouble. Linda gave the right hand tap a vicious twist and stepped under a spray of water that felt as if it had been refrigerated.

The treatment was drastic, but effective; she knew, from past experience, how effective. When she came out of the bathroom, she felt fairly human again, and by the time she was seated at the dressing table, with Anna's nimble fingers working at her hair, she was able to be cunning.

"I'm sorry I spoke to you as I did,"

she said, watching Anna's face in the mirror. "I'm always cross when I sleep in the afternoon. It was my own fault that I was late."

The sullen pink face did not change, nor the pale eyes move from their work.

"That's quite all right, madam," Anna said.

So much for that. There was no use trying to influence the girl now; she knew too much.

When Linda went down, she knew that she looked as good as skilled grooming and expensive clothes could make her look. But the black outfit had not, perhaps, been a wise choice. She liked the freedom of the wide black trousers, so full that they resembled a skirt except when the wearer was in motion; but the bodice left her arms and throat bare, and seemed to show more bone than flesh. She had had to send Anna to bore a new hole in the belt, and when it was buckled tightly it gathered the dress in unbecoming folds around the waist. *I'm too thin,* she thought, and then: *Pathos; I'm appealing to his sense of pity. Nice. And it probably won't work, either.*

The others were already assembled in

the drawing room, not in the library this time. Gordon did seem to get a perverse pleasure from Andrea's company; he loved baiting her. But he would never admit her into his sanctum.

As she went down the hall, Linda knew she was walking faster than usual, almost running. Something pulled at her like a magnet acting on a lodestone. She had felt it that morning, sensing his presence even before she saw him. Tonight the tug was even stronger. That was all it was so far, nothing reasoned or desired, only with a blind, mindless need. Like a fish on a line, she thought angrily, and shoved at the hangings over the doorway.

Andrea had already arrived. Sprawled with her usual lack of grace in an armchair near the fire, she raised a fat hand in greeting, and Linda saw her suddenly, not as the familiar friend, but as she must have appeared to a stranger, even one as tolerant and sophisticated as Michael Collins.

She was a very ugly old woman. Her ugliness was not the distinguished plainness some homely girls acquire in old age; it was plain, unvarnished, positive ugliness, strengthened by cultivated sloppiness. Her wrinkled face was overlaid with a thick coating of powder; her lipstick, applied in a wide slash without the aid of a mirror, always left smears on cigarettes and glasses. Her hair was another, clashing, shade of red, worn in a frizzy halo. Her dresses looked like the sort of thing that might be worn by a gypsy fortuneteller at a fair. Tonight, in honor of the occasion, she had added a few more yards of beads to the collection around her neck, and changed her long, full calico skirts for a magenta taffeta one of the same style. Long brass earrings dangled from her ears. In her left hand she held a jade cigarette holder.

I hate her, Linda thought. *Fat, ugly old woman . . .*

She knew a moment of despair so absolute that it felt like death. What had possessed her to ask Andrea to dinner? Some unformed idea of help, of support? But it wouldn't work that way. Andrea's weight would be on the other side of the scales, pushing them down, against her.

"Hello, Andrea," she said. "I hope the trip was successful."

"Darling girl," Andrea said effusively. She waved the cigarette holder, endangering her mop of hair. "Yes, I was just telling the boys about it. It was nasty, but I managed."

"A case of demonic possession," Gordon explained solemnly. "By—Beelzebub, was it, Andrea? Or Belial?"

"Oh, you nasty skeptic," Andrea said. She grinned at Gordon. The effect was hideous—white, unnaturally perfect teeth framed in smeary scarlet lipstick. "You know I'm never sure who it is. I just reel off a list of names and tell them all to get the hell out of the patient. It has to be one of the bunch."

Linda glanced at Michael. His expression was just what she had expected it to be—incredulity and amusement covered by a thin glaze of polite interest.

"Andrea, you are too much," she said irritably. "You sound like a charlatan."

"The fakers are the ones who bother with fancy words," said Andrea, flicking the ash off her cigarette. It landed on the Aubusson carpet, and she smeared it around with her foot. "I tell it like it is."

"Tell me," Michael said, leaning forward, "how do you go about exorcising an evil spirit? I know the Roman Church has a ritual for that purpose, but I don't imagine you—"

"No, I've got my own methods," Andrea said complacently. "Not that the other isn't effective enough. But it has to be performed by an ordained priest."

"That's right. I'd forgotten."

"You've studied the subject? Mm-hm. But you don't believe."

"No."

Reading their faces, Linda leaned back with a feeling of relief. Andrea's judgments of people were quick and violent—like or dislike, immediate and instinctive. Apparently she approved of Michael Collins. She grinned at him and he grinned back, remarking,

"At this point I'm supposed to say, 'Not that I haven't seen things, strange things, that were hard to explain by the normal laws of nature.' But I can't say that. I've never had the faintest flash of clairvoyance, nor seen a ghost."

"Never had the feeling that you'd been somewhere before, done the same thing at another time?"

"*Déjà vu?* Of course. Everyone has had that experience. It's easily explained in terms of subconscious resemblances, forgotten memories, without resorting to theories of precognition or reincarnation."

"*Touché,*" said Gordon softly, from the depths of his chair.

Andrea turned on him with a metallic jangle of jewelry.

"*Touché,* hell. Skeptics always drag that one out. They have an answer for everything—if you let them throw out half the evidence. I can quote you, offhand, a dozen cases of genuine precognition. Impressions of a scene, a house, a face—recorded and witnessed—which appeared at a later time."

It was the old familiar ground; they had been over it a dozen times, arguing in a perfectly good-humored way, which still made Linda queasy and nervous. Gordon was leading Andrea on again, not only for his own amusement but to entertain his guest. But now the conversation took an unexpected twist.

"Precognition, telepathy, clairvoyance," Michael said. "Aren't we wandering a bit from the track? ESP is one thing; demons are another. Or so it seems to me."

The room was brightly lit. One of Gordon's phobias was a dislike of darkness. There was no reason why Linda should have had the impression of something pale and shapeless stirring in a shadowy corner. There were no shadows; and the movement was only that of Jack Briggs, shifting in his chair. He was so quiet most of the time that his infrequent movements were startling.

"Your assumption is correct," he said in a precise, lisping voice, "if we accept your definition of normal and extranormal. But there is a single consistent hypothesis which accounts both for what you call clairvoyance, and for—demons."

Andrea gave him a queer look of mingled respect and hostility.

"That's right," she said reluctantly. "Look here, Mr. Collins, do you believe in God?"

Michael was silent. Andrea chuckled. Her laugh was not the dry cackle her appearance led one to expect, but a high-pitched, childish giggle.

"Funny," she said drily. "That question really gets people these days. They'll answer impertinent questions about their sex life and their emotional hang-ups, just to prove they're modern, emancipated intellectuals. But ask 'em about God and they squirm like a spinster when you mention virginity."

"*Touché* yourself," Michael said good-humoredly. "No, I was speechless out of ignorance, not embarrassment. I just don't know. That's as honest an answer as I can give."

Andrea nodded. Her face was grave, and not without a certain dignity.

"Fair enough. Let's avoid the embarrassing word, then. Do you believe in the existence of Good?"

"Philosophically, theologically, or historically?"

"Cut that out."

"All right," Michael said resignedly. "But you'll accuse me of equivocating again. Sometimes I do believe. Sometimes I have serious doubts."

Gordon leaned forward.

"No one who has studied history can believe in a benevolent creator," he said.

Michael looked at him curiously. Andrea ignored him.

"All right, Mr. Collins," she said. "You've already answered the next question, but I'll put it anyhow. Do you believe in the existence of Evil?"

Gordon, sensing his guest's discomfort, started to protest.

"Andrea, this is a ridiculous conversation. Can't we—"

"No," Linda interrupted. She had not meant to speak. The sound of her own voice startled her; it was harsh and peremptory, unlike her usual tones. "No. Let him answer."

"Of course," Michael said easily. "I'm enjoying this, Gordon. I'm just afraid of sounding like a fool. Philosophy was never one of my subjects."

"Philosophy be damned," Andrea said rudely. "I'm not interested in quibbles about Kant's categories of whatever the hell they are. Evil is a living, conscious force, operating in this world and the next. Anyone who denies that does sound like a fool."

"Evil deeds," Michael said. "Even evil men. But—Evil, with a capital E? An impersonal, active power?"

"There is nothing impersonal about Lucifer," said Briggs's soft voice.

The ensuing silence was broken by Gordon.

"Jack is inclined to be dogmatic about his faith."

He spoke to Michael, who smiled politely. Briggs laughed aloud.

"You needn't apologize for me, Gordon.

The orthodox believer must walk softly these days, it is true. But I feel sure that Mr. Collins is not offended by any expression of honest faith."

"That depends on the faith," Michael said drily. "Some beliefs are no less pernicious for being honest. But I don't see why I should be offended at an admission of belief in the devil."

Briggs chuckled again. His pudgy hand waved his half-full glass in a mocking salute. Linda realized that no one had offered her anything to drink. For once the thought did not preoccupy her. She was too engrossed in the greater need. *Ask him,* she begged silently, focusing her demand on Andrea. *Ask him, I can't. And I've got to know.*

"Then you don't believe in Satan—the powers of evil," Andrea persisted.

Gordon groaned, half humorously.

"Andrea, you have the subtlety of a pile driver. And the mindless persistence."

"And the directness," Michael said, smiling. "After the *double-entendres* of the literary world I find it refreshing. No, Miss Baker—Andrea, then, if you insist—I do not believe in Satan."

"Then how do you explain the existence of evil?"

"Do I have to explain it? I've got problems enough."

"Don't be frivolous."

"I beg your pardon." Michael sobered. "A number of explanations have been offered, have they not?"

"None make any sense." Andrea dismissed the garnered wisdom, philosophy, and theology of the world with a shrug. "Given the omnipotence of God and His complete unshadowed benevolence, you can't account for evil."

"The finite mind of man," Michael said, with the air of someone who is quoting, "cannot comprehend the eon-long plans of the Infinite."

"Baloney," Andrea said. Michael started at the word. "If our kindness is only a weak imitation of the supreme benevolence of God, and we gag at cruelty, how can He endure it, or condone it—much less perpetrate it, as He does, by your definitions?"

"Now wait a minute," Michael protested. "They aren't my definitions. I only said—"

"Baloney," Andrea repeated. The light was merciless on her face as she leaned forward. The wrinkled, cosmetic-caked skin looked like lava that had coincidentally congealed into the simulacrum of a human face. "The only hypothesis that accounts for evil is the existence of another Power, equal to the power of good and unalterably opposed to it."

"Manichaeism," Michael muttered. He glanced at Gordon. "Odd, we were talking about it earlier today."

If he was looking for help in changing the subject, he didn't get it. Gordon simply nodded.

"You're trying to snow me with words," Andrea said. "Think I'm a dumb old woman, don't you? Well, I know what Manichaeism is, it just so happens. They were on the right track; but they were wrong, just the same. Evil is! It exists! And you've got to fight it!"

Even Linda, tense and involved, had to admit that the choice of words was unfortunate; they sounded like a parody of a football cheer, and the muffled thud of Andrea's fist, pounding the arm of the sofa, was equally anticlimactic. Linda was the only one who didn't smile. Even Andrea looked, momentarily, as if her mouth might relax. But Briggs's oily chuckle tightened it again.

"You're the worst of the bunch," she said obscurely, glaring at the secretary. "You and your damned Lucifer!"

Briggs chortled again, and Michael's laugh echoed his.

"A singularly appropriate adjective," he said, grinning.

Linda couldn't stand it any longer. It was no use. Now she would have to try the other way. She jumped to her feet.

"Isn't it time for dinner?" she demanded; and without waiting for Gordon's answer, she went on wildly, "Of all the stupid, idiotic conversations . . . Let's talk about heroin, or the crime rate, or something pleasant. And someone get me a drink!"

By the time dinner was over, Linda felt better, except for the bad taste in her mouth, which no variety of food or drink was able to remove. They talked about heroin and the crime rate; about massacres in Iraq and starvation in India and poverty in Appalachia. Briggs gobbled and Andrea ate sloppily, scattering crumbs. Gordon ate almost nothing.

When they went back to the living room

for coffee, Andrea lingered, touching Linda's arm as if she wanted to exchange a word in private. Linda brushed past her. There was no use talking now. Andrea was a fool, like the others, a loud-mouthed, bragging fool. She had done more harm than good. No, there was nothing for it now but to try the only remaining means of approach.

It wasn't easy to arrange, though. Everyone seemed relaxed and lethargic after a heavy meal and an abundance of wine. Andrea flung herself down in her favorite corner of the sofa. Michael had chosen a chair by the fire; only his long legs and the top of his head were visible. Linda sat on the edge of her chair, nerves prickling. She didn't see how she was going to manage it. Unless, later . . . But that was dangerous, roaming the halls alone in the night. And it had to be to-night. He was leaving the next morning.

The fire crackled in the vast stone hearth, but its light was diffused and lost in the brightness of the lamps scattered around the room. The paneled walls and lovely stuccoed moldings of the beamed ceiling were another successful copy of an old English original. She had been unfair, of course, to attribute this artistic servility to Gordon. The house had been built by his grandfather, after his first trip abroad. He had been a parvenu, and *nouveau riche,* and all the other offensive French snob terms; but Linda supposed she ought to give the old man credit for realizing his own lack of taste. Rather than make a mistake, he had simply copied what he knew to be beyond criticism. It was a fault and a weakness in herself that she preferred to make her own mistakes.

Linda roused herself long enough to accept the brandy Briggs was handing around, and then slumped back into lethargy. They were at it again, Gordon and Andrea—not about demons, this time, but about gardening, which was their other major source of disagreement. If, as Gordon always said, you could call Andrea's mixture of superstition and random digging real gardening.

Characteristically, Michael was trying to keep the peace.

"I think science is now coming around to Andrea's point of view," he said. "Didn't I read somewhere that there may be a chemical present in the skin of certain people which stimulates plant growth?

The old green thumb made respectable?"

Gordon made a rude noise and Michael grinned amiably at him. Linda was accustomed to her husband's ability to charm; but he had succeeded even faster than usual in winning Michael. Slouched companionably in two chairs, side by side, they gave the impression of having known one another for years. To Linda's annoyance Andrea failed to see the amused sparkle in Michael's eyes, the reflection of Gordon's sly amusement. With loud cries of pleasure, the old woman amplified Michael's comment, adding, "You don't pay enough attention to these things, Gordon. If you'd listened to me, your marjoram would be in better shape."

Gordon laughed aloud, and Andrea finally realized that she was being made fun of. Her eyes narrowed angrily.

"I didn't know you had an herb garden, Gordon," Michael said. "How did I miss it today?"

"It's on the north side. Linda was the one who wanted an herb garden, so I had it laid out according to one of the old Elizabethan manuals. But Andrea is right. My marjoram is in wretched condition."

"I thought marjoram was a girl's

name," Michael admitted.

"It's a rather common plant. I've got a few of the rarer kinds that I'm quite proud of. Did you know that there are strict rules for the layout of such gardens—specific plants next to others, some which must be planted in borders, and so on? I've gotten quite fascinated by it, even though it was Linda's idea to begin with."

She felt their glances, but did not respond. Whose idea had it been? Hers, his—someone else's? Surely that was unimportant—except as another proof of her failing memory. Then, belatedly, she realized what they were talking about, and she sat up a little straighter. This might be the chance she had been waiting for.

". . . not like ordinary floodlights," Gordon was saying. "It's a new system. The effect is like very strong moonlight. No, it's no trouble; I had switches installed all over the house. And I love to show off my gadgets."

They were all at the window; Gordon was pulling back the heavy damask drapes. Linda turned in time to see Gordon touch the switch and the high oblong of black window turn silver as the outside lights went on.

Michael made appreciative noises.

"It does suggest moonlight," he said. "If I were ten years younger I'd turn it on at night and go for a moonlight stroll—tripping over things and reciting poetry."

"You can't see the herb garden, though," Gordon said, peering. "It's mostly hidden by the boxwood. Moonlight stroll? That's a good idea, Mike. It's a little chilly, but not too bad. Linda? Andrea?"

Out in the false moonlight, among the shrubbery, one person, or two, might casually wander away from the others. . . . Linda met her husband's eyes, and a cold, sobering shock ran through her. It was as if he could read her thoughts.

"No," she said. "I don't feel like it. But the rest of you go ahead."

When they had left—Andrea still arguing about marjoram, Briggs trailing his master in silent devotion—Linda got up and went to the window. The pale gray light did not suggest moonlight, not to her distorted imagination. It was a dull, unearthly light, like phosphorescence. It was bright enough; she could make out the tiny individual leaves on the boxwood hedges, twenty feet away. But instead of silvering objects as moonlight did, this light gave them a strange dead hue, between gray and green.

She shrank back into the concealment of the draperies as the others came into view, strolling slowly across the gray-washed grass. Andrea's floppy sleeves were wrapped around the upper part of her body. It must be pretty chilly outside. Gordon, as always the perfect host, spoke to the old woman and she shook her head vehemently—denying, Linda thought, any need for a wrap. Andrea prided herself on rising above physical needs. Old fool, Linda thought angrily.

After a time her mood improved. It was fun, watching people when they thought they were unobserved, studying faces and gestures undistracted by the added element of speech. Michael was a little taller than Gordon. He had a ridiculous way of walking, like—like a—her mind fumbled for an analogy and then, suddenly, she giggled. Like a camel. The same mixture of awkward angularity and inner dignity.

Gordon's head had been turned away from her. Now he turned, stretching out his arm to indicate some point of interest. His face was alive with the inner fire of personality that gave it its charm, and his sharp-cut features had a beauty even the ghastly light could not spoil. For the first time in months Linda's body responded with an inner twist that was more painful than a physical blow. Gordon, she thought. The name was like an incantation, loosening a flood of memories.

It hadn't been so long. Five years. Was that all? It seemed longer. . . . But she could still visualize Gordon as he had looked the first time she saw him, standing by the battered desk in Room 21 of Goddard Hall—the English Department. Only a dozen of them had signed up for the course, in the Art of the Novel; the departmental chairman had restricted it to seniors. But every eligible senior had registered. They were curious. A little skeptical, some of them, of a visiting professor who was only teaching one course, a non-academician, an intruder from the world of politics and inherited wealth. The Establishment—though they didn't call it that, then. But no one was contemptuous. Whatever his background, the fact remained that Gordon Randolph had written one of the big books of the decade, which had won every literary prize of its year.

If he sensed their curiosity and skepticism, he didn't show it. The tall, well-knit figure was relaxed, leaning against the desk; the handsome face smiled slightly, a smile that warmed the dark eyes. Even his clothing was perfect—loafers, dark slacks, tweed jacket. If the jacket had been cut by a tailor whose income was higher than that of any of the professors, it did not flaunt its ancestry. A stupider man might have had unnecessary patches added to the elbows, or affected a pipe. Gordon smoked cigarettes, from a crumpled pack that lay on the desk. That might have been affectation, but Linda didn't think so. In those days he smoked incessantly, one cigarette after another. That was before the doctors had started warning about cancer. Gordon quit then. . . .

It came back to her so vividly—the shabby old room, scarred and scuffed by generations of students; the dusty sunlight pouring in through streaked panes, brightening the colors of the girls' pastel sweaters and blouses, showing the uniformed contours of the boys' faces. . . . Beside Gordon's sure maturity they had seemed so young. Of course all the girls had fallen in love with him, even the ones who sneered at crushes on teachers. And the boys, after the initial antagonism, had succumbed in a different way. Linda could still feel the shock of incredulity when she realized that this god, this *man,* was looking at her with more than the smiling courtesy he displayed toward the others. That when he talked to her, his voice was different. That he really felt—

The vision was so real that the interruption made it waver and shake, like a film on a cracking screen. Linda turned with the bright shards of memory still close around her and blinked through dazzled eyes at the man whose arrival had disturbed her.

He was alone.

"Where—where are the others?" She stammered.

"Andrea's muttering incantations over some plants," Michael said with a smile. "Gordon was called to the telephone, and Briggs went with him."

"Oh."

Slowly Linda relaxed her cramped fingers, which had been clutching the edge of the drapes. Her mind began to function again. If Briggs had gone with Gordon, the telephone call must have been a business call, and it might take some time. Andrea in the garden, lost in her crazy spells . . .

You see, one of those disembodied voices murmured gently, *if you want something badly enough, it arranges itself.* . . .

She smiled, slowly, and saw the subtle response in Michael's face; she turned, slowly, slowly, and looked out into the palely lighted night. He would have to join her at the window; it would only be courteous. And from here she could see Andrea returning. She could hear, if she listened carefully, any footsteps approaching the room.

He came. She had known he would.

"Very effective," he said, after a moment.

Startled, Linda looked up at him. Just what had he meant by that ambiguous adjective? Whether he meant to refer to the lights or not, she would have to assume that he had.

"I don't really like it," she said. "The lighting."

"Why not?"

"Oh, I don't know. It bothers me, somehow."

"Because it's not real? You are bothered by pretense?"

This time she could not be mistaken. There was a slight but definite mocking tone in his voice.

"No," she said sharply. "I don't object to good imitations. But there's a tint in this light that is like a travesty of moonlight. Greenish. Don't you see it?"

Michael looked, frowning in concentration. That was one of the qualities that made him so attractive. He seriously considered new ideas. He might be prejudiced against her—that was inevitable—but he would not dismiss any reasonable question without thinking about it.

"You're right," he said finally. "You don't see it right away."

"No. It—grows on you."

Linda moved a little, shifting position. Her bare arm brushed his sleeve. She felt the slight recoil of his arm with satisfaction. He was not impervious. But then which of them was? Old and young, stupid and brilliant, sensitive and brutal—they were all alike in this one thing. If she couldn't reach the mind of the individual man, she would reach the male animal. But she would have to force it upon him. He was civilized enough, and cautious enough, to reject subtle advances. Some men would have responded before this.

She swayed, raising one hand to her face. Crude, this method, but time was short. Once she was in his arms, the rest would follow.

He had to put his arm around her; he couldn't let her crash to the floor at his feet.

"Feeling dizzy again?" he asked coolly. "You'd better sit down."

"No. I'll be all right in a minute."

Damn him, she thought. He was as rigid as a stick of wood. It was hard to resist his effort to move her toward a chair or couch, and still seem limp and helpless. She let go completely, clinging to him with both hands, her body against his.

There was a moment of resistance. He knew quite well what she was doing. Then it happened, as she had known it would. That the response was purely mechanical, a reflex that his mind rejected and resented, she did not care.

But as his arms tightened and his head bent, seeking her mouth, a strange thing happened. It was the first time for many months that a man had touched her in this way, and she had expected her body to respond with starved alacrity, all the more so because he was a man to whom she might have been attracted, normally, under normal circumstances. How abnormal these circumstances were she did not realize until she felt her head twist, avoiding the kiss she had invited, and sensed the pressure of her hands against his chest. His arms loosened; he could hardly escape feeling the mindless revulsion that filled her. And then, over the curve of his arm, she saw the eerily lighted window and the thing that stood outside, on the lawn, staring in at her.

Only once before had she seen it so distinctly. It stood quite still. Still as a statue, still as a figure painted by a child or a primitive artist—an outline sketched by a sharp pen and filled in, solidly, with black ink. Yet the individual hairs, bristling along the curve of the back, were distinct; so was the heavy, predatory muzzle and the thrust of the head. The only lights in the whole mass were the eyes—red, luminous, glowing like coals.

From a great distance Linda heard

Michael's voice repeating her name. She wasn't pretending now, and he knew it. But his voice was lost in the shrieking cacophony of the other voices, the voices that had haunted her for months, risen now to a whirl of mocking laughter: *We told you, we told you. Now it's too late. Too late, too late, too late . . .*

Then all the voices faded into blackness and silence.

Four

A sharp, stinging scent pierced Linda's lungs. She struggled, choking. Her face was all wet, cheeks and hands stung as if they had been slapped. Opening reluctant eyes, she saw a face near hers. It was not one of the faces she expected to see, and for a moment it was as unfamiliar as a total stranger's. A round, florid man's face, with horn-rimmed glasses and thick, iron-gray hair . . . Gold. Doctor Gold. Linda's eyes closed again.

"I'm all right," she muttered, as the doctor waved the horrible smelling thing under her nose again. "Don't . . ."

"Sure you're all right," he agreed smoothly. "Just fainted. Take it easy for a minute."

He patted her shoulder mechanically and stood up. Gordon must have dragged him away from a quiet evening at home; he was tireless, and pepper-and-salt stubble darkened his heavy jowls. As he moved away from her, Linda saw Andrea at the foot of the couch on which she was lying. The old woman was bent like a priest bowing before the Host; her hands wove patterns in the air and she crooned under her breath. A wave of feeble dislike swept Linda. How could she have such faith in the old witch? Not that Andrea didn't—know things. But she hadn't been much help so far. Her behavior tonight had been maddeningly wrong, evoking hostility instead of sympathy. What on earth did she think she was doing now—summoning her friend's wandering spirit back into her body?

Her ritual completed, Andrea caught Linda's eye. She leaned forward over the foot of the couch.

"What was it?" she hissed.

Linda shook her head. Stupid, Stupid . . . she couldn't talk about it here. Andrea knew that. But sooner or later she would have to tell Andrea about the latest appearance. Whom else could she talk to? No one else would believe her. Andrea only believed because she was half crazy herself.

Her eyes pulled away from the avid demand in the older woman's gaze. Michael was nowhere in sight; probably he had effaced himself, as any proper visitor would when the hostess was taken ill. Linda wondered where he was. She wondered why she cared—why this one man's absence from a room could make it feel empty. Especially now, after that unexpected fiasco at the window . . .

She forced herself to concentrate on the important presences. Gordon and Hank Gold made a significant little group, standing with their backs turned, talking in voices so low she could not make out the words. She didn't need to hear, she knew what they were saying. Once Gordon had made her visit Gold professionally. The doctor had poked every muscle in her body and taken samples of everything that was detachable. Then he had sat and talked. She had not been in good shape that day; the trend of the conversation had got away from her. Finally she had had to invent an excuse for leaving. It was a flight rather than departure, and Gold had been well aware of it. After that, she had refused to consult him again; had he not admitted that all her physical tests were normal? But she couldn't prevent Gordon from inviting his friend and neighbor to dinner occasionally. She couldn't always excuse herself on the grounds of a headache. She couldn't keep Gordon from telling him things.

And now—now she would have to fight. If there was the slightest hint, the least admission of what she thought she had seen . . . Panic twisted her stomach. Michael. Had she spoken to him in the last seconds, gasped out any damning description of the thing that stood glaring outside the window? There was no need to wonder whether he had seen it. No one saw it except she herself. Once, when she was showing Hank Gold the gardens, it had passed through the darkening twilight like a flash of black fog. Turning, at her startled exclamation, he had denied seeing anything except a shadow. That made it all the more important that she should not mention the word now—that deadly, ominous common noun.

The conference ended. They turned and came to her, Gordon first, the doctor following, scratching at his chin.

"Bed for you, baby," Gordon said,

with a forced smile. "Hank says you'll be fine after a good night's sleep."

Linda gathered her wits together.

"Hank probably hates both of us," she said. "Dragging him out in the middle of the night just because I fainted."

Gordon's smile faded.

"I couldn't get you out of it," he said. "This can't go on, Linda. You must agree—"

A hand on his arm stopped him. Gold was smiling, but his eyes gave him away.

"This girl needs rest, Gordon, not a lecture. We'll discuss it in the morning."

"Sorry," Gordon muttered.

"Nothing to be sorry about." It was farcical, the contrast between Gold's smile, his casual voice, and his intent, betraying stare. "Here, Linda, pop one of these down. Then off you go. I'll see you in the morning."

It appeared as if by legerdemain, a small white capsule lost in the vast pink reaches of his hand.

"What is it?" Linda asked.

"Just a mild sedative. So you can sleep."

Trapped, Linda looked from the little pill to Gold's face—pink, smiling and inexorable.

Silently she took the capsule. What was the use?

When she had swallowed it, both men seemed to heave a simultaneous sigh of relief. They expected more of a fight, Linda thought, and derived a faint, grim satisfaction from fooling them even that much. This was right; this was how she had to behave from now on. She had been wrong, before, to struggle openly.

"I'll carry you," Gordon said.

She waved him off.

"Up all those stairs? I can walk perfectly well."

The room wavered as she sat up and Gold came to her assistance. She was glad to lean on the arm he offered. It was better than some of the other possibilities. Now that she was standing, she could see Michael, near the door. She walked slowly toward him, leaning on the doctor's arm.

It was impossible for her to tell from his carefully controlled face, what he might have heard—or repeated. But she had to know.

"What made me faint, Hank?" she asked, in a sweet, worried voice.

"I can't be sure, my dear, until we

run a few tests."

Linda stopped, pulling on his arm.

"But you gave me every test you could think of. You said I was fine." Her voice rose; with an effort, she got control of herself. "I hate being jabbed with needles," she said meekly.

"Many people do." Gold's chuckle would have deceived most listeners. "My own nurse—would you believe it, I've got to give her a tranquilizer before I can take a blood sample. I think you're very good about it, Linda."

"But if the other tests were normal—"

"My dear, that was just a routine physical. There are rare diseases and deficiencies that require specific analysis. I may have missed something."

"Such as what?"

She didn't look at the doctor; she looked at Michael, now only a few feet away. And she knew.

"My dear child, I can't possibly speculate. It could be anything from an allergy to a chemical deficiency. Perhaps you can give me the clue—something you ate or drank, something you did today. . . . Come along, now, you ought to be in bed; we'll talk about it tomorrow."

The pressure of his arm increased and Linda went with it, no longer resisting. She had found out what she needed to know. During Gold's final speech, Michael's eyes had met hers. There must be some truth to this business of ESP, she thought. She had asked, silently; and he had answered, in equal silence.

As she went through the doorway, Michael seemed far away from her. She was tired; so tired she could hardly move her feet. The doctor's strong arm half lifted her up the stairs. As she went, through the thickening mists of sleep, she heard Gordon speak his guest's name, and knew that they would be settling down for a long talk as soon as Andrea left. The pill, the damned sleeping pill; she wouldn't be able to creep downstairs to listen, as she had listened to other conversations. But it didn't matter. She knew what they would say as well as if she were in the room, invisible and percipient.

II

"Thanks, yes," Michael said. "I could use a drink."

Gordon nodded and went to the bar, which was concealed in what had been a Hepplewhite sideboard. Glancing around the room, in the mental equivalent of a man brushing himself off after a crawl through the woods, Michael reorganized his shaken faculties. The secretary, Briggs, wasn't in the room; that was why Gordon was doing his own bartending. Come to think of it, Briggs had not reappeared after fetching the doctor. The man must have some idea of tact after all.

Andrea was still very much with them, though, and Michael wondered how Gordon planned to get rid of the old woman. The man's need to talk crackled in the air like electricity, but Michael thought he would not bare his soul in front of the witch. Witch . . . It wasn't so hard to believe, seeing Andrea as she looked now. Excitement and the damp night air had loosened her frizzled hair so that it hung in limp locks across her cheeks. Witch locks . . . another appropriate word whose meaning he had never considered.

"One for the road, Andrea?" Gordon spoke without turning from the bar.

"Subtle as a brick wall," the old woman cackled. "Forget it, Gordon, I can take a hint without being primed like a pump. I'm going."

She heaved herself up from the couch in a mammoth flutter of skirts and jangle of beads. She was too good an actress, Michael thought, to leave without a good exit line. Gordon seemed to feel the same way; he turned with a glass in each hand and stood watching Andrea. Andrea did not disappoint them. Drawing herself up to her full height, she thrust out an arm and pointed a finger at Gordon.

"You jeered at me tonight, Gordon Randolph, for fighting the powers of darkness. Take care—for They are not mocked. The time may come when you will beg on your knees for the help you despise now. Be sure that I will not deny you."

She spun on her heel, her skirts belling out like a monstrous purple flower, and stalked toward the door. Michael arranged his facial muscles into a conciliatory smile, but Andrea was not disarmed. She had a parting word for him, too.

"As for you—you are a mocker and a doubter. . . ."

An uncanny transformation came over voice and face, as the first trailed off into silence and the other lost its rigid anger. The old woman's throat worked hideously as she struggled to speak. When the words finally came, they were shocking because of their softness—faint and whispering, like a child's voice calling out in the terror of a nightmare.

"Help," Andrea said. "Please . . . help . . ."

Too amazed to move, Michael stood rooted, staring at her, and in another second the act was over. The wrinkled face snapped back into its malevolent expression and Andrea stamped out of the room, leaving a silence that vibrated.

"Whew," Michael said feebly. "She's really something, isn't she?"

Gordon removed himself from the sideboard, against which he had been leaning, and sauntered toward Michael, holding out one of the glasses. The incident, which had shaken Michael, seemed to have removed some of Gordon's tension. He was clearly amused.

"Sit down and have a drink, in that order. That's what I love about Andrea. She always provides me with an excuse to have another drink."

Michael laughed and followed his

host's suggestions.

"How does she get home?" he asked.

He was about to add the obvious witticism, but there was no need; his eyes met Gordon's and they both grinned.

"Not by broomstick," Gordon said. "Believe it or not. No, she walks everywhere she goes; the old bitch is as tough as they come. I'd have ordered the car out for her if I hadn't known, from past experience, that she'd refuse it. With commentary."

"That I can believe. Why does she dislike you so much?"

"I can think of about ten good reasons," Gordon said promptly. "Six pathological, three socioeconomic, and one—well, maybe it's psychotic too." He tilted his head back and finished his drink in one long swallow, rising as soon as it was gone. "Another?"

"No, thanks."

Michael contemplated his barely touched glass with some constraint. It was coming now; and he couldn't refuse to listen. Just as one human being to another, he owed Gordon that much. And as a potential biographer . . . Maybe the best thing he could do for Gordon was get him started talking.

"She hates you because of Mrs. Randolph."

"Why not call her Linda?" Gordon came back to the couch and sat down. "You're a perceptive young man, aren't you?"

"It doesn't require much perception to see that."

"No, you're right. It sticks out like a sore thumb." Gordon's shoulders relaxed as if an invisible burden had been lifted from them. The glance he gave Michael was a compound of apology and relief. "Sorry I said that."

"I'm not looking for juicy tidbits for a best seller."

"I know. Thanks."

They sat in silence for a few minutes, and then Gordon sat up straighter.

"Okay. Professionally or otherwise it's damned good of you to listen to this. Frankly, I'm at my wits' end. I don't know what to do—and this is one thing I must do right."

"I understand."

"I think you do. You see," Gordon said, staring down at his glass, "I love her." He gave a queer, smothered laugh.

"The oldest, tritest cliché in the language. From a writer, at that, a man who's supposed to know something about words. But that's it. That's what it comes down to, when you strip away all the verbiage. I love her and I won't let her go."

"Go?"

"Not physically. Although she has tried . . . I mean retreat, withdraw into some dark world of her own. That's what she's trying to do."

"Neurotic? Or psychotic?"

"Words, words, words," Gordon snapped; his suave courtesy had left him, and Michael liked him all the better for it. "A psychiatrist can think up labels. I can't. But I know, better than anyone else can. She's pulling away, moving back; and now the world she's invented is becoming real, for her. She—sees things."

"Interesting," Michael said carefully. "How that phrase, which has a perfectly matter-of-fact meaning, can suggest so much that isn't at all matter-of-fact. I gather you mean she has hallucinations?"

Gordon's swift glance at his guest was not friendly; but Michael returned it equably, and after a moment the queer empathy between the two men had re-established itself. Gordon laughed suddenly and leaned back, putting his glass down on the table.

"Thanks again. That's my greatest danger, I guess—becoming mystical myself. We all do, when catastrophe strikes. What has brought this curse upon me?—that kind of thinking. And it is, to say the least, nonconstructive. Yes, she has hallucinations."

Michael nodded silently. He was afflicted with an unusual constriction of the brain. Three words. That was all she had said—groaned, rather—just before she slid through his fumbling hands in a genuine faint. But those words, coupled with the similar incident in the grove earlier that day, had told him enough. He was on the verge of repeating his knowledge to Gordon when something made him hesitate. After a moment, Gordon went on.

"The hallucinations are only part of the problem, but to me—and to Hank Gold, whom I've consulted—they seem a particularly alarming symptom. It seems to be an animal of some kind that she fancies she sees—a dog, perhaps. Why it should throw her into such a frantic state . . ."

The black dog.

The words formed themselves in Michael's mind so clearly that for a moment he thought he had spoken them aloud. He did not; nor did he stop to analyze the reasons for his continued silence on this point. Instead, he said, "It seems to be an animal? Don't you know?"

Gordon laughed again; this time the sound made Michael wince.

"No, I don't know. Don't you understand? Whatever her fear is, I'm part of it. I'm the one she hates, Mike."

It all came out, then, like a flood from behind a broken dam. Michael sensed that this had been building up for a long time, with no outlet. Now he was the outlet. He listened in silence. Comment would have been unnecessary.

"Linda was barely twenty-one when I met her," Gordon said. "She was a student, taking the course I taught that one year—you know about that, I suppose. It was an experiment; I thought perhaps teaching might give me something I had failed to find in other pursuits. It didn't. But it gave me something that meant more.

"She was beautiful. She never knew, nor did any of the clods around her, how beautiful she really was. You can see it still, though it's contaminated now, faded. What you may not realize is that she was also one of the most brilliant human beings . . . Oh, hell, that's the wrong word; why can't I find the right words when I talk about Linda? Intelligent—yes, surely. Original, creative, one of those rare minds that sees through a problem to its essentials, whether the problem is social, arithmetical, or moral. But there's an additional quality. . . . Wisdom? Maybe that gives you a clue, even if it's not quite right. The quality of love. You know how I mean the word—'And the greatest of these . . .' I know, I'm making her sound like a saint. She wasn't. She was still young, crude in some ways, impatient in others, but that quality was there, ready to be developed, drawing . . .

"It drew me. God, how it drew me! I couldn't sleep nights. I sat around waiting for that damned class to meet, three days a week, so that I could see her. I had every adolescent symptom you've ever heard of, including humility. It took me four months to realize that I didn't have to wait for class, or skulk around the library and the coffee shop, hoping for a glimpse of her. . . . You aren't laughing. I wouldn't blame you if you did. I mean, I wasn't precisely the greatest lover that ever lived, but I'd had some experience; there's not another woman alive or dead that I'd have dithered over for four months before I got up the courage to ask her to have dinner with me.

"After that," Gordon said softly, "it went quickly. We were married six weeks later."

He relapsed into silence, staring dreamily at the fire. Michael said nothing. He knew there was more to come.

"Linda's background," Gordon said suddenly. "I suppose, if you follow the current theories, that it accounts for what is happening to her now. I can't see it myself. Maybe I'm too close.

"Her father was a policeman, just an ordinary run-of-the-mill cop on the beat. He was killed in a gunfight when she was thirteen, shot dead on the spot by a nervous burglar he was trying to arrest. Posthumous medal, citation—and a collection taken up by the appreciative citizens which kept the widow and three orphans eating for about six months.

"It seems fairly clear that her father was the only member of the family with whom Linda had any emotional ties, so his death hit even harder than it would ordinarily hit a girl of that age. Her mother I've never met; she remarried and moved to some damned hole like Saskatchewan when Linda was sixteen. Linda refused to invite her to the wedding; she showed me the letter her mother wrote when she read of our engagement in the newspapers. It was fairly sickening, full of effusions about how well her baby had done for her little self, and suggestions as to how she could share the wealth with the rest of the family. Linda threw it in the fire. She must have written her mother; an absence of response wouldn't be enough to choke off that sort of greedy stupidity. Whatever she said, it was effective. We haven't heard from the mother-in-law since, nor from the two brothers. One is a merchant seaman, the other is in one of the trades out west—carpenter, plumber, I don't know what.

"That's what makes the phenomenon of Linda so hard to believe—that she could have emerged from that mess of normal, grubby people. Her father must have been an unusual person. Or else she's a throwback to something in the remote family past . . . you never know. She's always refused to let me look up her genealogy. Not that it matters, of course, but I was curious, strictly from a scientific point of view.

"So, she loved her father and hated her mother; nice, straightforward Oedipus complex. And she married me because I was a good father figure, older, successful, supportive. Christ, Mike, you don't need to nod at me; I know all this, I've been over it, to myself and with professionals, a dozen times. But the reason why psychiatry fails to satisfy me is because it invents its own data..You act in a particular way because you hate your father. You admit you hate him—fine and dandy. You say you don't hate him, you really love him? You're kidding yourself, buddy, because I know better; you wouldn't be acting this way if you loved him. You hate him. But, in a way, you hate him, too, because of that thing called ambivalence. What good is that sort of thing to me, Mike? It gives too many answers."

He waited. This time he wanted a response.

Michael didn't know what to say. He never did know, when people talked this way. What do you say to a man who has cut his heart out and put it on the table in front of you? "Nice, well-shaped specimen. There seems to be a hole in it, right here. . . ."

"It doesn't give simple answers," he said carefully.

"The question is simple."

"Is it really?"

"Why does my wife hate me?"

Michael made an impatient movement.

"Any question can be stated in simple terms. 'Why do men fight wars?' 'If we can send a man to the moon, why can't we solve the problem of poverty?' 'God is good; how can He permit evil?' That sort of simplicity is a semantic trick. You don't alter the complex structure of the problem by reducing it to basic English."

Gordon did not reply, and for some minutes the two men sat in silence, listening to the hiss of the dying fire. That sound, and Gordon's soft breathing, were the only sounds in the room. Michael realized that it must be very late. He was conscious of a deep fatigue—the sodden, futile exhaustion that resulted from wallowing in other people's emotional troubles. Too much goddamned empathy, he thought sourly. He thought also of the comfortable guest room upstairs, with its nice, soft mattress and its well-placed reading light. But he couldn't leave, not while Gordon wanted an audience. And there was something else that had to be said.

"Gordon."

"Hmmm?" Gordon stirred; he looked as if he had come back from a great distance.

"I'm wondering. Whether I should go ahead with this project."

"What do you mean?" The confessional was closed; Gordon's dark eyes were searching.

"Probing the emotional problems of a man who's been dead for a century is one thing. Obviously I can't lacerate your private emotions in that way. And I'm not sure that I can do anything worthwhile with your life without considering them, not any longer."

"I wondered too. Whether you'd say that."

Gordon stood up, stretching like a big cat. Michael noted the smooth play of muscle and the lean lines of his body, and a fleeting thought ran through his mind:

I'd hate to tangle with him, even if he is forty.

"Another drink?" Gordon asked.

"No, thanks."

"I'll bet you're beat. You can go to bed in a minute, Mike. I appreciate all this. . . . But first I want to make a confession, and a request."

"You want me to go ahead with the biography."

"Yes."

"And the confession?"

"I hate to admit it, it's so childish." Gordon didn't look embarrassed; hands in his pockets, he stood gazing down at Michael with a faint smile. "But you are a perceptive devil, Mike. I wasn't aware of this, consciously; but I guess one of the reasons why I allowed this project to get underway was that I hoped you might come up with some burst of insight into my problem. Something I can't see because I'm too close to it."

"Something the best professionals can't see either?"

"I told you my misgivings about psychiatry. And even if the head shrinkers could help, Linda won't let them. She's refused even to see a neurologist."

"You overwhelm me," Michael said helplessly. He meant it literally; he felt as if Randolph had just dumped a load of bricks on him. He was flattened and breathless under the heap of responsibility. He was also annoyed. It was too much to ask of any man, much less a poor feeble writer.

"No, no, don't feel that way. I don't expect a thing. I just . . . hope. Look, Mike, I understand your scruples and your doubts, completely. Try it. Just try it. Work on the book for a couple of weeks, a month, see how it goes. Then we'll talk again."

"Okay."

Michael stood up. He felt stiff and queasy and in no mood to argue.

"We'll leave it that way," he said. "Damn it, Gordon, I can't help but feel that you're exaggerating. Your wife doesn't hate you."

"No?" They faced each other across the hearthrug. Gordon, hands still in his pockets, rocked gently back and forth as if limbering up for a fight. His eyes were brilliant. "Six months ago she tried to kill me."

III

Rain fell, heavily enough to keep the windshield wipers busy and make the oily surface of the highway dangerously slick. The weekend drivers were pouring back into the city. Michael had to pay close attention to his driving. A long night's sleep had left him oddly unrefreshed; he had started out tired, and two hours on one of the nation's most expensive death traps didn't exactly help. By the time he reached his apartment he could barely drag himself upstairs. There were four flights of stairs. The old building had no elevator.

After the Randolph mansion, his two rooms and kitchenette should have looked grubby and plebeian, but Michael heaved an involuntary sigh of pleasure at the sight of his worn rugs and tattered upholstery. His desk was overflowing with unfinished work. He had left the dishes in the sink. Even so, the place felt warm and cozy compared to the atmosphere of the big handsome house in the country.

He selected two cans, more or less at random, from the collection on the kitchen shelves, and started to heat up the contents. Napoleon had been and gone; his dish on the floor was empty, but he was nowhere in sight. The kitchen window was open its usual three inches. It still amazed Michael that a cat the size of Napoleon, the scarred, muscled terror of the alleys, could get through an opening that narrow, but he had seen him do it often enough, sometimes with the speed and accuracy of a rocket.

Once he had tried shutting Napoleon in the apartment while he was away for the weekend. Napoleon had expressed his opinion of that with his usual economy of effort; he had left neat piles of the said opinions every few feet down the hall, through the living room, culminating, in the most impressive pile of all, in the center of Michael's unmade bed. Michael hadn't even bothered to speak to him about it. He was only grateful to Napoleon for skipping his desk. After that he left the window slightly open and took his chances with burglars. A closed window wouldn't deter anyone who really wanted to get in. There wasn't anything in the place worth stealing anyhow.

When the soup was hot, he carried the pan into the living room and sat down, putting his feet up on the coffee table, which bore the marks of other such moments of relaxation. He ate out of the pan, remembering, with a wry smile, the smooth, unobtrusive service of the breakfast he had eaten that morning, complete with butler and antique silver chafing dishes. Then his smile faded into an even wrier frown, as the thoughts he had successfully avoided all day forced their way into his consciousness.

Gordon Randolph had excelled at half a dozen different careers. Michael wondered why he had never gone on the stage. He had an actor's instinct for a good, punchy line of dialogue.

Then Michael shook his head, as his habitual sense of fairness reproached him. Gordon didn't have to dramatize the situation. It was theatrical enough. And he, Michael, had provoked that simple, shocking punch line. He had more or less set it up. Nobody could resist a line like that one.

"Six months ago she tried to kill me."

The man has guts, Michael thought. He's still there—not only in the same house, but right in the next room.

Gordon's description of that incredible

event hadn't been theatrical at all; if anything, it had been understated. But Michael's writer's imagination had not required any details. He could picture it only too vividly; to wake from a sound sleep to see, standing over you, a figure out of a nightmare—or out of a Greek tragedy, a figure with the terrifying beauty and malignancy of Medea, arm upraised, knife poised to strike—and to know that the would-be killer was your own adored wife. . . . No wonder primitive people had believed in demoniacal possession.

Because he had the muscles of an athlete and the quickness of a cat, Randolph had survived the encounter, but he still bore the mark of it, a long, puckered scar along his forearm. Michael's insistent imagination presented him with another picture that was even worse than the first. To wrestle for your very life with some Thing that had the cunning and strength of the insane, and yet the familiar soft body of the woman you loved; held back by fear of hurting the beloved, but knowing that if you failed to hold her, the Other would have your life. Demoniac possession? God, yes, surely that was how you would think of it, despite the centuries of rational skepticism that had supposedly killed that superstition.

The soup on the bottom of the pan was scorched. Michael's food always was; he cooked everything at top heat. He ate absently, without noticing the taste. There was a bad taste in his mouth anyhow. That house—that sick, evil house . . .

He paused, the spoon dripping unnoticed onto his knee, as his mind grappled with this new and absorbing notion. Evil. Now why had he thought of that word? It was a concept he avoided because it was at once too simple and too complex—meaningless, he would have said once. And yet, during that whole weekend, the word had come up again and again. They had all used it, talked about it.

A thud and then a clatter came from the dark kitchen, and Michael jumped and swore as he noticed the puddle of soup on his trouser leg. He put the spoon back into the pan and swabbed ineffectually at the spot with his hand. That only made it worse. Then he looked up, glaring, as the pad of heavy paws announced the arrival of Napoleon.

The cat stood in the doorway, returning Michael's glare with interest. He was an enormous animal, as big as a small dog, and uglier than any dog Michael had ever met. His ancestry must have included cats of every color, for his fur was a hideous blend of every hue permitted to felines—orange, black, brown, white, gray, yellow, in incoherent patches. Now he looked leprous, having lost a good deal of fur in his encounters with other tomcats. One ear was pretty well gone, and a scar on one side of his whiskered countenance had fixed his jaw into a permanent maniacal grin. From the glow in his yellow eyes, Michael deduced that he had just returned from another victory. After a moment, Napoleon nodded to himself, sat down, lifted his back leg into an impossible position, and began licking his flank.

"Don't bleed on the rug," Michael said automatically.

Napoleon looked up from his first aid, gave Michael a contemptuous stare, and returned to his labors. Michael returned to his thoughts, which were considerably less pleasant than Napoleon's.

Homicidal mania. They didn't call it that nowadays, did they? Paranoia? Schizophrenia? He shook his head disgustedly. Gordon was right: words, words, words.

They meant nothing to a man whose wife had tried to kill him.

Evil. Another word, but it was a word rooted deep in human experience; it satisfied the demand for understanding more than did the artificial composites of a new discipline. It had the solid backing of centuries of emotional connotations. It brought back references from every literary source from Holy Writ to Fu Manchu. Out of this accumulation of literary and racial memory, one quotation came to Michael's mind:

> By the pricking of my thumbs,
> Something evil this way comes.

Nobody ever expressed an idea quite as aptly as Shakespeare. But in this case the evil was not approaching. It was already there—in that house.

Napoleon finished his ablutions and stalked over to lean heavily on Michael's leg. It was his only means of expressing an emotion, which Michael, in his softer moments, liked to interpret as affection. Someone had once said of that hard-bitten monarch, Henry VII, that he was not, to put it mildly, uxorious. In the same vein of irony one might say of Napoleon that he was not a lap cat. He did lean, occasionally, and his weight being what it was, the effect was noticeable. Michael got up with a weary sigh and extracted a can of cat food from the supply on the shelf. Affection? Gluttony, rather. Napoleon applied himself to supper with uncouth gulps, and Michael wandered back to the couch.

Not even the cat, for whom he felt a sneaking fondness compounded with envy, could distract him from the black current of his thoughts. How the hell could he write a biography of a man who was as hag-ridden as Gordon Randolph without tearing the man's soul to bloody shreds? Especially if he went on in this vein of half-baked mysticism. Evil deeds, evil men, he had said—but Evil, in the abstract? If there was evil in the beautiful house, it had to emanate from some living individual.

There weren't that many candidates. The revolting old woman, Andrea, was one of them; she was a constant visitor, and she was crazy as a loon. Michael wondered how genuine her belief in witchcraft was. Ninety-nine percent, he thought. What other hang-ups did she have? Certainly the old woman's blend of malice and superstition was not a healthy influence; but how profoundly had it really affected Linda Randolph? Had Andrea implanted her own insane ideas, or merely strengthened neuroses that had already begun to form? Even insanity has its own brand of logic. The paranoid schizophrenic may kill a complete stranger, suddenly and seemingly without cause; but in terms of the murderer's delusion, his action makes perfectly good sense. As the object of a widespread conspiracy aimed at his life and reason, he is only acting in self-defense when he kills one of the conspirators. Was that why Linda had attacked her husband? Could such a delusion have been planted by a third party—such as Andrea?

Then there was Briggs, the fat little man who looked like a moribund pig. Physiognomy was not a science. Under his pale, pudgy facade, Briggs might have the soul of a saint. But Michael doubted it. Briggs's feelings toward the Randolphs were obvious. He idolized his employer and resented—because he desired—his employer's wife. Which was natural. Randolph had been modestly vague about the circumstances that had brought Briggs to his present post, but Michael had got the impression of persecution, a miscarriage of justice, the loss of a profession for which the man had prepared all his life. Briggs wasn't the type to square his shoulders and march back out into the arena after someone had kicked him where it hurt. Randolph's offer of a job might, literally, have saved his life. No wonder the little man admired his boss. His attitude toward Linda was equally comprehensible, if less attractive. Malice—plenty of it. Michael wondered whether Gordon was too damned high-minded to see how his secretary felt about his beautiful wife. But Briggs's brand of feeble frustration was not evil, not in the sense Michael meant.

Randolph? Michael dismissed that hypothesis not because of Randolph's charm and talent but because of a fact that stood as solidly as Mount Everest. Randolph was genuinely, desperately, in love with his wife. Although Michael had interviewed a lot of people, he couldn't always tell the truth from the assumed; but in this case he would have staked his reputation on the genuineness of Randolph's feelings.

All of which led straight back to the

most obvious source of evil. Linda herself.

Now, there, surely, he was out of his depth and could candidly admit the fact. God damn it, he wasn't a psychiatrist. Nobody but a professional had the right to speculate about a mental condition as severe as Linda's. He couldn't even consult a professional. It would be an unforgivable violation of friendship.

But the idea remained, dangling like a shiny toy in the forefront of his mind, and for a few minutes he played with it. Often in his biographical research he had talked to Galen Rosenberg about the personalities of his subjects. Rosenberg had been one of his father's best friends, and Michael would have appreciated his pithy comments even if he had not been one of the top psychiatrists in the east. His humility and his sardonic sense of humor were as great as his all-embracing tolerance. It was a pity Gordon couldn't convince his wife to see Galen. If anyone could help her . . .

Michael shook his head. He was busybodying again, and if he had learned anything in the course of his thirty-three years, it was the futility of trying to force help on people who didn't want it. No, he couldn't discuss the case with Galen, not even under pseudonyms. His problem was not Linda's neuroses, it was a question of his own professional competence. Could he do a decent job with Randolph's life without mentioning the fact that Randolph's wife had tried to kill him? Another of those simple questions that weren't simple at all.

The answer, like the question, could be phrased with paradoxical simplicity. Michael realized, with a slight shock, that the answer was not the one he had hoped to get. He was a professional, and a good one; on that theme he had no false modesty whatever. Already sentences were framing themselves in his mind, possible lines of investigation were taking shape; the subject fascinated him as a problem, all personal ties aside. Oh, sure, there would be sticky moments, places where he would have to walk carefully, but they were only part of the challenge of the job. He could do it, all right. And he wanted to do it. And he didn't want to do it.

Michael bounded to his feet with a snarl, knocking two issues of *Mad,* an *American Historical Review,* and approximately two weeks of the *New York Times* off the coffee table, and evoking an answering growl from Napoleon, who was crouched on the rug by the front door. It was his favorite place. What he was waiting for, Michael never knew, though he wasted a lot of time speculating. Other cats? Not people. Napoleon hated people, all people, and departed via the window whenever a visitor approached.

"Why the hell I don't get a nice friendly dog, I don't know," Michael said aloud. "I could talk to it and get an answer now and then. I can't even kick you to relieve my spleen. You'd wait till I was asleep and then come in and tear my throat out. Who do you think you are, squatting there by the door? A watchdog? A lion? A vulture? God damn it, I hope that old saw about animals reflecting the personalities of their owners isn't true. You make me look like some kind of nut."

Having thus relieved his spleen, he stalked toward the bedroom, shedding coat, tie, and shirt as he went. Napoleon settled back on his haunches muttering to himself. The eerie sound followed Michael all the way into the bedroom, and he kicked the dresser in passing. Why couldn't the cat purr like an ordinary feline? This sound wasn't quite a growl, but it certainly wasn't a purr; Napoleon never expressed approval in that traditional fashion. He never expressed approval at all. He just sat around muttering to himself. A helluva pet for a poor miserable bachelor . . .

No pets. No animals at all, on the whole expansive twenty acres of Randolph's estate. Surely that was not coincidental. You'd expect a man like Randolph to ride and hunt, to keep dogs.

Michael turned out the light and pulled the crumpled sheet up to his chin. He liked to consider himself above such considerations as physical comfort, but his uncooperative body remembered the smoothness of the sheets at the Randolph house, and the yielding yet firm surface of the mattress. Surely this mattress had grown another lump since the last time he slept on it. He wriggled, trying to find a smooth spot. No use. The damned mattress grew tumors, like protoplasm. . . .

There was no clue to Randolph's personality in the absence of animals; that was a pretty corny old cliché. A lot of nice people didn't like dogs. There were such things as allergies, too. And . . . of course. Linda Randolph's neurosis had to do with animals. Randolph couldn't have a dog on the place when the sight of an imaginary one sent his wife into fits. So much for the subtle analytical biographer's insight.

Michael gave up his search for comfort and lay staring up at the ceiling, hands clasped under his head. The dirty yellow light from the street filtered in through panes grimy with city dirt, past the cracks in the wooden slats of the ancient blind. Sounds filtered in, too—the soft drizzle of the rain and the hooting, honking blare of traffic. Even at this late hour there were cars on the city streets. Soon the trucks would begin their nightly deliveries, but he wouldn't hear them; his ears had become inured to the grind of brakes and the vibration that was gradually eroding the fabric of buildings and pavements. He was used to the sounds and the grime and the press of human beings. They were part of his habits; without them he probably couldn't work. Yearning for apple blossoms and fresh country air and crocuses (crocuses?) pushing their tender green tips through the damp brown earth—sentimental nonsense, that was what it was. A nice place to visit, but I wouldn't want to live there.

Soothed and comforted by the familiar cacophony and the friendly dirt, he was drifting off to sleep when he remembered something else. He hadn't paid much attention at the time to Randolph's remark; he had been tired and confused, and the remark hadn't made any sense anyhow. Now he remembered it, and the utter illogic of it brought him out of his doze, wide awake and staring.

"If she should come to you," Randolph had said, "try to get her to see a doctor. Maybe you can do it."

Had Gordon Randolph really said that? Of all the weird, crazy things to say . . . And he had simply nodded and muttered, "Sure, of course; be glad to."

Michael groaned aloud. What had he got himself into this time? What kind of tacit admission could be read into that acquiescing mumble of his? He was always doing things like that, agreeing to propositions without listening to them, letting his mind wander off into byways and returning to a conversation to find that he had committed himself to ideas he violently opposed or plans that he had no intention of carrying out. But this was his worst fiasco yet. Did Randolph really think . . .?

Of course there had been those two episodes. When a man walks into a room and finds his wife in another man's arms, he may be excused for thinking there is something between them. Was Linda Randolph a nymphomaniac as well as an alcoholic?

Michael groaned again, so heartily that it provoked a loud response from Napoleon, out by the front door; but at the same moment he denied the thought. He had spotted Linda as a heavy drinker the first time he saw her. The symptoms of the other were just as obvious, and she wasn't . . . No, indeed, she wasn't. His face burned, in the darkness, as he remembered the strength with which she had held him off.

So, all right, he told his wounded male ego—so you made a mistake. You got carried away. Perfectly natural. But the girl really was sick, she had passed out cold.

"If she should come to you . . ."

Damn it, why didn't he listen to what

people said? He should have rejected the preposterous suggestion. He shouldn't have seemed to accept any such possibility.

Then the most disturbing thought of all forced its way into his reluctant mind. Had he failed to deny the proposition because, in reality, it had not seemed so incredible? Did he, unconsciously, want Randolph's wife to seek him out—for help, for anything? He pushed the idea away, outraged; but it came back. If a desire was really unconscious, he wouldn't know it himself. If he really wanted . . .

"Oh, damn it," Michael said helplessly. There was only one thing to do with an idea like that one. He turned over and went to sleep.

Five

The fantasies and self-doubts of the night were easy to dismiss in the cold light of dawn—which was not only cold, but gray, rainy, and sooty. But it was several days before Michael could make himself stop listening for footsteps coming toward his door.

He threw himself into work as a cure for mental degeneration, and found that after a while he didn't have to force himself; the hunt was up, and as usual it gradually gripped him. Even the inevitable frustrations were minor challenges, to be overcome.

One such challenge was Randolph's book. Michael could have sworn he owned a copy of *The Smoke of Her Burning;* it took two hours of disorganized search before he would admit that he no longer owned it. He kept meaning to get his books arranged in some kind of order, but they wouldn't let themselves be arranged; every time he started the project, he ended up with piles all over the floor and himself sitting cross-legged in the middle of the debris, deep in some fascinating volume he had forgotten he owned. The bookshelves were as motley as the volumes they housed; he had always meant to have some bookcases built in.

What had he done with Randolph's book? Damn it, he had to read Randolph's book, that was the least a biographer could do. Standing in the middle of the floor, like a pillar in the midst of a forum paved with literature, Michael scratched his chin. He must have given it to someone. Why hadn't he read it himself? That was not unusual, though; he was a compulsive book buyer, and his collection included a deplorably large group that he had never had time to read. He would just have to buy another copy of *The Smoke of Her Burning*.

But it wasn't that easy. The book was out of print. After all, as the third bookdealer pointed out waspishly, the printing presses of America poured out thousands of new books every year. You couldn't expect them to keep every old title in stock. Oh, sure, *The Smoke of Her Burning* had been an important book. But you couldn't expect . . .

So Michael tried the secondhand bookstores and encountered another snare; he could waste days in such places. He finally found the book, but not until he had loaded himself with old masterpieces he hadn't been looking for and probably wouldn't read—including, for reasons he refused to consider, a worn copy of somebody's *History of Witchcraft*. By the time he got home, he had transferred his annoyance to Gordon's book, and no longer wanted to read it.

There were plenty of other things to be done. He spent two afternoons in the newspaper morgues reading about the public exploits of Gordon Randolph. It was an unexpectedly depressing activity. Some of the yellowed, crumbling clippings were over twenty years old; the face of a young Gordon Randolph mummified by antique newsprint made any attempt at immortality seem futile.

The clippings came from sports pages, literary columns, and the general-news sections, but there was one significant omission. Randolph's name did not appear in the gossip columns. Rarely, there might be a mention of his presence at some charity affair or concert, but he never escorted a lady who was not impeccable in reputation and social status. Either Randolph's private life was arranged with a circumspection that verged on Top Secret, or he was abnormally well behaved. Not a wild oat in the whole field.

His marriage had rated a long column, and the lady reporter gave it the Cinderella approach—Professor Weds Student, Millionaire Marries Policeman's Daughter. They had been married at the college chapel. There was a picture of Linda Randolph in her wedding dress, and Michael found it more depressing, for different reasons, than Gordon's photographs. Poor as the print was, it conveyed something of that quality Randolph had vainly tried to describe. It conveyed something else—happiness. She glowed with it, even through cheap paper and smeary ink. From that, Michael thought, to what I saw three days ago. He turned the page quickly.

All of it, sports achievements, literary kudos, political successes, were dry bones.

This was just the beginning. The next step was to talk to people who knew Randolph. So, on Wednesday, Michael got his car out and drove up to the campus of the well-known Ivy League school where Randolph had matriculated.

He had taken the precaution of providing himself with a general letter of introduction, and it finally got him into the sanctum of a Vice-President in charge of something. Public Relations, to judge from the gray-haired gentleman's suave manner. The President of the university was unavailable. Probably away on a fund-raising campaign, Michael thought—or building barricades in preparation for the spring campaign of the SDS. Not that it mattered. Anything the President would say about one of his most illustrious alumni wouldn't be worth peanuts. The same thing was true of the Vice-President. Michael only needed him as a source of references.

"I'm afraid there are very few of Mr. Randolph's former professors available," the Vice-President explained winsomely. "Now although I was not myself in residence at the time, I have followed Mr. Randolph's career with interest, and I might say . . ."

He recapitulated Randolph's public career, which Michael could have recited from memory, for ten minutes before Michael could stop him.

"I want to talk to people who actually knew him," Michael explained.

The Vice-President hesitated, torn between irritation and caution. How these pompous asses did love to see their names in print, Michael thought. The man was smart enough to know that if he vexed the biographer, his name might appear amid adjectives that would make him writhe. The pungent style of the periodical that had commissioned the biographer was well known.

"Well, of course, this was twenty years ago," the V.P. said, with a slight sniff. "Most of our professors are mature men when they are at the height of their careers; by now the majority are retired or—hem—deceased. And, while people tend to think of the academic profession as static, there is in actual fact—"

"A lot of job shifting," Michael interrupted. "I know that. I'll do the tracking down myself. All I really need are the names of Randolph's professors and their current addresses, if they are available."

"Well, if you insist, Mr.—"

Michael insisted. When the file was produced, the Vice-President brooded over it.

"Physics; Professor Kraus. Emeritus, now, of course; I believe he returned to Germany or Austria. If he's still alive . . . Sociology; that would be Professor Smith, he is now at Elm College, in the—er—Midwest somewhere."

"Chicago," Michael said.

"Somewhere of that sort, yes. I don't know that he would be of much help to you; Mr. Randolph only took one of his courses. Now his major, naturally, was English; the chairman at that time was Professor—"

He looked up, his eyes widening, and Michael nodded.

"Collins. He was my father. He's dead. Ten years ago."

"I'm sorry. . . . Well, then, let me see, there was Doctor Wilkes. . . ."

Not a single one of Randolph's former professors was still in residence. Michael finally escaped with a very short list. Four of the men were still living, two in Europe and one at Harvard, plus the unfortunate exile in the Midwest. Michael went home and wrote letters. He couldn't go traipsing off to Munich to interview a man who had taught Randolph algebra twenty years ago. The man at Harvard was on sabbatical leave.

He had begun his investigations with the academic world not only because it was more in line with his own interests but because he believed in the importance of that period in character formation. Sooner or later, he would have to interview Randolph's business associates. Talk about a subject being outside your field; he wasn't even sure what Randolph's business was. One of those massive conglomerates that included manufacturing, investments, oil wells, and God knows what else. But there were offices someplace in the city; if there wasn't a Randolph Building, it was presumably only because Randolph hadn't got around to constructing one. Yes, eventually he'd have to talk to the inhabitants of the business world, but he had no illusions about that; no one who worked for Randolph was going to tell him anything interesting.

So the next step was the college where Randolph had taught. It was in Pennsylvania; not a long drive, but he decided to plan to stay overnight, since that particular episode was fairly recent, and there ought to be a number of witnesses still available—possibly even a few students working for advanced degrees.

A sullen sun sulked above the skyscrapers when he left the city, but it wasn't until he had bypassed Philadelphia that he felt any awareness of spring. The Main Line suburbs reminded him of the countryside around Randolph's home—manicured lawns and smug, neat houses, flowers and kids playing in the front yard. Things were blooming.

This time he had taken the precaution of setting up an interview in advance, by phone, and he saw, not a Vice-President, but the Vice-Chancellor. Michael had read too much history to have much faith in revolution as a means of social progress; but every time he met a college administrator, he was aware of a sneaking sympathy for the militant students. The Vice-Chancellor might have been a brother of the Vice-President—the same graying hair and discreet tie, the same canny brown eyes. Michael sniffed. Yes; they even used the same scent. Christ, he thought; and placed a look of intelligent interest in his face as the Vice-Chancellor lectured.

"I was a mere Assistant Professor at the time," he explained with a deprecating smile. "Nor was Gordon in my department. Economics is my field."

"Then you didn't know him well?"

"We had several interesting chats at the Faculty Club."

In a pig's eyes, Michael thought crudely.

"What did you talk about? Economics?"

"Among other things. He was very well informed for a layman, very much so. A brilliant mind, of course. And capable in a wide range of subjects. That is of course the outstanding factor in his personality. And that's what you're interested in, isn't it, my dear fellow? His personality. I'm sure everyone who knew Gordon was struck by that—the breadth of his interests."

It went on in this vein for some time. Michael had suspected from the first that this pompous ass could not have won Gordon's friendship, and after half an hour of name dropping and burbling generalities, he was sure of it. It took him another half hour to extract the information he wanted. When he left, the Vice-Chancellor sent his regards to dear old Gordon.

On the steps of the Administration Building, Michael saw a bearded youth attired in a red plaid poncho selling copies of the school paper. He bought a copy. The picture on the front was a scurrilous caricature, badly drawn but recognizable, of the Vice-Chancellor. Michael turned back.

"Contribution to the cause," he said, and went on his way leaving the hairy young man looking in bewilderment at the five-dollar bill in his hand.

It took Michael the rest of the day to find one of the teachers who had been Randolph's colleagues. Though they all had offices and office hours, nobody seemed to be in his office at the specified time—or, if he was, he refused to answer the door. (Michael could have sworn he heard harried breathing inside one locked and unresponsive room.) What were they afraid of? he wondered. Students? Which wasn't so funny, nowadays . . . He finally caught one man as he was making a surreptitious exit, and when Martin Buchsbaum found he was not a student, he invited him in.

Buchsbaum was a youngish man, chubby and pink, with a nose that looked as if it had once been broken, and a cherubic smile.

"Randolph? Sure, I met him. But I never knew the guy, not to talk to. I had just made my Assistant Professorship, didn't even have tenure. He was one of the sheep, and I was the lowest of the goats. You know, the sheep and the—"

"I know. My father was a teacher."

"Then you do know. The gulf between the tenured and the non-tenured is wider than the one between the Elect and the Damned. I'm sorry, friend, but I can't tell you anything about the Great Man. He was lionized, idolized—"

"Even canonized?"

"Man can't even plagiarize a quotation these days," said Buchsbaum amiably. "What did your old man teach, English Lit?"

"Right."

"It doesn't follow, though. I threw a chunk of Andrew Marvell at a cop once. He not only capped the quote, he went ahead and gave me a ticket."

"A mere traffic ticket? Weren't you

out there hurling obscenities and bricks at the police last fall?''

"I was." Buchsbaum's face was glum. "I slipped and fell and sprained my sacroiliac while I was running away. Cost me seventy-eight bucks for doctor bills. After that I decided I was too old and too underpaid to be a liberal."

Michael laughed. He got up to go a little reluctantly; Buchsbaum was a pleasant change from the Vice-Chancellor.

"Stick around," Buchsbaum suggested. "A man who knows his Fry is a man worth knowing. Or, better still, come home, meet the wife, have a beer. I'll try you on the more obscure metaphysical poets."

"If I didn't have eight more people to track down today, I'd accept with pleasure. I used to enjoy this sort of thing, in my younger days. You ivory-tower boys have a nice life."

"You are viewing it with the rosy glow of old age remembering lost youth. Don't kid yourself. Why do you think I skulk around the halls with my collar turned up like James Bond? Students, committees, secretaries wanting lists of things, parents, students . . ."

"Without the students you wouldn't have a job."

"Don't give me that; I've quit being a liberal." Buchsbaum put his feet up on the desk and adjusted them so that he could look between them at Michael. "We all hate students. Most of my peers aren't that blunt about it; they blather on about the book they haven't been able to finish and the vital research they can't carry out because of their onerous teaching load. The majority of them couldn't write a book if you dictated it to them. What they mean is, they hate students. Like me."

"What about Linda Randolph? Did you know her?"

Later, Michael was to wonder what made him ask the question. He had meant to throw out some feelers about Linda; this was where Randolph had met her. But she was not his main interest.

"I knew her," Buchsbaum said.

"That romance must have caused a lot of comment."

"You could say that."

"I've met her. She's charming, isn't she?"

"Is she?" The feet were still on the desk, the stout body as relaxed; but the pink face wasn't friendly any longer. Feeling idiotically rebuffed, Michael turned toward the door. Buchsbaum said suddenly,

"Sit down, Collins. Don't go away mad. I'm sorry if I sounded . . . Hell, I was in love with the girl, of course."

"Of course?"

"Most of her teachers were."

"Not the students?"

"Oddly enough, no. Caviar to the general, you know."

"Cut that out."

"Sorry, it's a bad habit. No; I think she put the kids off a bit—the callow youth. She was bright as they come, and the juvenile male doesn't care for that kind of challenge. But . . ."

He was silent for a time, staring reflectively at the tip of his left shoe; and Michael was reminded of Gordon, groping in the same way for words to describe his wife. When Buchsbaum began to speak, his voice was soft and abstracted, as if he were talking to himself.

"We make cynical remarks about the lousy students. Most of them are, you know. They don't give a damn—they lack motivation, in the current jargon—and even if they have motivation, they don't have the intelligence of a medium-bright porpoise. Day after day you stand up there on your podium and you strip your brain and throw it out, into a sea of dead faces, and it falls flat on the floor and dies there. But now and then—once a year, once out of a thousand students, if you're lucky—you look around and see a face that isn't a flat doughy mass with the right number of holes in it for eyes and nose and mouth. It's a face, a real face. The eyes are alive, the mouth responds to the things you say. When you make a joke, the eyes shine. When you throw out an idea that takes a little cogitation, the forehead actually wrinkles—something is going on behind it, some gears are really meshing. When you say something that—that moves her, the mouth curves at the corners, not much, just a little up or down depending on whether she's moved to laughter or to tenderness. . . ."

The pronoun had slipped out, but Buchsbaum didn't try to retract it. His eyes moved from his shoe to Michael's face, and he smiled.

"The Reminiscences of a Middle-Aged Loser," he said wryly. "It's true, though;

every teacher knows about it. The quality of the response differs. Hers was unique. I won't say that I wasn't affected by the fact that she was also a gorgeous dish."

"I'm sorry," Michael said, realizing that the revelations were finished. "I didn't mean to probe into your private affairs."

"Sure you did." Buchsbaum took his feet off the desk and stood up. It was dismissal. He was friendly, but guarded, now. "Only you wanted me to talk about Gordon, not his wife. Sorry I can't help you."

"Have you read his book?"

"Naturally. It's brilliant. Like everything else the man has done." Buchsbaum beamed at his visitor. "I hate his bloody guts. You noticed that."

II

"I hate his bloody guts."

"If it hadn't been for him, I'd have killed myself that night."

"A desperately unhappy man."

Three interviews, three different comments.

Pacing the dark streets of the town in

search of a restaurant that promised something more suited to an over-thirty stomach than pizza or oliveburgers, Michael pondered the results of his day. He had located one other teacher, and one student. The latter, Tommy Scarinski, was on the last leg of his doctorate, having taken off several years because of illness. Michael was fairly sure that the illness had been what is referred to as a nervous breakdown. The boy still twitched. He was a pale, very fair youth, slender as a girl, looking much younger than his twenty-four years. He had idolized Randolph—canonized him, in fact. Michael didn't doubt that he had contemplated suicide. The impulse was far more common in this age group than most people realized. With the majority of the kids it was only an impulse. Some of them liked to believe the influence of a friend or lover had been the catalytic agent that deterred them from that most final of all gestures of protest. In this case, though, Michael rather thought that Tommy—it was a mark of his immaturity that he still called himself by the diminutive—did owe his life to Randolph. He had been at the age, and at the stage of mental deterioration, when the influence of an idol could make or break his mind. But—my God, what a responsibility. What a delicate, damnable job. Chalk one up for Randolph.

There was a sign, down the block, that said "Restaurant." Michael opened the door and saw a dim interior, not too crowded. A waiter appeared promptly. He ordered a drink and a steak and let himself relax against the imitation leather of the booth.

Buchsbaum's comment wasn't really a mark against Gordon. It was another example of the man's sophomoric attempt at wry humor, with strong touches of masochism. Buchsbaum had never been Gordon's rival, in the ordinary sense of the word; he was the sort of man who would always prefer a romantic illusion to a possible rejection. Most probably he didn't even dislike Gordon.

And why, Michael wondered irritably, should he be thinking in terms of pluses and minuses? He wasn't trying to defend Gordon or play the part of Devil's Advocate; that wasn't the way he worked. He wanted the truth—and he knew it was never a single isolated fact, but a patchwork of differing, sometimes contradictory, views.

The waiter arrived with the drink, and Michael took a hearty swig of it. He made a wry face. Should have specified the brand; this tasted like something out of a still. But it was better than nothing.

The third interview had been the least productive, for all its verbiage. Professor Seldon was almost at the compulsory retirement age of sixty-five; a diminutive, dapper old man with a mop of white hair and a goatee and beard of the same silky hue. He talked fluently; God, Michael thought with an inner grin, how he did talk! He had been dependent on clichés for so long that he couldn't have said "Good morning" if Shakespeare or Milton hadn't happened to say it first. And he was Chairman of the English Department.

Seldon's comments on Gordon were about as useful as the newspaper accounts had been. Reflex reactions. The remark about Gordon's tragic unhappiness had some normal human spite behind it, though Professor Seldon would have been genuinely indignant if you pointed that out. He was a third-rate scholar and a second-rate human being; envy of a better man could not be openly expressed, so it masked itself under the guise of benevolent pity. Translated, his remark simply meant: *This man has everything I would like to have. Nobody ought to be that happy—except me. So he must be miserable, down deep underneath, where it doesn't show.*

And, ironically, the old man was right. Randolph was an unhappy man. There was a serpent in his Eden, though that was a cliché worthy of Seldon himself. But Seldon had no knowledge of Gordon's private life. His assessment of Gordon might have come straight out of the high school Class Prophecy; "Bright, intelligent, friendly; bound to succeed."

Michael caught the waiter's eyes and nodded. The mellowing effect of the whiskey wasn't quite complete, he could stand another one. Frustration of this sort was normal, he knew that. Most people weren't perceptive about other people. Wrapped up in their own miseries, they had no energy to spare for the problems of others; anyhow, they tended to pigeonhole people as they did ideas, and reacted to deviations from a wholly imaginary picture with astonishment and annoyance. "Good old Sam wouldn't do a thing like that." "Mary, of all the people in the world; she must have changed a lot since I knew her." Whereas, of course, Mary hadn't changed at all. Mary, like everyone else, was not one Mary but a dozen. Her astonished friend had just not happened to see the Mary who finally broke out.

Then why, Michael wondered, was he so irritated by his failure to get an instant, comprehensible picture of a man as complex as Gordon Randolph? Was it because he wasn't getting any picture at all, not even a misleading one? Hadn't Randolph had any friends, only associates and disciples?

No. He had not. That was the only useful point Michael had obtained from Seldon.

"Oh, no, Randolph didn't associate with . . . us," he said. Mentally supplying the three missing words, Michael suppressed a smile. "I presume he passed his leisure hours with friends in the city. Except—yes. I recall being surprised, at the time . . . He spent a good deal of time with the students."

The emotion that colored his voice—one of the few times that genuine feeling was allowed to show—was simple astonishment. Remembering Buchsbaum's conversation, and some of the student complaints he had seen published in recent months, Michael understood. His internal amusement, this time, was rather sour. By God, things had changed. He remembered the big, echoing old house where he had grown up; the front door always open and the carpet in the hall worn threadbare with the tread of students' feet, in and out, at all hours of the day and night. His father had a funny notion of a teacher's role. . . . Professor Seldon would probably never know why Michael left so abruptly.

But it was that very lead that had led to his present frustration. The student-teacher relationship, if it was a good one, could be one of the most important in life. He had expected some interesting material from Randolph's students. Having gone, posthaste, to look up the enrollment for Randolph's class, he was delighted to find that one of the top students was still around. Tommy Scarinski.

Maybe his reasoning had been fallacious. But he didn't think so, he was inclined to cross Tommy off as an isolated aberration. The best students in the class, the ones who got the highest grades—they still gave letter grades in those bad old days—might not necessarily be the people who had most attracted Gordon, but it was far more likely that his favorites would be found among that group than among the kids whose work had been too poor to rate Gordon's approval. Besides, the class file included Randolph's comments—terse, sympathetic, and intelligent. The four "A" students had received the most favorable comments—with one exception. Miss Alison Dupuis had been dismissed with a curt: "Idiot savant; but how can you flunk a calculating machine?" With the other three, Randolph had obviously enjoyed a personal friendship.

One of the three had been Linda.

The second, Joseph Something or Other, had dropped out of sight. The vinegary spinster at the Registrar's office could tell him only that Joseph was no longer registered. Well, that was something he could do tomorrow; he had been too pleased at the availability of Tommy Scarinski to check the other records, to see whether Joseph X had matriculated, or transferred to another institution. Graduate school somewhere was a likely possibility, in view of his scholastic record and his teacher's praise. What had Gordon said? "Genuine creativity and drive—a rare combination." Yes, Joseph was worth tracking down. The evaluation of a brain like that, sharpened by several years of maturity and by absence from his former mentor, would be valuable. That was why Tommy had been so disappointing: The years hadn't sharpened his brain, it was still mushy. . . . Poor devil.

The waiter brought his steak, and Michael finished his drink and his deliberations. As he ate he glanced around the room in search of distraction from thoughts that were becoming stale and futile. It was a pleasant, undistinguished little place, like a thousand other restaurants in a hundred other towns. The only thing that made it different was the fact that it was in a college town. There were a lot of students present, mostly couples, and they definitely brightened the scene. The voices were shrill, but they were alive; they got loud with excitement, they vibrated with laughter. Collegiate styles were undoubtedly picturesque. Floppy pants, beads and pendants, clothes that dangled, and jingled, and blazed with color. Michael approved of beards; at least you could tell the boys from the girls that way, and the Renaissance look appealed to him. A couple at a table next to the booth he occupied might have posed as models for the New Look—the boy had long brown hair, and hair over most of the rest of his face; a red kerchief was knotted around his throat. Michael's eyes lingered longer on his date. The long, straight blond hair obscured her face most of the time, but her legs were in full view. They were booted up to the knee, and what she wore above them, if anything, was hidden by the tablecloth.

Michael signaled the waiter for his coffee. The man lingered, swabbing unnecessarily at the table, and Michael resigned himself.

"Stranger in town?"

"Yes. I'm just here overnight."

"You busy tonight?"

"No," Michael admitted, wondering what form the conventional offer would take this time.

"You like music?"

"Well—some kinds," Michael said, surprised and curious.

"Stick around then, have another cup of coffee. Kwame is due in a few minutes.

He's not bad, if you like that kind of music."

"Kwame?"

The waiter, a tired-looking man with receding hair, grinned.

"That's what he calls himself. Real name's Joe Schwartz."

"What does he play? The sitar? The viola d'amore?"

"Just the guitar. But, like I said, he's not bad. If you like that kind of music."

He moved on to the next table, leaving Michael feeling ashamed of his cynicism. Maybe he ought to get out of the big city more often. It was a hell of a note when you were surprised by ordinary human amiability. The conversation was a lesson for him in another way; it emphasized his point about personality stereotypes. The weary middle-aged waiter was not the sort of person you'd expect to enjoy the music produced by somebody named Kwame, even if he didn't play the sitar.

His newfound friend was on the alert, and signaled him with a jerk of his head when the performer appeared, but Michael didn't need the signal. Even in this crowd he would have spotted Kwame.

Such is the power of suggestion that

Michael had unconsciously expected the performer to be black—with a name like Joe Schwartz, yet, he told himself. But the sparse expanses of skin visible were of the sickly tan that people choose, for some obscure reason, to call white. The hair was extensive; it made the efforts of the other boys look epicene. Now that, Michael thought admiringly, is a beard!

It swept down in undulating, shining ripples to the boy's diaphragm, where it mingled with the waves of long brown hair. Although the night was chill and damp, Kwame wore only jeans and a sleeveless embroidered vest, which flopped open with each step, displaying a cadaverous chest. He was barefoot. But his guitar had been carefully swathed against the damp. It was a twelve-string guitar, with a shining surface that might have been produced by Stradivarius or Amati. Expensive, loved, used, and tended like a baby.

There was a tiny podium or stage, about the size of a dining-room table, at the far end of the room, and at another gesture from the waiter, Michael took his cup and moved down to an unoccupied booth near the stage. The other habitués were doing the same thing. Kwame, who had seated himself cross-legged on the floor, placed the guitar across his lap and sat waiting. His eyes moved incuriously around the room, and as they met Michael's, the latter was conscious of an odd shock. Drugs. The eyes were unmistakable. . . . And why, he wondered cynically, was he shocked? He read the newspapers.

There was no announcement, no introduction. When everyone had seated himself, and silence had become profound, Kwame began to play.

Michael's first reaction was negative. Kwame's harsh voice had little appeal for a post-adolescent square who concealed a secret weakness for old Perry Como records, and Kwame's playing, though competent, was not remarkable. The songs were a mixture of legitimate folk music and modern rock imitations of folk music; a few of them sounded vaguely familiar, but Michael was not sufficiently knowledgeable about the popular repertoire to identify them. All had one theme in common: peace, love, innocence, and the annihilation of all these by man's cruelty. The mushroom cloud billowing up around the kids playing in the daisy field, the blast of an explosion annihilating the kids in the Sunday School . . . Kevin Barry lost his young life again, and the lambs were all a-crying. But it was effective. The images were sure fire, they couldn't miss.

Two of the songs were different. Kwame ended his recital with them, and by that time Michael had succumbed to the same spell that held the rest of the audience. He couldn't have explained why he was spellbound, none of the elements of the performance were that good. But in combination . . .

Then Kwame swept his fingers across all twelve strings in a crashing dissonant chord, and broke into a vicious, and extremely funny, satire on the Congress of the United States. Like the others, Michael ached with containing his laughter; he didn't want to miss the next line. At the same time the cruelty of the satire made him wince, even when he shared Kwame's opinion of that particular victim. The laughter burst out explosively at the end of the song.

Kwame didn't give it time to die, but went right into the next number. It was a very quiet song. It was about love, too, and about peace and innocence; but these verses allowed beauty to survive and triumph. The words were very simple, but they were selected with such skill that they struck straight home, into the heart of every compassionate hope. They were articulated with meticulous precision; and as he listened, Michael felt sure that Kwame had written the song himself—and the one that had preceded it. The boy was a magician with words. He made strong music, did Joe Schwartz. . . . And then, with the suddenness of a blow, Michael realized who Kwame was.

The performance ended as it had begun. Kwame simply stopped playing. Some fans came over to talk to him; and Michael looked up, blinking, to see the waiter standing by him.

"Thanks for telling me," he said. "I enjoyed that."

"He's a good kid," the waiter said.

"Do you suppose I could buy him a drink, or—"

"He don't drink."

". . . a cup of coffee? Or maybe a steak?" Michael eyed the protruding ribs of Kwame.

The waiter grinned.

"This isn't Manhattan," he said obscurely. "He'll talk to anybody. Hey, Kwame—friend of mine wants to meet you."

Kwame looked up. He saw Michael, and his beard divided in a sweet smile.

"Sure," he said. His speaking voice was as harsh as the one he used for singing, but several tones higher. Two of his fans trailed him as he approached the booth and he gestured toward them, still smiling. "Okay?"

"Sure," Michael said. "Join me."

They settled themselves, Kwame placing his guitar tenderly on a serving table against the wall, where it would not be jostled by passers-by. The waiter lingered.

"You haven't had dessert," he said, giving Michael a significant glance.

"Oh. Oh! That's right, I haven't. Will you all join me?"

They would, and their orders left Michael feeling old and decrepit. Banana split, chocolate cake a la mode with hot fudge sauce, and a double strawberry frappé sundae for Kwame. Michael ordered apple pie and gave the waiter a nod of thanks as he departed. He ought to have realized that Kwame would be a vegetarian, and he was glad to have been saved from the gaffe of asking the boy if he'd like a steak. It would have been tantamount to offering someone else a nice thick slice off his Uncle Harry.

The food was a useful icebreaker, conversation, at first, was difficult. Kwame spoke hardly at all. Smiling dreamily, he was far out, someplace else. His friends, a blond girl (were they all blondes these days?) and her escort, who had a long cavalry-style moustache, treated Michael with such wary deference that he felt he ought to have a long white beard—and a whip. Yes, that was what they reminded him of—two captured spies in the enemies' clutches, refusing to speak for fear of giving away vital information. Name, rank, and serial number only . . .

They loosened up after a while, as Michael plied them with coffee and sympathy, and he began to enjoy himself. They weren't any more articulate, or sincere, than his generation had been; but they sure as hell were better informed. The much-maligned boob tube, perhaps? More sophisticated, superficially, yes, the little blonde was discussing contraceptives with a wealth of detail his contemporaries had never used in mixed company. Which was okay with him; his hang-ups on that subject weren't deep seated. He wondered, though, if basically these youngsters were any wiser than he had been at their age. They knew the facts; but they didn't know what to do with them, any more than he did. Maybe he was just old and cynical. He felt old. When he looked at Kwame, he felt even older.

Time, and the double frappé, had had their effect; whatever drug it was that Kwame had taken, it was beginning to wear off. He sat up straighter and began to join in the conversation. His comments had no particular profundity. But the young pair responded like disciples to the utterances of the prophet. When Kwame cleared his throat, they stopped talking, sometimes in the middle of a word, and listened with wide, respectful eyes.

Michael, whose mental age was rapidly approaching the century mark, found himself strangely reluctant to introduce the subject he wanted to discuss. He was relieved when Kwame gave him an opening.

"You're twenty-five now? You must have been a student, six years ago."

"Bright," Kwame said. The blonde

giggled appreciatively.

"You were here when Gordon Randolph was teaching here."

"Right . . ."

The response wasn't quite so prompt.

"I'm doing a biography of him."

"Groovy," Kwame said.

Michael persisted.

"I've been interviewing people who knew him because I have a weird notion that personality, or character, or whatever, isn't an objective, coherent whole. It's a composite, a patchwork of reflections of the man as he appeared to others."

That interested them. The blond girl nodded, smoothing her hair, and Kwame's dreamy eyes narrowed.

"Personality, maybe," he said. "But not character. Two different things."

"How do you mean?"

"Character, you call it—soul, inner essence—not a patchwork. One integrated essence."

"All part of the Infinite Consciousness?"

Kwame shook his head. The beard swayed.

"I don't dig that Zen stuff. All part of an infinite something. Names don't name, words don't define. You've gotta feel it, not talk about it."

"Hmm." The collegiate atmosphere must be getting him, Michael thought; he had to resist the temptation to plunge down that fascinating side track. "But that inner core, the integrated essence—that's beyond the grasp of a finite worm like myself. All I'm trying to get is the personality. I'm hung up on words."

"All hung up on words," Kwame murmured.

"So you can't tell me anything about Randolph?"

"Man, I can't tell you anything about anything."

This was evidently one of the proverbs of the Master. The blonde looked beatific, and her escort exhaled deeply through his nostrils, fixing his eyes on Kwame. Michael turned to them with the feeling that he was fighting his way through a web of gauze.

"Neither of you knew him, I suppose?"

"My sister was here then," the blonde said. She sighed. "She said he was the sexiest man she ever saw."

"Great," Michael muttered. "Haven't any of you read his book? It's a study of one of the problems that concern you—

decadence, decay, the collapse of a society's moral fiber."

Even as he spoke, he knew he was dropping words into a vacuum. They professed concern about certain issues, but the only opinions they allowed were the opinions of their contemporaries and those of a few selected "in" writers. Many of them rejected the very idea that any generation but their own had searched for universal truths. Unaccountably irritated, Michael turned to Kwame, who was nodding dreamily in rhythm to a tune only he could hear.

"If you're not hung up on words, why do you use them? You use them well. A couple of those songs were—remarkable. You wrote them, didn't you? Words as well as music?"

Kwame stopped swaying, but he didn't answer for several seconds. When he turned dark, dilated eyes on Michael, the latter felt an uneasy shock run through him. He had reached Kwame, all right; he felt, illogically, as if he had said something deeply insulting or obscene.

"Only two," Kwame said. "I only wrote two of them."

"They were the best," Michael said.

"You ought to perform more of your compositions."

A spasm contorted Kwame's face.

"I don't write songs now. Not for a long time."

"Why not?"

"I can't anymore."

Kwame put his head down on the table and began to cry.

The other two were staring at Michael with naked hostility, but he hardly noticed. The fact that he did not understand Kwame's distress did not lessen his feeling of guilt at having somehow provoked it. He felt as if he had struck out blindly with a club and maimed something small and helpless, something that responded with a shriek of pain.

"I'm sorry," he said quickly. "I didn't mean—"

Kwame raised his head. The top fringes of his beard were damp, and tears still filled his eyes; but he made no move to wipe them away.

"You don't know what you mean," he whispered. "You see the shadows on the wall of the cave and you think they're real. Man, you don't know what's out there, in the dark, on the other side of the fire."

So they still read the old-fashioned philosophers. Michael recognized the allusion, it was one of the few images that remained from his enforced study of Plato. Humanity squatting in the cave, compelled to view the shadows cast on the wall by a flickering fire as the real world, never seeing the Reality that cast the shadows. . . . But his original reading had not evoked the chill horror that gripped him at Kwame's words. What Beings, indeed, might stalk the darkness outside the world, and cast distorted shadows? Whatever They were, Kwame knew about them. Michael had the irrational feeling that if he looked long enough into the boy's wide, liquid eyes, he would begin to see what Kwame had seen. . . .

Drugs, he told himself. Drug-induced hallucinations . . . His incantation of the conventional dispelled the shadows, and he said gently, "It's all right. I'm sorry. Forget the whole thing."

Kwame shook his head.

"Can't forget . . . anything. I need something. Need . . ." His eyes turned toward the others, silent, defensive, watching. "You got anything? Grass? Acid?"

The blonde gulped, glancing at Michael. The boy, who seemed to have better control of himself, said calmly, "Nobody carries the stuff, Kwame, you know that. Not in here, anyhow."

"Then let's go someplace." Kwame shoved futilely at the table and tried to stand. "Let's go—"

The flutter of agitation had spread out beyond their table; other patrons were staring.

Michael sat perfectly still. Kwame's agitation was beyond reassurance; all he could do was refrain from any move or comment that might seem to threaten or condemn. In fact he felt no sense of condemnation, only a profound pity. After a moment, Kwame relaxed. There was perspiration on his forehead.

"Sorry," he said, giving Michael another of those sweet smiles. "We've gotta go now."

"I've enjoyed talking to you," Michael said. "And I enjoyed your performance. You're really good."

"Sorry I couldn't help you."

"That's all right."

"And thanks for the food."

"It was a pleasure."

The other two were standing, looking nervous as singed cats. But Kwame seemed to be bogged down in a mass of conventionalities.

"Sorry I couldn't—"

"It doesn't matter."

Kwame brooded.

"I knew her," he said suddenly.

"Who? Oh . . ." Michael knew how a policeman must feel when confronting, single-handed, a hopped-up addict with a gun. He didn't know what was safe to say. Kwame spared him the trouble.

"Linda. She's his wife now."

"I know."

"Beautiful," Kwame said; Michael knew he was not referring to Linda's face or figure. "A beautiful human being. We tripped together."

Balanced between caution and curiosity, Michael still hesitated to speak. Why hadn't he thought of that? Drugs might help to explain . . . Kwame seemed to sense what he was thinking.

"Not pot, nothing like that. She didn't need it. She was on a perpetual trip." He sighed. "Beautiful human being."

"Yes," Michael ventured. "Did Randolph take—"

Kwame shook his head.

"Oh, no," he said gravely. "Not him. He didn't need it either."

He started to walk away, his companions falling in behind him like a guard of honor. Then he turned back to Michael.

"He always knew about it."

"About what?"

"The dark," Kwame said impatiently. "The dark on the other side."

Six

Michael shoved at the typewriter. Glued to the table top by a two-year accumulation of dirt, spilled coffee, and other debris, it did not move; but the movement jarred the table, which proceeded to tip half a dozen books, an empty coffee cup, and a box of paper clips onto the floor.

Michael spoke aloud, warmly. The only response was a growl from Napoleon, crouched before the door. He pushed his chair back, slumped down in it, and moodily contemplated the single sheet of paper before him.

It was raining in the city again. He could hear rain pounding on the windowpane and see the dirty trickles that slid down the glass inside, where the caulking had dried and flaked and never been replaced.

Rain. Like all words, this one had its accumulated hoard of images. Sweet spring rain, freshening the earth and washing the grubby face of the world . . . The trickles on his window were jet-black. There was enough dirt on the window, but God only knew what color the rain had been to begin with.

The desk lamp flickered ominously, and Michael cursed again. He had forgotten to buy light bulbs. There wasn't one in the apartment. He had already taken the bulb out of the kitchen.

It might not be the bulb, of course. It might be the damned fuses in the damned antiquated building, or some other failure of the outmoded and overloaded electrical system.

From the dark kitchen came a pervasive stench of scorched food. In his mental anguish over the typewriter, he had forgotten about the pan of stew till it burned to a charred mass. One more pan in the trash can. . . . He stubbed his toe groping through the dark kitchen. The broken coffee cup was not one of the ones from the dime store, it was a tender memento of something or other Sandra had given him. Sandra? Joan? Hell.

The paper, the sole product of an afternoon of creative effort, brought no comfort. It was filled from top to bottom with a series of disconnected phrases that weren't even passable prose.

I hate his bloody guts.
He saved my life.
A desperately unhappy man.
A brilliant scholar.
Sexiest man she ever met.
All-around competence.
Wonderful guy, a real chip off the old block.
Keen, incisive business brain.
Almost too sensitive.
After Budge, one of the greatest backhands I've ever seen.
Brilliant . . . brilliant . . . brilliant . . .

And, at the very bottom of the page, dug deep into the paper by the pressure of his fingers on the keys:

He always knew about it. The dark on the other side.

Damn the words, and damn the doped-up infantile little hippie who had produced them, Michael thought. But this verbal incantation didn't bring relief. He saw his words too clearly for the empty things they were. They didn't describe Kwame, and they didn't cancel the impact of the words Kwame had used. He makes bigger magic than I do, Michael thought sourly. Heap strong magic . . . The words haunted him; last night he had dreamed of shadows and waked in a cold sweat, tangled in bedclothes as if he had spent the eight hours battling an invisible attacker.

Still. Dismiss Kwame as a talented junkie, and what did you have left? A series of epigrams, and damned dull ones at that. He was heartily sick of that word "brilliant."

Yet as the inconclusive interviews had proceeded, one concept began to take shape. One thing about Randolph that was significant, and hard to explain. Incompleteness.

Yet you couldn't say he didn't finish what he began. He finished his book. As a writer, Michael knew the importance of that; for every completed book there are a thousand beginnings. He had finished teaching his course and he had apparently taught it well, even brilliantly—damn that word! He had not abandoned tennis or swimming until he had mastered both skills, and his retirement from politics had followed a series of almost uncontested victories.

He mastered a skill, and then he stopped. Was it because he found all of them too easy? No challenge? Or was it because, under the façade of competence, he was somehow unsure of his ability? That wasn't as ridiculous as it sounded. The severest critic was internal. If a man couldn't satisfy that, paeans of praise from the outer world couldn't convince him of his worth. He had to keep on trying, fighting, accomplishing, and never succeeding, because the inner critic was insatiable. So—eventually, suicide, alcoholism, drugs. It had happened before.

But not, Michael thought, to Gordon Randolph. His life had not followed that pattern. If he had quit competing, it was not in the spirit of defeat. He had not retreated into any of the standard forms of suicide. He seemed—yes, damn it, he was—a happy man, except for one thing, the one thing in which he had not succeeded. The one thing for which he cared most desperately. And none of the pat phrases on that sheet of paper gave any clue to his successes, or to his one great failure.

Michael reached for another sheet of paper and inserted it into the typewriter. At the top of the page he wrote:

His wife tried to kill him.

Was that why he couldn't make any sense out of the man who was Gordon Randolph? Because, like so many of the others who had known her, he was becoming obsessed by Randolph's wife?

In her way, Linda was an even greater enigma than Gordon. Not because the coalescing picture was incoherent. A beautiful human being—they all agreed on the content of that, if not in the exact words, including Randolph himself. He had groped for words and so had Buchsbaum, but poor old Kwame had caught it. Then what had turned her from a saint into a devil, from a beautiful human being into an alcoholic, a haunted psychotic?

If I were writing a novel, Michael thought, they would have a common cause —Gordon's incompleteness, his wife's madness. But life is rarely so tidy or so simple. Or, if it is, the connections are too complex for us to see.

The light bulb flickered again. Napoleon

muttered. The rain poured down harder. Michael got up and went into the kitchen. He stubbed his toe—the same toe.

A moving streak shot past him, into the sink and out through the slit in the window, its passage marked by a crash of breaking crockery, which was Michael's last saucer. Nursing his throbbing toe, Michael restrained his curses and listened. He knew what Napoleon's abrupt departure heralded. After a moment it came. A knock on the door; simple and ordinary. There was no reason why the sound should have made an anticipatory shiver run down his spine.

II

Linda watched the rain ripple against the window of the bus. The downpour was so heavy, it didn't look like rain, but rather like a solid wall of water against the window of a submarine. The warm, stuffy bus was a self-contained, miniature universe; and the dark on the other side of the window might have been the vacuum of outer space. A few scattered lights, blurred by the rain, were as remote as distant suns.

The bus was not crowded. Not many people would come into the city in such weather and at such an hour, too late for the theaters or for dinner. The seat next to hers was occupied by a young sailor. He had come straight to it, like an arrow into a target. When he tried to strike up a conversation, she looked at him—just once. He hadn't tried again. He hadn't changed seats, though; maybe he didn't want to seem rude.

Linda didn't care whether he moved or not. She was aware of his presence only as a physical bulk; nothing else about him could penetrate the shell of her basic need. Even her physical discomfort was barely felt. Her shoes were still soaking wet and muddy. She had squelched through the ooze of Andrea's unpaved lane, hoping against hope, even though she knew she would have seen lights from the road if anyone had been at home. She had even pounded on the door, hearing nothing except the yowl of Andrea's pride of cats. Linda knew she could get into the house without any trouble, but with Andrea gone, there was no safety there. It was the first place they would look. Only a senseless desperation had taken her to Andrea in the first place. She wasn't running to anything or anybody; she was running away.

The impulse which had got her onto the bus was equally senseless. She had a little money, not much, and no luggage. If she paid in advance, she could get a room in a hotel; but how long would it be before Gordon found her? If he didn't want to call the police in, there were other, more discreet, ways of tracking her down. Anna would know what clothes she was wearing. There were hundreds of hotels; but Gordon could afford to hire hundreds of searchers. She wished the bus would go on and on forever, without stopping. Then she wouldn't have to decide what to do next.

When the bus reached the terminal, she sat unmoving until all the other passengers had got off, until the driver turned and yelled. She squeezed her feet back into the sodden leather of her shoes. Another stupid move; the driver would remember her, now that she had lingered and made herself conspicuous. He wanted to clear the bus and go home; he stood by the door tapping his fingers irritably on the back of the seat.

Linda walked through the terminal and out onto the street. It was still raining. She walked. She walked a long way. In her mind was the vague idea of confusing the trail by not taking a taxi directly from the bus station. Not that it mattered; he would find her sooner or later. But she had to keep trying.

Finally she came to a brightly lighted street where there were many people. Cars, too, on the pavement. Taxis . . . Yes, this might be a good place from which to take a cab. She stood by the curb and lifted her hand. Cars rushed by, splashing water. Some had little lights on top. None of them stopped. Linda blinked vacantly as the water ran down off her hair into her eyes. Rain. That meant taxis would be hard to find. She remembered that fact from some obliterated past.

A taxi skidded to a stop a few feet beyond her and she walked toward it, but before she could reach it a man darted out, opened the door, and jumped in. The taxi started up, splashing her feet and calves with water. She stood staring after it. Another car stopped, almost at her elbow. The driver leaned out and flung the door open.

"Okay, okay, lady; if you want it, grab it. Hop in."

She got in, sat down.

"Where to?"

The address was written down on a slip of paper inside her purse, but she didn't need to look at it. She had known, all along, that she meant to go there.

"Must be from out of town," the driver said, pulling out into the street. "Figured you were, that's why I stopped right by you so nobody could beat you to it. Chivalry's been dead for a long time, lady. You gotta move fast if you wanta survive."

"It was nice of you," Linda said politely. "Thank you."

She didn't have to talk, he talked all the rest of the way. She remembered to tip him; it was an obvious thing, but to-night nothing was obvious, every move-ment and every idea was a long, arduous effort. What she did not remember until it was too late was that she had meant to leave the taxi at some indeterminate corner and walk the rest of the way. Too late now . . .

The street was dimly lighted, lined with buildings. In the rain and the dark, everything looked black—sky, buildings, windows. She dragged herself up the flight of steps, her shoes squelching.

There was no list of tenants' names outside the door, and no lobby—only a small square of hallway, with the stairs rising up out of it, and two doors, one on either side. Cards were affixed to the doors. She squinted at them through the rain on her lashes. Neither bore the name she sought. She went up the stairs.

Not the second floor, not the third. Another floor, surely it must be the last. There was no elevator; it had not occurred to her to look for one. She went on climbing. The wood of the stair rail felt rough and splintery under her fingers. The whole structure, stairs and rail, felt alive; it yielded, protesting with faint sighs, to the pressure of hands and feet.

The light was dim, a single naked bulb on each landing. Luckily for her, she reached the topmost landing before they failed, every light in the building simultaneously, plunging the place into abysmal darkness.

Linda threw herself to one side, feeling for the wall, for any solid substance in the darkness, heard a door flung open and felt the rush of something past her. Something plunged down the stairs, sliding from stair to stair but never quite losing its footing, never quite failing. It sobbed as it went.

III

So much for premonitions, Michael thought.

It was Gordon Randolph who had knocked at his door. Not Gordon's wife.

Randolph's dark hair was plastered flat to his head; the ends dripped water. The shoulders of his tan trench coat were black with wet. Wordlessly Michael stepped back, inviting Randolph in with a gesture of his hand. Closing the door, he wondered what he ought to offer first. Coffee, a drink, dry clothes . . . But one look at his guest told him that any offer would be ignored, probably unheard. Randolph stood stock still in the middle of the rug. Only his eyes moved, darting from one side of the room to the other, questioning the darkened doorways.

"She's gone," he said.

Michael nodded. He had realized that

nothing less than catastrophe would have brought Randolph here in this condition. He felt profound pity for the tragic figure that stood dripping on his rug; but a less noble emotion prompted his comment.

"Why here?" he demanded.

"I went to Andrea's place first. Nobody was there. I searched the house."

"You searched—"

"Briggs is checking the hotels. Private detectives. But I thought maybe—"

Michael took a deep breath.

"Give me your coat," he said. "You're soaking wet. I'll get you a drink."

"Thanks. I don't want a drink."

"Well, I do."

Ordinarily, the relief of movement would have given him time to collect his thoughts, but fumbling around in the dark kitchen was only another irritant. When he came back into the living room, carrying two glasses, Randolph was standing in the same position, staring fixedly at the bedroom door. Michael thrust a glass into his hand.

"Now," he said, "you can tell me why you think your wife might have come here. And make it good."

For a second he thought Randolph was

going to swing at him. Then the taut arm relaxed, and Randolph's pale face twitched into a smile.

"All right," he said. "I had that coming to me. Get this straight, Mike. There is not in my mind the slightest shred of doubt about you and your intentions toward Linda. This is a pattern."

"You mean—this has happened before?"

Even from the little he knew, Michael should not have been surprised. He was. He was also, though he could not have said why, repelled.

"Twice before. Both friends of mine. It isn't you, you know." Randolph glanced at something and added hastily, "Damn it. I seem to be saying all the wrong things. You, and the others, are symbols of something, God only knows what; if I knew, I'd be a lot closer understanding what is wrong with her. I'm grateful that you're the kind of man you are. You wouldn't take advantage of her sickness."

"Not in the sense you mean, no. I have several old-fashioned prejudices," Michael said wryly. "Well, you can see for yourself that she isn't here. What precisely do you want me to do?"

The lamp chose that moment to give a

longer, more ominous flicker. It was symptomatic of the state of Randolph's nerves that he jumped like a nervous rabbit.

"The bulb's about to go," Michael said.

"Not the bulb, that reading lamp flickered too. I hope we're not in for another of those city-wide power failures."

Randolph's face was white. Michael thought he understood the reason for the man's terror. The thought of Linda, lost and confused, wandering the blacked-out streets, disturbed him too.

"If she should show up, I'll call you at once. Where?"

Randolph shook his head.

"I'll be on the move. And she's wary and suspicious. If she overheard you speaking to me, she'd run. You couldn't detain her unless you—"

"Uh-huh." He didn't have to be specific. Michael could see the picture—the struggle, the screams, the neighbors, the cops . . . "A nice mess that would be," he muttered. "Then what the hell do you want me to do?"

"The ideal thing, of course, would be to get her to see a doctor."

The prompt reply dispelled any lingering doubts Michael may have had. Though why he should have had any, he didn't know.

"Ideal but difficult, if she's suspicious as you say."

"She's suspicious of me," Gordon said. "That's why she rejects every doctor I suggest. From you she might accept it,"

"Well, I could try," Michael said dubiously. "Be sure to let me know, will you, when you find her."

"Of course."

He seemed to have nothing more to say; yet, despite his concern, he was in no hurry to leave. He stood, holding the glass he had not even sipped, his head cocked as if he were listening for something. My God, Michael thought incredulously; he does expect her. At any second. Does he walk through life that way, listening for her footsteps?

"Well," he said again, "I'll do as you suggest—if she does show up, which I don't believe she will. And if I do get a chance to telephone, you'll be . . .?"

"I've an apartment in town," Randolph said vaguely. "Maybe you could leave a message."

He put his glass down on the desk;

and then, with the suddenness of a thunderclap, without even the usual preliminary flicker of warning, every light in the apartment went out.

The effect was frightening, disorienting. There was a faint glow from the window —so the blackout was not city-wide—but in the first moment of shock Michael didn't see that, and neither, obviously, did Randolph. Michael heard his voice, but he recognized it only because it was not his own. The sound was something between a scream and a sob, and it raised the hairs on the back of Michael's neck. Before he could move or speak, Randolph had blundered toward the door. Michael heard the sound of the door being flung open, and the rush of a body out onto the landing and down the stairs. He moved then, trying to shout a warning; the old, worn steps were treacherous enough in the light, he could visualize Gordon sprawled at the bottom with a broken neck. The anticipated slither and crash never came. The sounds of frantic movement diminished, and ended in the slam of the front door.

Then, in the ringing silence that followed, Michael saw the glow of the street lights through the window. He let out his breath with an explosive sigh. Once Randolph got outside, he would realize that his worst fear was unfounded. The man's nerves were in a shocking state. Not surprising; it was bad enough to worry about what might be happening to your wife, adrift in every sense in a blacked-out city; worse to worry about what she might be doing to others.

The lights chose that moment to restore themselves, and Michael blinked and cursed them absentmindedly. He had just had another thought, no more reassuring than the others he had been thinking. Linda had tried once to commit murder. Gordon spoke of a pattern. She had run away before; and what, Michael wondered, had she done on those other occasions? Michael had no illusions about one thing. Gordon might be the most altruistic of men, but on one subject he was beyond ethics. He would protect his wife at any cost—even if the cost were another life.

It was not a cheerful thought, especially if he accepted Gordon's assumption that he himself was Linda's next quarry. Michael shivered. There was a chill draft from the door, which Gordon had left open. He turned; and saw Linda staring at him from the doorway.

Her face was alarmingly like the one he had pictured in his latest fantasy—white and drawn, with eyes dilated to blackness. The only thing missing was the knife he had placed in the imaginary woman's hand.

For a moment they stood frozen, staring at one another. Then Michael got a grip on himself.

"You sure are wet," he said conversationally. "You'd better come in and dry off before you catch pneumonia."

One small, soaked shoe slid slyly back a few inches, as if bracing itself for a sudden movement. Michael didn't stir.

"He was here," she said. "Looking for me."

"Yes."

How long had she been standing out there in the hall? She must have come up after Gordon arrived, but before he left; that blind rush of his would have knocked her flat if she had been on the stairs, and there hadn't been time for her to climb them afterward. So she had been outside the door when Gordon fled, concealed by his agitation and the coincidental darkness.

"You didn't tell him I was here?"

she persisted.

"How could I? You weren't here."

She nodded.

"Are you going to call him now?"

"Not if you don't want me to."

"I don't want you to."

"Then I won't."

The conversation was unreal. Michael couldn't remember what it reminded him of—Lewis Carroll, something existentialist? No. It was of a conversation he had had with the four-year-old son of a friend, some weeks earlier. The directness, the repetition of the obvious . . . Carefully he took a step, not toward the pitiable, shivering figure in the doorway, but back, away from her.

"You might as well come in and dry off," he said. "I'll make some coffee. Something hot."

"If I ran you could chase me," she said.

"Through all this rain?" He smiled, "I'm too lazy."

Her foot moved uncertainly. It took a step; then another and another. Michael let his breath out slowly. She was in. Safe. Now why did that word come into his mind?

IV

Linda knew she wasn't safe, not even there, where she had wanted to come. But there was nowhere else to go.

She stood and sat and moved like an obedient child, while Michael helped her off with her coat and took off her wet shoes and dried her feet on something that looked suspiciously like a shirt. He made coffee; his movements in the dark kitchen were interspersed with bumps and crashes and repressed exclamations. She could hear every move he made. In a place this small, he wouldn't have a telephone extension in the kitchen, surely. The phone in the living room was on the table that served as his desk. She could see it from where she was sitting, and she watched it as if it were alive, a black, coiled shape that might spring into sudden, serpentine threat.

When he came back, carrying two cups, he was limping slightly.

"I keep stubbing my toe," he said with an apologetic grin, as she looked at his stockinged feet.

"Why don't you turn on the light? Or wear shoes?"

Michael looked surprised. It was an endearing expression; Linda wished she could simply enjoy it, instead of wondering what lay behind it. Probably he was surprised that she could frame a sensible question.

"I'm sort of a slob," Michael admitted, handing her one of the cups. "See, no saucers. No shoes. They're around here somewhere. . . . The place is a mess. I should be ashamed, entertaining guests in a hole like this."

"You weren't expecting company," she said drily. The heat of the cup, between her hands, began to seep through her whole body. Even her mind felt clearer.

"No," he said; and then, as if anxious to change the subject, "How long has it been since you've eaten? What about a sandwich? Or some soup? That's about the extent of my talents as a cook."

"It sounds good."

"I'll see what I've got on hand."

Another period of bumping and crashing in the kitchen followed. Linda sat back, closing her eyes, and then straightened up again. The warmth and the illusion of refuge were dangerous. She mustn't give in to them. From now on she had to be on the alert every second. There was still a chance, slim but worth trying, because it was the only chance. But if he failed her, she must be ready to act, instantly. In self-defense.

There was a louder crash from the kitchen. Michael's comment had a different tone, as if he were addressing another person instead of swearing to himself. Linda started, the empty cup wavering in her hands. Then Michael reappeared, carrying a plate. At his heels was another figure. Linda stared at it in comprehension and relief.

"Hope we didn't startle you," Michael said guilelessly. "He always comes in through the window, and through anything else that may be in his way. He just broke my last decent glass."

The cat, a monstrous, ugly animal, sat down, so abruptly that Michael tripped over it and nearly dropped the plate.

"Here," he said. "Take it quick, before he gets it. I was out of bread. I'm afraid the eggs got a little burned. . . ."

There were two fried eggs on the plate. The yolks wobbled weakly, but there was a half-inch rim of brown around the whites. For the first time in weeks Linda felt like laughing.

"They look lovely," she said, and glanced nervously at the cat, who was eyeing the plate with avid interest.

"His name is Napoleon," Michael said. "He hates people. But I've never known him to actually attack anyone."

"You don't sound as if you like him very much."

"We loathe each other."

"Then why do you keep him as a pet?"

"Pet? Keep? *Me* keep *him!*"

"I see what you mean."

She finished the eggs. They tasted terrible, but she needed the energy, in case . . . Lunch. Had she eaten any? Napoleon began to make a noise like a rusty buzz saw, and she looked at him apprehensively.

"I don't know what it means," Michael said gloomily. "He isn't purring, that's for sure. But he does it to me, so don't take it personally."

"I won't. Michael—"

"Wait," he said quickly. "We'll talk. We'll talk all you like. But not just yet, not until you're comfortable and dry. I won't call Gordon, not unless you tell me to. That's a promise."

"I believe you."

"Thank you." His eyes shifted. "Oh, hell, I forgot, I'm expecting someone to drop in this evening—an old friend of mine. Shall I call and try to put him off?"

"Maybe that would be better," Linda said slowly.

"All right. It may be too late, but I'll see what I can do. In the meantime, your clothes are wet and you look like a drowned rabbit. The bathroom is through there. See if you can find my bathrobe someplace. It's in the bedroom—on the floor, probably."

He was smiling at her, his eyes as candid as a child's. Linda wished desperately that she could trust him. But she didn't dare trust anyone. The risks were too great.

"Thank you," she said. She stood up. She reached for her purse. "I won't be long," she said.

Michael followed her into the bedroom, switching on the light. Like the living room, it was big and high-ceilinged. Automatically Linda's eyes assessed the exits. One big window. No window in the bathroom, which looked as if it might have started life as a closet when the building had stood in its newly constructed elegance. An enormous carved wardrobe now served the functions of a closet. There were two doors, one into the living room and one into the bathroom. All the furniture, including the wardrobe, was battered and nondescript. Interior decoration was clearly not one of Michael's interests. Every inch of wall space, except that which was occupied by the wardrobe and the doors and windows, was covered with bookcases; even the bed had been moved out into the middle of the floor to allow more space for books. The bed was not made.

Michael ambled around muttering apologies, picking up socks and underwear and books and old letters, and heaping them unceremoniously on the single chair. His face brightened as he lifted a drab garment from the floor.

"Here's my bathrobe," he said, shaking it out. "Gosh, I'm afraid it's pretty wrinkled."

"Wait a minute." He darted into the bathroom, gathered up shaving equipment, towels, and more books. "There should be a clean towel someplace. . . ."

They found one, finally, on top of one of the bookcases. Linda closed the bathroom door and turned the shower on full force. She put her ear to the door and listened. The bedroom door closed with a bang, which probably represented one of Michael's attempts at tact, or reassurance.

Linda opened the bathroom door just wide enough to slip out, and eased it shut behind her. There was a telephone extension on the bookcase by the bed. She eased the instrument out of its cradle, her fingers on the button underneath. There was a slight click; but with luck he wouldn't notice it.

The click was lost in the ringing. She had moved so quickly that he had barely had time to dial the number. She waited, her hand over the mouthpiece, so that he could not hear the sound of her ragged breathing.

Finally the receiver at the other end was picked up. She knew, from the first syllable, that the voice was not the one she feared; and the relief was so great she almost lost the words.

"Let me speak to him," Michael said; and then, after a pause, "Galen? It's me, Michael."

He had been telling the truth. Her astonishment and joy were so great that she did not concentrate on Michael's next statement: something about "said you'd drop in tonight."

"But, Michael. I'm just leaving for—" the other man said.

Michael cut him off.

"Yes, I know. Hold on a second, Galen."

That was all the warning she had, and it was barely enough. She eased the receiver back down into its slot with a care and speed she had not expected her unsteady hands to know, and then dropped down, flat on the floor beside the bed, as the bedroom door opened.

The bathroom door was closed and the rush of water was unchanged. The thud of her heart sounded like thunder in her ears, but she knew Michael could not hear it. He stood motionless for a few seconds. Then the door closed.

Linda got to her knees. She didn't dare pick up the telephone again. She didn't have to. There was something wrong, or he wouldn't have bothered to check on her before proceeding with the conversation. And now she remembered what the person on the other end of the wire had said, at first, "This is Dr.

Rosenberg's residence."

The mammoth volumes of the city telephone directory were where she might have expected them to be—on the floor. She scooped up the classified directory and ran into the bathroom. On her knees on the floor, she began turning pages. "Department Stores . . . Hardware . . . Machinery . . . Physicians." And there he was. Rosenberg, Galen. A conscientious member of the medical profession; four separate numbers were listed, including his home phone. Most doctors avoided giving that one out. But her eyes were riveted to the one word that mattered, the word that told which medical specialty Dr. Galen Rosenberg practiced.

It might be a coincidence. Presumably even psychiatrists had friends, like other people. But if Rosenberg had intended to visit his friend Michael, why did Michael care whether she overheard the conversation? And why had he interrupted the other man at that particular moment? On his way to—where? Not, she thought, to Michael's apartment. Not then. He was clever, Michael Collins, but not quite clever enough.

Her mind worked with the mechanical

precision it developed in moments of emergency. Coat, bag—she had those. Shoes—they were still in the living room. That was bad. Well, she would just have to leave them.

Stripping off her dress, she opened the bathroom door and walked boldly across the bedroom. The door was still closed. She opened it a crack, and called, "Would it be all right if I washed my hair? It feels horrible."

"Sure." Michael's footsteps approached the door. It started to open, but she was ready; she pushed it back, making sure he saw her bare arm and shoulder.

"Hey," she said, putting a faint amusement into her voice.

"Oh, sorry. There should be some shampoo, someplace. . . ."

"I found it. Just wanted to let you know I wasn't drowned."

"Oh. Thanks."

He sounded embarrassed. She pictured him standing outside the door, his long, thin face alert and compassionate. Linda's mouth tightened.

"Your friend," she said, through the crack. "Did you reach him?"

"Friend? Oh, I'm afraid I wasn't able

to put him off. He won't stay long. Don't worry. I'll tell him something."

I'm sure you will, she thought.

"Okay," she said, and closed the door.

So that was that. Naïve of her to expect anything else.

Letting the water run, Linda closed the bathroom door and slipped into her dress. The skirt was still damp; it felt clammy and cold against her skin. Gathering up coat and bag, she went to the window of the bedroom.

For several terrifying minutes, she was afraid she couldn't open it. The latch was a flimsy, old-fashioned thing, but the frame refused to yield to her frantic shoves. Outside, dim through the filthy glass, the angular black shape of a fire escape mocked her efforts. When the window finally gave, it went up with such a rush that she almost fell out.

Sprawled across the sill, she lay still for a moment, with the rain beating down on her head and the cold air in her face. Then she pulled herself back. Folding her coat, she went across the room to the wardrobe and opened its double doors.

The bedroom door opened, and Michael's

voice called, with hideous cheerfulness, "Linda? Hey, are you decent? Friend of mine wants to meet you."

Huddled in the back of the wardrobe, behind a heap of old newspapers and dirty laundry, Linda held her breath. Not that she needed to; when the truth dawned on him, Michael made enough noise to drown out a squad of heavy snorers—bellowing for his friend, splashing around in the bathroom as if he expected to find her submerged in the tub, and then rushing to the open window.

"She's gone," he kept repeating. "Damn it, Galen, she's gone."

Linda heard the other man's deep voice for the first time. They had talked in the other room for some minutes, but they had kept their voices so low, they were only murmurs.

"Out through the window? That's a hell of a route, Michael. I wouldn't have thought that old rattletrap of a fire escape would hold any weight."

"It obviously did. The dust on the windowsill is smeared where she crawled out. And—yes, her coat's gone. Her purse too. But—wait a minute—" Linda heard him run out and return. "Her shoes are still here! She went out in the rain, barefoot. . . . She's out there now, somewhere. Oh, God. I muffed it, Galen. If she gets hurt, it's my fault."

"Calm yourself. You sound like a bad performer trying out for Hamlet."

"Sorry," Michael muttered. "Damn it, Galen, I don't see how she knew. I was so careful—"

"There's a telephone extension in here. If she's as intelligent as you say, she could have managed."

"You mean it isn't that hard to outsmart me. And you're right."

"Cunning and intelligence are two different things. But before you go flying off in all directions again, let's stop and figure this out. Are you sure that fire escape is still functional. She may be out there still, halfway down. Or lying below, with something broken."

Michael rejected the last suggestion with a wordless sound; but Linda scarcely heard it. Her eyes were fixed, in horror, on the doors of the wardrobe. They were old and warped and did not close completely; a narrow line of yellow had announced the switching on of the light when Michael entered the bedroom. Now the crack altered its shape, widening and narrowing in turn. Someone was trying to open the door.

Her attention flickering wildly from the attempt on the door to the conversation, she realized what the older man, the one named Galen, was saying. My God, she thought; he knows I'm here. He's smarter than Michael, smarter and tougher; he knows I'd be afraid to step out on that fire escape. He must be leaning against the doors, making them move, just to frighten me.

Then the door opened and she saw the source of her terror. Not the doctor. Something worse. The cat, the damned cat. She was afraid of the cat. It looked like a diabolical animal, and it hated people; Michael had said so. It would take one look at her and yowl or spit, and back out, and then they would know where—

Linda saw its eyes shine with that eerie fire, which is, scientifically, due to a perfectly normal phenomenon of light refraction. Then the eyes disappeared. Deliberately the animal sat down, its back to her, and began washing its tail.

"There's nothing in the alley," Michael

said, with a loud sigh of relief.

"And no signs of her having gone that way, either."

"A flashlight doesn't show that much detail from up here. What did you expect, a glove draped daintily over a garbage can? Damn it, Galen, she had to go that way. There's no place to hide in here. I was in the kitchen the whole time, she couldn't have gotten past me."

A small contorted shape in the corner of the wardrobe, Linda could almost feel the other man's gaze, moving thoughtfully around the room. Oh, yes, he was much smarter than Michael. It never occurred to that innocent idiot that she hadn't left. But he knew, the doctor—he had had considerable experience with people like her.

Whether he actually bent over to look under the bed, she did not know; a snort of amused disgust from Michael might have been his response to such a gesture. But she knew when the doctor's searching eyes lit on the wardrobe—the only other place in the room where a person might be concealed.

"There's Napoleon. Still as unsociable as ever?"

"He hates everybody," Michael said

absently. "Likes it in there, though. . . . Galen, what am I going to do?"

Napoleon finished washing his tail, turned around, and prepared to go to sleep. After the first knowing look, he had not glanced in Linda's direction.

"Well," the doctor said finally, "let's sit down and talk about it. Your original account was somewhat abbreviated."

"Have you got time?"

"Sixteen minutes. Then I'll have to drive like hell. I must catch that plane."

They went out, talking about the medical conference the doctor was going to attend. Linda let her head fall back against one of Michael's coats. Against the light from the half-open door of the wardrobe she saw the solid, unmoving black lump that was Napoleon. An odd smile curved her mouth. How very appropriate, she thought.

For the moment, at least, she was safe, reprieved by the hallowed familiar of legend, by the animal sacred to the powers of evil. What would happen next she neither knew nor cared; she still had to get out of the apartment, but she would worry about that later. Now she could relax, for a little time, enjoying the omen, and listening intently to the conversation, which was clearly audible through the open door.

"I wonder," the doctor said, "why she should come to you. Is she in love with you? Or you with her?"

"I don't know what the word means," Michael said quietly.

"No more do I."

"Then why the hell did you bring it up? No, I don't think she's running to anyone, or anything—unless it's safety. She's running away from something. Not her husband—"

"How do you know?"

"Well, for God's sake! Modern women don't run away from husbands, they divorce them. Besides, he—he's devoted to her. Desperately worried about her. He's out in this filthy rain now, looking for her. He was here, not five minutes before she came."

"He was?"

"I wish to God you people could carry on a normal conversation instead of trying to make it into a Socratic dialogue," Michael said irritably. "Yes, he was. And before you can ask, I'll tell you. I don't know why he should expect to find her here—that's the truth, Galen. But he did. He says she's run away before—to other men."

"What other men?"

"How the hell should I know? I didn't ask."

"I think I might have asked," the doctor said thoughtfully. "If a nervous husband told me I was number three on any list, I'd be curious about my predecessors. All right, never mind that. She runs away. He pursues."

"You make it sound . . . Galen, I tell you the girl is off her head."

"How do you know?"

"Oh, for—"

"All I'm trying to indicate is the stupidity of jumping to conclusions. As a writer you ought to know that a single set of observed facts may be capable of varying interpretations. And you know the human tendency to misinterpret evidence in terms of a preconceived theory. So far, all you've conveyed to me is that the woman is running away from something she fears. Either her husband is the source of her fear, or he is closely connected with it. Certainly it's possible that her fears are unjustified or imaginary; that she is, as you so elegantly put it, off her head. But it is also possible that she fears a real danger, one which even you would admit to be a legitimate cause of fear if you knew what it was. Just because you can't see it doesn't mean it isn't there."

"I know what she's afraid of," Michael said reluctantly. "And it—isn't there."

"What is it?"

"A dog. A black dog. She saw it one night and it terrified her so badly she went into a fainting fit."

"You didn't see it?"

"It happens that I didn't see it. But if I had, if it was real and not a figment of her imagination—so what? The cause is inadequate to explain her response. I tell you, the girl was frantic with fear."

The doctor did not respond at once. Linda, who had followed the discussion with growing hope, sagged back. For a while he had sounded like a possibility, a potential convert. But Michael's last statement was unarguable.

"I could argue that," the doctor said after a while. "But I'll accept your hypothesis, if only to keep you from bellowing at me."

"My hypothesis? I haven't one."

"You sure as hell have. And it's time you dragged it out into the open and had a look at it. Your voice, when you said, 'A black dog,' was significant. What does that phrase suggest to you? No fair thinking about it—give me some images."

"The Hound of the Baskervilles," Michael said promptly. "Luminous eyes, jaws dripping with phosphorescence . . . The black dog of the Celts, that presages doom . . . A grisly story I read when I was a kid, about a werewolf. . . ."

"Now I," said Galen, "had a black dog once. A big black mutt who followed me everywhere I went and chewed up my shoes and hid under the bed when my mother scolded him."

"All right," Michael muttered. "I see your point, damn your eyes. None of my dogs was black. But it's not just a personal bias, Galen. It's partly the emotional atmosphere in that damned house. There are so many sick feelings—between Linda and that foul secretary, between Linda and the old hag who calls herself a white witch. When I looked back on the weekend, it seems to me that we talked of nothing but evil, and demonology, and

Satan. The house is big and brightly lit, it has every modern luxury; but it stinks of ugly emotions. It's a sick house. Now laugh."

"Why should I? That's the most important thing you've said yet. You are neither stupid nor insensitive—"

"Thanks a lot."

"—and emotional atmospheres can be felt. I'd never deny that. The origins of the feeling are another matter."

"I know. And since I don't believe in mental telepathy, I've been trying to remember what small, unnoticed clues I must have seen. There must have been something; I don't ordinarily come over psychic."

The springs of the armchair creaked.

"I must go," the doctor said. "I'll barely make it as it is. I'll call you when I get back, Michael."

"But what am I going to do?"

"What are you looking for, free advice? It's your problem."

"Consoling as always."

"You've already made up your mind what to do. You just want me to agree with you. You're planning to telephone the bereaved husband and tell him his wife was here?"

"I have no choice about that."

"Perhaps not. Good-bye, Michael."

"Here's your briefcase. . . . Your Olympian detachment is all very well, but this isn't a remote, academic problem. She's on the loose right this minute, contracting pneumonia by walking around in the rain without any shoes on, if nothing worse. I don't like the role of informer; but for her own safety I must tell Randolph that she was here. Maybe he can—"

"Randolph?"

Linda heard the sound of the front door opening. The voices had gotten fainter; but the change in the doctor's tone came from some other cause than distance.

"This is Gordon Randolph's wife you've been talking about?"

"I thought I shouldn't mention names."

"No . . . Damn it, I'm late now. I'll break my usual rule, Michael, and give you one word of advice, if you'll walk downstairs with me. If you should hear anything . . ."

Linda was on her knees, oblivious of the danger of discovery; but strain as she might, she could make out no further words, only a mutter of voices as the two men descended the stairs. She crawled out of her hiding place, over the prostrate form of Napoleon, who snarled affably at her as she passed. Her cramped muscles complained as she stood upright. Overriding physical discomfort was the agony of indecision that racked her mind.

She went to the door and looked warily out into the empty living room. The lights still burned and the front door stood open. Michael was a trusting soul. . . . From below, amplified by the funnel of the stairwell, the rumble of voices floated up.

Briefly she fought the wild, dangerous urge to rush down the stairs and catch him before he left. But she knew she couldn't take the chance. They all talked that way, the ones who considered themselves liberal and sophisticated; but when it came to action, they balked at the final conclusion. If she could only talk to him at her leisure, with some means of escape at hand in case he turned out to be the broken reed all the others had been. . . . Too late for that now. Too late for anything but escape.

In her arms she still clutched the coat and purse, which she had been holding for so long. Darting across the room, she scooped up her shoes and went out the door. She reached the floor below just before Michael's head came into view, and cowered in the shadow of the stairs as he went past. If he had turned his head he would have seen her; but he went quickly, intent on his next move. The telephone; Gordon. And Gordon would see through her trick. He knew her habits and he wouldn't accept the obvious without checking. She would have to hurry. Gordon would come. Hurry . . .

The door above slammed shut and Linda fled down the stairs, her stockinged feet making no sound. The front door of the building opened and closed, and a slight dark form blended with the darkness of the night, and disappeared.

Seven

When Michael discovered the trick she had played on him, his first reaction was anger —not at his own stupidity, but at Linda. Gordon, who had just come back after an inspection of the alley under the fire escape, smiled wryly at his expression.

"I know just how you feel, but don't let it get you."

"You told me she was intelligent," Michael said, recovering. "I should have believed you."

Gordon's smile faded.

"The operative word is not intelligence. There's a special kind of cunning developed by people in her condition. . . . Oh, hell, Mike, I'm still trying to mince words. I'm sorrier than I can say that you got dragged into this mess; but now that you are involved, it would be stupid of me to hold anything back.''

Michael couldn't help remembering that it was Gordon who had dragged him into the mess. Then his annoyed vanity faded at the sight of Gordon's tormented face, and he shrugged.

''I feel very bad about letting her get away. If I had realized how sick she was—''

''Precisely why you shouldn't feel guilty. It was my fault for understating the problem. Let's forget that and go on to something constructive.''

''Shouldn't we be trying to trace her? There's a subway station in the next block; cabs aren't too frequent around here. . . .''

''Briggs is already on that,'' Gordon said.

''Oh. Sure.''

Another unwelcome memory recurred to Michael—the look of unconcealed repugnance on Linda's face whenever she saw Briggs. Surely he wasn't the best person to send after a frightened woman. . . . He shrugged the doubt away. It was none of his business.

''How about a drink?''

''No, thanks; I'd better get moving.''

But Gordon appeared to be in no hurry; drawing on his gloves with deliberate care, he managed to look poised and aristocratic in spite of his obvious worry. By just standing there he made the shabby little room look shabbier. His keen black eyes moved around, lingering on the paper-strewn desk.

"How do you feel about the biography now?" he asked.

"I don't know. I've put quite a bit of work into it. . . ."

"Have you really?" Gordon's dark gaze swung back to Michael. "Whom have you talked to? Or should I ask that?"

"Oh, sure, why not? I started with the colleges. You made quite an impression at both of them."

"They all mouth the conventional academic baloney," Gordon said cynically. "Wait till you talk to my former political cohorts. They won't be so complimentary."

"They were somewhat annoyed at your retirement, I suppose."

"A euphemism." Gordon smiled. "But by all means talk with them; you'll get an interesting view of my personality. Well. I'll be in touch, Mike."

"Please do. I'm concerned too."

When Gordon finally left, Michael dropped into the big overstuffed chair and put all ten fingers in his hair.

She had looked so young.

The glamorous hostess in her expensive gowns had seemed mature; the shrewish wife had a woman's cruelty. But she wasn't that many years out of college; she must be ten, even fifteen, years younger than Gordon. And when she sat huddled in his big chair, with the rain dripping down onto her pale cheeks, she had looked about sixteen. Her hands and feet were as fragile as a child's; the sodden shoes had been no longer than his hands.

Yes, he reminded himself, and she had presence of mind enough to take those pathetic little slippers with her when she outfoxed him. Poor little Cinderella? Rich little Lucrezea Borgia was more like it. But still he sat motionless, head in his hands, his fingers contracting as if their pressure could force from his mind the picture that persisted through every conscious doubt—the picture of a slight, dark figure running down a dusky corridor, growing smaller and more tenuous as it fled, until it finally vanished into air.

II

Next morning Michael went around and heckled his agent. Sam Cohen was not noted for his equable disposition; after half an hour of querulous dithering, he exploded.

"What the hell do you mean, you don't know whether you want to write it or not? You've got to write it. We've got a contract!"

"I didn't sign it in my own blood," Michael snarled.

Sam recognized the signs; he was used to them, but he got writer's temperament so seldom from Michael that it took him by surprise. After a blink of his scanty eyelashes, he went into the routine.

"Mike, you know this is the best deal I've ever gotten for you. It's too good to pass up, even if you don't care about the damage you could do your professional reputation if you renege on a formal contract. Hell, we may have a best seller on our hands if this rumor about Randolph's going back into politics is true."

Michael sat up in his chair.

"Where did you hear that?"

"The essential criterion of a rumor is

that nobody knows how it started. But I've heard it mentioned more than once."

"Hmph. I didn't know you could do that. Get back into the game, I mean."

"Why not? He never lost an election, you know. With his money and charm, the party bosses would jump at him. Sure, it will take a little time to get his name before the public again, but—didn't you ever wonder why he agreed to this biography when he's refused even an interview for years?"

"I guess I am naïve," Michael said slowly. "He's a nice guy, you know. The idea of his using me—"

"Naïve is right," Sam snorted. "So how is he using you? Making you rich is all. Does that make him any less of a nice guy? Oh, get out of here, and let me work. And do some work yourself."

Michael grinned and wandered out. On the street he stood blinking at the feeble sunshine and wondering what he wanted to do. He had called Gordon that morning, when the latter had failed to call him. Linda was still missing. The sunshine was anemic. The smog was heavier than usual. It was a lousy day. He was in a lousy mood.

So he spent the day doing nothing. He made a feeble attempt to clean up the apartment, a chore which was weeks overdue, but he knew his real motive was to be at home in case Gordon called. He did manage to get the dirty laundry collected; there were socks under the cushion of the chair and a sock on the kitchen table. Rooting around in the bottom of the wardrobe, he found a pile of dirty shirts. On top of them lay a small, crumpled black glove.

Straightening up, with the glove in his hand, Michael abandoned the shirts. So that was where she had been; obviously, there wasn't any other place. Then he remembered something, and, turning, he bellowed loudly for the cat. Napoleon was gone. Deprived of an audience, Michael muttered to himself. The animal was obviously getting senile. Or else there was something about Linda Randolph that appealed to him. A nasty thought, that one . . .

By evening, when the phone still refused to ring, Michael was desperate. He straightened his desk. He managed to cram half the books that had been on it into one bookshelf or another, but there was no place for the rest. He needed another bookcase. Only, where was he going to put it? Every inch of wall space in living room and bedroom was already taken up. Maybe the bathroom . . . Then, on the bottom of a pile, he found the book that he had bought and then ignored. Randolph's masterpiece. With a snort, Michael threw himself into a chair and began to read.

He came to three hours later when Napoleon bit him on the ankle, milder attempts to gain attention having failed. Still carrying the book, he stumbled out into the kitchen. He gave Napoleon the hamburger he had intended for his own dinner, an error he didn't even notice till the next day. He went on reading.

At four in the morning, he finished the book, and fell groggily into bed in a state of mingled exaltation and rage. The pathetic little mental image of Gordon's wife had developed a set of fangs. Anyone who could write a book like that when he was still in his twenties . . . The man needed encouragement, admiration, an atmosphere of peace and quiet—not a crazy wife who probably resented his superior talent. Lying awake in the darkness, Michael could see the ghosts of Gordon's unwritten books, laid out in a row like murdered babies. Murdered *in utero* by Gordon's wife.

This partisan mood carried Michael through the next few days. He didn't call Gordon, but Gordon called him and reported that Linda had not yet been found. He sounded less edgy. Of course, if she had been hurt or killed, she would have been heard of by this time, Michael thought. Personally, he no longer gave a damn.

He spent two infuriating days trying to track down some of Gordon's political associates, knowing full well that he would never reach the hidden men who made the real decisions, and discovering that politicians were even more peripatetic than academicians and just as impressed with their own importance. Yet through the platitudes and glittering generalities, an impression gradually formed. He believed the rumors of Gordon's return to politics. It was ridiculous, of course, to resent Gordon's failure to take him into his confidence. Maybe he hadn't made up his mind yet.

Michael found himself curious to read some of Gordon's political speeches. They were not easy to locate; the big-city newspapers had not followed out-of-state local campaigns in detail. Finally he managed to find back issues of the leading newspaper of Gordon's state.

Even in cold print the speeches were impressive. Michael could imagine their effectiveness when they were delivered with the full force of Gordon's dynamic personality. He had wondered what kind of political speech might be composed by the man who wrote that fantastic book. Now he knew. Of course the media were completely different; a political speech was not a novel. But the similarity was there, not in phrasing or in content so much as in an underlying integrity, the product of a particular kind of mind.

Gordon's candidacy had been supported by the newspaper. It got a lot of coverage, and the not-so-subtle slant in the reporting, compared with the tone taken toward Gordon's unfortunate opponent, made Michael's mouth twist in wry amusement. Politics, he thought, with the comfortable contempt of a man who has never run for office. Well, you couldn't blame

Gordon for the traditional dirtiness of the game. . . . He kicked himself mentally. Blame, hell, you don't condemn or approve, he reminded himself. You just read. And write, if possible.

It was pure accident that he saw the item at all. It was on the front page, but it was hidden down in the lowest left-hand corner, and Gordon's name was mentioned only once, in small print.

There was a photograph, and he studied the inexpressive features of the young man with interest. Copied from a formal studio portrait, the face was not distinctive. High forehead, hair and eyes of some determinate dark color, horn-rimmed glasses so big that they reduced the features to unimportance. Gordon's campaign manager, William S. Wilson.

The name was familiar. Michael groped through his mental card file on Randolph for several seconds before he realized that the familiarity had nothing to do with contemporary events. The name was that of Edgar Allan Poe's character. A nice, cheerful story that one, about a man haunted by his own ghost.

The analogy was nonexistent. Accidental death, the police believed—the strain of an exciting campaign, and too many sleeping pills. There was no reason why the young, successful assistant of a rising politician should take his own life.

Michael was curious enough to pursue the story. The next installment had retreated from page one to page fourteen, reasonably enough, since there were no dramatic developments. The assumption of accidental death was confirmed by all the evidence the police had been able to turn up. So much for William Wilson.

Michael didn't know, then, that the seed had been planted. It had not yet taken root; it just sat there in the darkness of his subconscious mind, rubbing a little, but beginning to be encased, like a grain of sand in an oyster, by layers of protective preconceptions. But the intrusion was a seed, not a sterile piece of grit. The telephone call he got the next day started it growing.

Typically, Galen didn't waste any words. "Have you resolved your latest problem?" he asked, as soon as he had identified himself to his surprised listener.

"No, she's still missing. Where are you?"

"Paris, of course. I told you I'd be here

till the end of this week. Michael, I want you to go over to my office and—"

"You're calling me from Paris? Why?"

"If you'll be quiet for a minute, I'll tell you. I'm due at a symposium in about four and a half minutes. Go over to my office and pick up an envelope my secretary has for you. I've already spoken to her."

"You want me to mail it to you?" Michael asked, groping.

"If I wanted something mailed to me, I'd have my secretary mail it," Galen said impatiently. "The envelope is for you. Go and get it now. Don't make any decisions until you've read the contents."

"What the hell are you talking about?"

"I don't believe I've used any words of over three syllables, have I? I must go now. I'll be in touch with you as soon as I get back. And remember, don't do anything drastic until you've seen that envelope."

The receiver went down with a decisive click. Galen never bothered with hellos and good-byes.

Michael hung up. There was no use trying to call back. He didn't know what hotel Galen was staying at, and it was more than likely that Galen would refuse to add anything to his enigmatic message even if he could be located. He was never obscure except by choice.

Michael got up and wandered over to the window. It was raining again. The sky, what little he could see of it, was a dirty gray, and the puddles in the alley reflected the sallow light with a sheen of oily iridescence. Even on the fourth floor, with the window closed, he could hear the snarl of bumper-to-bumper traffic on the street. Absently, Michael drew his initials in the smeary film on the inside of the pane. The hell with it. He wasn't going all the way across town on a day like this just to pick up an envelope.

The foul evening darkened, the rain beat a peremptory tattoo against the window. Michael wandered the apartment like a caged lion, unable to settle down or even to understand the strange sense of uneasiness that grew, slowly but steadily. Unable to concentrate and unwilling to go out, he puttered with small jobs he had been putting off; he put a new light bulb in the kitchen and started to cook himself something to eat. It was then that he discovered he had given Napoleon the hamburger. There was nothing else fit to eat except various things in cans, and he realized he wasn't hungry anyhow. He was too nervous to eat.

Nervous. Slowly Michael let himself down into a chair and considered the word. He reviewed the symptoms: taut muscles, mildly queasy stomach, restlessness, general malaise of mind. Yes, that was his trouble; he was as nervous as a cat. . . . He gave the somnolent Napoleon a look of hate, and revised the figure of speech. He hadn't had the symptoms for years, that was why he had been so slow to recognize them—not since college exams, or the early days of his working career, when a particular interview, or letter, or telephone call might make or break his new-hatched confidence in himself. So why now, when there was nothing hanging over him that really mattered?

The thing hit him with the violence of an earthquake, but it was nothing physical, nothing that any of the conventional senses would have recognized. Yet it was as peremptory as the sudden shrilling of a telephone in a silent room. It summoned, like a shout; it tugged at the mind like a grasping hand. It lasted for only a second or two, in measurable time; but while it lasted, the room faded out and gray fog closed in around him. He was conscious of nothing except the calling. Even the hard seat of the chair under him and the solidity of the floor beneath his feet seemed to dissolve. It stopped as abruptly as it had begun. There was no fading out, merely a cessation.

Michael found himself on his feet. His face was wet with perspiration, and his knees were weak. Blinking like a man who has emerged from a cave into bright sunshine, he looked around the familiar kitchen, and found its very normalcy an affront. The table was still a table; it rocked slightly under the pressure of his hand as it always did. It ought to have changed into an elephant or a tortoise. The view from the kitchen window should not be the normal view of night darkness; it ought to show an alien sun over some weird landscape. The thing that had invaded his mind was as shattering and as inexplicable as any such transformation.

But the most incredible thing about the experience was that he accepted it. He knew, not only what the calling was, but who had sent it. Knew? The verb was too weak; there was no word in the language for the absolute, suprarational conviction that filled his mind.

He was still a little unsteady on his feet as he crossed the room. He noticed that Napoleon was no longer in his favorite place by the door. Evidently the cat had left, and he hadn't even heard him go.

His desk was covered with papers, notes, books. Michael didn't touch any of them. Slumped in his chair, his eyes fixed on vacancy, he thought. It was one of the hardest jobs he had ever done in his life; methodically, he examined and demolished all the guideposts he had established in the past ten days—as well as a few mental monuments that had been standing a lot longer. It left his conscious mind pretty bare. He didn't try to construct any new theories to fill it up. He couldn't yet.

The urgent impulse that still gripped him, even though its stimulus had vanished, did not interfere with his thinking; it occupied a level much more basic than reason or conscious thought. It was rather like an overpowering hunger or thirst. But he couldn't yield to it yet; a man who walks along a contaminated stream knows, even though his throat is a dusty agony, that he cannot relieve the pain until he finds clear water.

Why hadn't he gone out, that afternoon, to get the envelope Galen wanted him to have? The office was closed now, and he didn't know the secretary's last name, or address.

The contents of that envelope must concern Randolph, and they must be important. That conclusion wasn't intuitive; it was the result of logic. Galen's reaction that night, when he learned the identity of the fugitive, had been markedly peculiar. He hadn't been merely surprised; he had been worried. That last, hasty spate of advice had also been uncharacteristic: *Don't do anything, don't take any action whatsoever. I'll discuss it with you when I get back.*

But Galen had decided the matter couldn't wait. That oblique reference at the beginning of the telephone conversation indicated that he had been thinking about the Randolphs, and strongly suggested that the rest of the conversation concerned them. Galen thought nothing of trans-Atlantic telephone calls, or any other obstacle that stood in the way of what he wanted done, but he did not extend himself over a mere whim. The material must be important. And if it were favorable, noncontroversial, Galen wouldn't be so cautious about it.

Unless one of the Randolphs had been Galen's patient. Michael dismissed that theory at once. Under no circumstances would Galen discuss a patient's case with him. No, the connection had to be something else; and Michael had a pretty good idea as to what it must be.

He tried to remember his first impressions of Galen, but he couldn't pin them down; Galen had just been one of the Old Man's friends, too antique to be interesting. Galen must be over sixty—he had to be, if he and the Old Man had been at school together in Europe, before the last big war. He didn't look it. Physical fitness was something of a fetish with him. Not surprising, perhaps, after the two-year hell of a concentration camp and the desperate years of underground fighting that had preceded the camp. More surprising was Galen's mental stability. There was a certain ruthlessness under that passionless exterior of his, but he was as free of bitterness as he was free of optimism. It was revealing, perhaps, that he never spoke of the war years, or of the wife and small son who had been devoured by the holocaust. His reference to his boyhood pet was one of the few times Michael had ever heard him mention his childhood. His parents, too . . .

It was Michael's father who had been primarily responsible for getting Galen out of the chaos of postwar Germany; the kind of help the old man had given during those years had never been made explicit to Michael, by either man; but after his father's death, Galen was—there. Silent, withdrawn, unsentimental—but there.

Michael shook himself mentally. This was a sidetrack, a waste of time. There was no point in speculating when, in a few hours, he would have the answer in his hands. In the meantime . . .

He thought for another hour. At the end of that time he finally moved, but not much; when he finished, there was on the table a single sheet of paper. It contained only four names, in Michael's cramped writing, but he contemplated the meager results of his labors with grim satisfaction.

Then he picked up the pen and added a phrase after three of the names.

William Wilson. Dead. Suicide?
Tommy Scarinski. Nervous breakdown; attempted suicide.
Joseph Schwartz. Breakdown; drugs.

He paused, pen poised, studying the list. Incredulity was hard to conquer. It seemed so unlikely. . . . Yet there they were, four of the people who had been closest to Gordon Randolph in his adult life. His campaign manager and friend, and his three prize students during that single year as a teacher—a position, surely, that gives a man or woman enormous influence over younger minds. And of those three, one was still a nervous wreck, and another had retreated from a promising career into a world of drug-induced terrors. And the third . . .

The third was Randolph's wife.

III

Threading a tempestuous path through a mammoth traffic jam, Michael blasphemed the beautiful weather and the long weekend. The balmy sunshine had infected half the inhabitants of the city with the urge to flee to Nature. Galen's secretary was one of them. It was after ten that morning when the answering service told him the office wouldn't be open, and he had wasted more time in a futile attempt to track down Galen's secretary. Finally he drove to Galen's house and harassed his manservant until the poor devil consented to open up the office and help him search. That had taken several more hours—the harassment, not the search. Whatever her other failings, Galen's secretary did what she was told. The envelope, with Michael's name typed neatly on it, was in the top drawer of her desk.

Badly as he wanted to examine the contents, another need was stronger. He had wakened that morning with a renewed uneasiness, not so demolishing as the call that had summoned him the night before, but constant and peremptory. He was on his way now to answer it.

He braked, swearing, as a blue Volkswagen roared blithely past on the left and ducked into the nice legal margin between Michael's car and the rear of the one ahead of him. He couldn't even think in this chaos; driving took too much concentration, with so many morons on the road.

He resisted the childish desire to drive right up onto the back fender of the Volkswagen. Today, of all days, he couldn't take any chances. The afternoon was far gone; but he would reach his destination in two or three hours, and by that time he had to have a clearer idea of what he meant to do when he got there. So far the demand had been strong and basic, blotting out all thoughts but one: Get there. Sooner or later, though, he would have to make a plan. He couldn't stand on Andrea's doorstep waiting for another message from Beyond.

Linda must be at Andrea's. It was the only place she knew, the only potential ally who had not failed her. Michael had reached that conclusion logically; direction was one of the elements the mental call had lacked. Gordon had already searched the witch's cottage, which did not lessen the probability of Linda's being there now; the safest hiding place is one that has already been investigated. But she would be wary of visitors in general and hostile toward Michael in particular. Remembering the telephone book, open to the page with Galen's name, Michael felt the same mixture of shame and chagrin that had moved him originally. He wasn't proud of his performance that night. To say the least, it had been stupid. She probably thought of it as betrayal. No, she wouldn't let him into the house, not unless the days of loneliness and fear had reduced her courage to the breaking point. He might have to break into the house—a prospect he faced with surprising equanimity. For such a purpose, darkness would be useful.

But when he stopped at a restaurant in the next town, it was not only because of the need to kill a little more time. He couldn't wait any longer to see what was in Galen's envelope.

It was a big Manila envelope and it was sealed not only by tape but by a heavy wad of sealing wax. The wax was fresh and the envelope clean, which meant that the material it contained must have been gathered together only recently. It was not one of those envelopes so dear to writers of sensational fiction, which has been moldering for years in a secret hiding place until the *deus ex machina* of the book produces it just in time to foil the villain. The envelope was not bulky. It could not contain more than a dozen sheets of paper.

When he had the papers in his hand, Michael sat staring blindly at them for a while before he started to read. He had been expecting what he found; it was, after all, the most logical connecting link between Galen and Randolph. But it was still something of a shock to see again the sprawling, angular handwriting that had once been as familiar as his own.

A letter a week for almost seven years, arriving every Tuesday morning. Careless and unmethodical as his father was about other things, he wrote every Sunday. Michael never kept personal letters after he answered them; there certainly had been no particular point in saving his father's. They were good letters, informative and amusing because of their acidulous comments on people, books, and events. So far as he could remember, the old man had never mentioned Randolph. Which was not surprising; by the time he had left home, Randolph was no longer a student.

His father had written less frequently to Galen, but he had kept up a regular correspondence with his old friend. Galen never threw anything away. These letters were only a small part of the mass of materials that were docketed, labeled, and filed—both in the neat cabinets filling several rooms of Galen's house, and in the latter's capacious memory. Galen had not kept these letters because of a premonition. But he would not have produced them now unless they had significance.

After these optimistic deductions, the first letter was a disappointment. It didn't even mention Randolph's name.

Professor Collins rambled on for two pages about the petty gossip and activities of the university. Michael knew that some of the ivory towers were rat infested, but he had forgotten how largely small malices can loom, even to a mind that is supposed to wander in the airy realms of ideas. Cheating on examinations, unexpected pregnancies, a rumor of students dabbling in black magic . . . Nothing was new on the campuses. There was only one name mentioned in the letter, that of a student for whom his father had high hopes. His name was Randolph.

Puzzled and deflated, Michael put the letter aside. Maybe Galen's secretary had made a mistake, or else Galen had told her to include all the letters dated to a particular year. He could hardly quote specific identifying details over the telephone, especially when he hadn't read the letters for over ten years.

Michael felt sure of this hypothesis when he started the next letter and found Randolph's name in the opening paragraph. The context was not precisely what he had come to expect of Gordon Randolph.

"These sporadic flashes of brilliance baffle me," his father had written of the school's star athlete and president of the student body. "I expected great things of the boy, he's already a school legend, but he never happened to take any of my courses until this year—which is his last. I'd say that literature simply wasn't his field, if it weren't for that rare outstanding essay."

The rest was inconsequential, for Michael's purposes. There was another reference to the devil worshipers, whose existence was now a well-established rumor. His father found them exasperating, whoever they were: "They've been reading about the Hellfire Club and decided to imitate that bunch of nasty-minded little——"

The next word was indecipherable; which, Michael thought, with a reminiscent grin, was probably just as well. His father's collection of epithets and expletives were drawn from the riper Restoration dramatists; some of them had curled his hair even in his supercilious high school days.

As he read on, his sentimental nostalgia increased; but so did his bewilderment. There were eight letters in all. One of them didn't even mention Randolph, the others contained more references to his father's pet student—what was the kid's name?—Al Something—than to Gordon. Poor old Dad must have been losing his grip, Michael thought. Gordon was only a few years away from his great book; according to the publisher's blurb, parts of it had actually been written while he was in college. If his father hadn't spotted a talent of that magnitude . . .

The last letter was no more informative, but it was something of a shocker. His father's handwriting was shakier than usual, and his sentences were so garbled by emotion as to be relatively incoherent in parts. The feeble idiocy of the campus

Hellfire Club had exploded into scandal and disaster; one student was dead as a result of an occult experiment, which his father's Victorian inhibitions had kept him from describing in detail. And that student was the boy for whom he had had such hopes—Alfred Green.

Large as the affair had been in the minuscule world of the university, it hadn't made much of a splash in the press. Michael remembered hearing something about it, but the influential board of trustees had succeeded in suppressing the details. Still, reading between the lines, it must have been a nasty business. The word was his father's. It kept recurring, through the scribbled agitation of the lines: nasty, foul, disgusting. It would seem that way to him, Michael thought. Then, at the end of the letter, came a hasty postscript.

"Young Randolph came by this evening, to express his regrets. Alfred was one of his closest friends. It was kind of the boy, and perceptive, to know that this has hurt me worse than an ordinary scandal would have done. Perhaps I haven't been fair to him. Antipathy is an odd thing."

Michael sat staring at the last page for

a long time, while the cigarette burned down between his lax fingers and his second cup of coffee grew cold. He felt completely deflated. He had expected a complete, startling answer to the enigma that had begun as a simple problem of character, and which had now taken on such ominous outlines. But there was no answer in these letters, only new questions. In the back of his mind the mental call still pulled, confusing what wits he had left.

It was not until he was trudging through a blue twilight on his way to the place where he had left the car that he realized what the letters had told him. Another death. Randolph's triumphant career seemed to be unnecessarily littered with corpses.

He forgot this new piece of the puzzle, which was merely an addition to his list rather than a clue as to why the list existed, as he drove through the streets of the village near Randolph's estate. The street lights had come on and the houses looked peaceful and homey, with lights twinkling through the gathering darkness. The temperature had dropped, though; the wind that tossed the boughs was sharp. He rolled up the car window.

He hit a snag when he turned into the curving streets of the suburb. He had already observed that the inhabitants of Brentwood liked their privacy. There were no quaint mailboxes with names on them along the curving drives and walled estates. There weren't many street lights, either. Maybe the rich didn't need them. They had their own methods of guarding against crime—burglar alarms, dogs, even private guards.

Nor did Andrea court publicity. Michael found the house at last only because it was at the end of the sole road that was unpaved and unlandscaped. A survival from a simpler past, he thought, jouncing down the rutty lane. If there was a house down here, it was well hidden. Mud squelched under the tires, and he had visions of being thoroughly stuck, at the end of a road that petered out into forest.

As the thought formed, the road ended. The dark shapes of trees loomed up, and Michael jammed on the brakes, skidding. He saw the gate, and knew that he had arrived.

It was the sort of gate Andrea might have had constructed to her specifications if she had set up shop as a newly certified witch—wooden, rickety, sagging on rusted hinges. Thick, untrimmed shrubs concealed the path beyond and leaned out over the fence like watchful sentries. The house beyond was visible only as a crazy shape of roofs and chimneys that cut off a section of starry sky. There was no light, and no sign of human life.

Shapes other than man-made cut off the starlight. Half the sky was curtained by clouds. The wind lifted Michael's hair from his forehead and turned the boughs of the tall shrubs into armed appendages, which thrust out in abrupt challenge. The clouds hung heaviest toward the east. As Michael watched, distracted from his search by the eerie movement of the night, a glow of light flickered above the tops of the pines, like the ghost of a sick sunset. It was followed by a slow, far-off roll of thunder.

Practical considerations intruded on the fascination of the approaching storm. This trek might turn out to be more disastrous than a plain old wild-goose chase. The road was already gluey with mud; another heavy rain could maroon him in this abandoned lane. He had better check the house.

The mental call that had brought him a hundred miles was gone.

When it had left—if it had ever existed, save in his imagination—he could not remember. But its absence left him feeling blind or deaf, bereft of a sense that had, even in so short a time, become something he depended on as uncritically as he accepted the use of his eyes. For the first time in nearly twenty-four hours he examined his activities in the cold light of reason, and found them folly. Only his inborn stubbornness brought his hand to the latch of the gate.

It screeched rustily. He had half expected that it would, but the sound, shattering the quiet night, made him jump. As he took a tentative step forward, something streaked across the path in front of him. He grabbed instinctively at the branch of the shrub, stabbed his thumb on something sharp, and let out a yell. The shrub had thorns.

The darting streak that crossed his path hadn't triggered any fantasies, though; he knew what it was—a cat, one of the dozen that Andrea was reputed to keep. He wondered where the others were, and what arrangements Andrea made for their comfort while she was off on her frequent trips. Then he realized that all the shrubbery was alive with movement. The action of the wind made the foliage mutter; but there were other sounds. Small, ground-level movements rustled branches and made leaves whisper. He saw something glow into life at the base of a bush near the house—two small round dots of red fire. The cats prowled.

He went down the path, feeling with feet and extended hands. The clouds had grown heavier; there was no moon, and even the faint starlight became increasingly obscured. He found the house by running into it, literally. By daylight it was probably attractive; there was a low porch, flanked by pillars and draped with vines. He had banged his head on one of the pillars. The roof hung low, almost brushing his head. He made his way to the door and fumbled for a bell or a knocker.

This was the moment of low ebb. The expedition seemed utterly futile, his mood of the last few hours a wild delusion. The door did not seem to have a bell, and even if he found some means of making his presence known, he did not expect an answer. Then lightning split the sky—nearer now, a thin sword of light instead of a far-off glow. For a split second he saw the details of the door starkly outlined—brass knocker shaped like a frog's head, small leaded window, even the splinters in the wooden panels where impatient cats had demanded entry. Then the light vanished, leaving his eyes blinded. But his muscles remembered, and his hand found the knocker.

The damn thing made a sound like a brass drum. Echoes rolled into the windy night; he heard them mutter and die inside, beyond the door. Then the panels moved.

The inside of the house was darker than the night. He saw only the pale oval of her face, suspended in blackness. He never doubted her identity, even though she seemed smaller than he remembered, as small as a child, as small as a bent old woman.

"I knew it was you," she said, in a breathy whisper.

Michael nodded, than realized that she could see no more of him than he could see of her.

"I figured you'd be here."

"Why didn't you come before?"

"It wasn't until last night that I got your—" Michael stopped; it was hard enough to mention his fantastic experience, but the phrase he had been about to use reduced it to insanity, as if the thing he had received had been a telegram or phone call.

Then he realized she was not listening. She was looking past him, out into the dark garden.

He was slower to perceive. He realized first that the wind had died; leaf and bough hung motionless, as if in apprehension of what was coming. He thought, *This is going to be one hell of a storm.* And he knew the thought for what it was —the desperate defense of the commonplace against a phenomenon it was afraid to admit. For the stillness was abnormal. Linda's hand gripped his arm, her fingers digging in like claws. At the same instant the silence burst. He recognized the sounds, but they sounded different, here, than they had coming from the back alleys of the city. Cats. The howls and snarls seemed to come from more than a dozen feline throats. The shrubbery was animate with glowing eyes and flying bodies.

The fury of the cats might have warned him, if he had had time to think. The next flash of lightning came too quickly; it caught him unprepared. The storm was moving in. All the horizon was dark with boiling masses of cloud, and the thunderclap came close on the heels of the light, booming like a cannon's roar. In the ghastly gray-blue light he saw it. Standing stiff-legged and huge, it might have been only a monstrous image, cut out of basalt or obsidian. But the pricked, listening ears were alive, and so were the eyes, glowing with an inner fire. When the darkness returned, he felt as if every light in the world had failed, and the darkness was worse than the vision itself, because he knew it was still out there, waiting—the black dog.

Eight

Linda knew it would be better there. Since the thing first appeared to her, she had developed a special sensitivity; she didn't have to see it now, to know it was coming. It was a tension in her very bones, like fear, a stench like the foulness of decay. But familiarity did not breed contempt, or acceptance. Every time she saw it, the feeling was worse. She would have stood there, frozen, if Michael had not pushed her into the house and slammed the door.

Two inches of wood were a frail barrier against the thing in the garden. But it seemed to cut off some of the aura of terror that enveloped it. Only then did she realize the enormous importance of what had happened.

"You saw it," she gasped. "Oh, God,

oh, God—*you* saw it!''

''I saw it.'' His voice was queer; she thought that the emotion that made it shake was fear, until he went on, ''God forgive me. I thought you were imagining it.''

He caught her to him, holding her so tightly that breathing was an effort. For a long moment she stood quiescent in his arms, recognizing the impulse for what it was, a desire untouched by ordinary physical passion. She felt it too—the reassurance of contact with another living human body.

''You're not afraid,'' she murmured.

''Like hell I'm not,'' Michael said promptly. ''Linda—what is it?''

''You saw it.''

''Yes, and I know too well that eyesight is a damned unreliable witness. We can't stand here all night. Are you sure it can't get into the house?''

''I'm not sure what it can do.''

''That's comforting. Aren't there any lights in this hole? I'd be happier if I could see what was coming at me. I think.''

''Of course there are lights. I was afraid to use them, before.''

As she switched the lights on, Michael turned from the door. He had been peering out through the small window, and he answered her question before she could voice it aloud.

"Nothing there now. I could see clearly during that last big flash."

"It's gone," she said. "Not—vanished. Withdrawn."

"You can feel it? Sense it? Damn the language, it's inadequate."

"I can tell when it's coming, sometimes. But not long in advance."

Michael laughed, a short, explosive sound that held no amusement. The antique wall sconce, which was the sole source of light in the hall, held pink bulbs shaped like candle flames—one of Andrea's cuter affectations. The rosy light gave Michael's cheeks a healthy flush, but she knew, by the shape of the lines around his mouth, that he was badly shaken.

"We're talking about it as if it were susceptible to natural laws," he muttered. "Damn it, I'm still not ready to admit that it isn't. It was the shock of seeing it like that, when I hadn't . . . And you've been living with that for—how long?"

"I don't know. . . . Months."

"And you've held on to your sanity."

"By the width of a fingernail," she said. "By the breadth of a hair."

Separated from her by the width of the hall, Michael did not move; but the steady dark eyes held hers with a look that was as palpable as a touch, and as expressive as a page of print. Linda knew the look; no woman with a single normal instinct could have failed to read it. Her eyes fell before his, and after a moment he spoke in a casual tone.

"As a companion in a haunted house you're not very cheering. You look like a little ghost yourself. How long has it been since you've had any sleep, or a decent meal? And speaking of food, I'm starved. Is there anything in the house except toad-stools and henbane?"

"Yes, of course. Come out to the kitchen."

While she made coffee and scraped together a scanty meal, Michael wandered around the kitchen making casual remarks. This was an interlude of comparative sanity in the midst of madness; both of them recognized its artificiality, just as they recognized the need for a breathing space. But she knew that he looked out the window each time he passed it, and she did not miss the fleeting glance he gave the door. It was bolted and chained; Andrea had left it that way, and she had checked those bolts daily, knowing their inadequacy but knowing, as well, that no precaution could be neglected. Only once did he refer to the thing that loomed large in both their minds.

"The cats," he exclaimed, as a tabby-striped tom appeared, demanding sustenance. "How do they get in and out?"

"One of those pet doors, in the cellar. No," she said, as he made an involuntary movement of alarm. "It's too small for anything but a cat. You know how they can compress themselves—like rubber—"

"Yes, I know," he said.

The meal was a poor one—she had depleted Andrea's stock of food—but Linda ate ravenously. She hadn't had much appetite the last few days. Michael watched her with satisfaction, eating little himself. She didn't blame him; canned lima beans and tuna fish were unappealing unless you were half starved. When she pushed her empty plate away and looked up, she found him braced and ready.

"Talk to me," he said. "I don't know how much time we have."

"About—it?" She made a helpless gesture with her hands. "How can I? How do you talk about something that is either supernatural or else a—"

"Delusion? You still believe that?"

"At first, when you saw it too, I thought . . . But Michael, you've heard of collective hallucinations."

"The fact that you can still admit that possibility is a good indication of your sanity," Michael said. "I'm willing to admit it myself, but only as one theory among others. Linda, are you sure that damned thing isn't real? That it isn't an actual, living dog?"

"There is no such animal in the neighborhood. Believe me, I made sure."

"A wild dog? Even a wolf? It sounds unlikely, I know, but—"

"Even a wolf can't live without food. Sooner or later it would rob a poultry yard, or attack a pet animal. It might not be seen, but its presence would certainly be known."

"And no one else has seen it?"

"No . . ." She found it hard to meet his eyes after that admission, but he seemed undismayed.

"Not Andrea?"

"She knows about it," Linda admitted. "She believes in it. But she's never seen it."

"Odd," Michael muttered. "That she hasn't seen it. She believes it's supernatural, of course."

"Of course. But don't make the obvious mistake about Andrea. For all her superstitions, she has a hard core of common sense. She can believe in various fantastic phenomena, but she doesn't imagine things. There's a difference."

"I know what you mean. I could believe in flying saucers without too much effort; there has been a certain amount of evidence. But I can't believe that I saw one land, and a bunch of little green guys get out of it, unless I have a screw loose somewhere."

"None of Andrea's screws are loose. She has some screws in unusual places, though."

Michael laughed.

"Then you and I are the only ones who have seen the dog," he said. "When did you see it first?"

"It's hard to remember exactly. . . .

About a year ago, I guess. I remember the occasion very clearly, though."

"I can see why you might."

"I went for a walk, at twilight. I like that time of day—at least I used to. I wasn't in a very happy mood. There had been . . . words, with Gordon. I walked out under the trees, just wandering around. The ground was wet and soggy, but everything smelled so fresh and sweet. The sky was a pale greenish blue, there was a new moon. I went down that avenue of cherry trees. It ends, if you remember, at a fence; there's a pretty view from that point, out across the pastures.

"I was leaning on the fence, thinking, when—there it was. I saw it quite distinctly; the light was fading, but it seemed to stand out, as if something shone behind it. I was frightened, but only because it appeared so suddenly, out of nowhere, and because it was a fierce-looking dog and a stranger. Honestly, Michael, I couldn't be mistaken about that, I really like dogs, I was friends with all the neighbors' pets. . . . Well, I knew better than to run, but I retreated as quickly as I could. It didn't follow me. Not until later did I realize that it hadn't moved, or made a sound, the whole time. It just stood there, looking at me. . . .''

''When did you start to think that it might not be a real dog?''

''Not that time. Not even when a search failed to turn up any sign of such an animal. Gordon was alarmed when I told him,'' she said expressionlessly. ''He insisted on looking for it, right then, even though it was almost dark. He and the yard servants searched again next morning, and he called all the neighbors, and the police, to see if anyone else had reported seeing it. No one had. But the worst was . . . I told you the ground was soft and wet. When they searched the field where I had seen it, they found no prints.''

From Michael's expression, she realized that, despite his comments, he had been clinging to the hope that the creature was material. This piece of news hit him hard.

''How could prints show on grass?''

''There were large bare patches,'' she said inexorably. ''Something would have shown, somewhere.''

''I see. But that wouldn't be enough, in itself, to convince you that you were having hallucinations.''

''No. I didn't start thinking that until

Jack Briggs failed to see it, the next time it came."

"If he wasn't looking . . ."

"It ran straight across the terrace while we were looking out the drawing-room window. It went fast, but it was in sight for several seconds. That's a long time, Michael."

"Long enough. Any other non-witnesses?"

"Several. My maid, for one. That was from an upstairs window, of course, and it was pretty dark."

"Not easy to see in that kind of light, especially if she had already been told you were suffering from hallucinations. Most people see only what they expect to see."

"Gordon told her something," Linda said doubtfully. "I think he must have warned all the servants about me. They started treating me peculiarly about that time. But God knows I was acting pretty peculiarly anyhow."

"I imagine he pays excellent salaries, doesn't he? Yes; money, and his famous charm, could convince them of anything he wanted them to believe."

The room was full of cats by this time —fat cats, thin cats, striped, spotted, and

Siamese. One of them jumped onto the table, with that uncanny suggestion of teleportation that surrounds a cat's suave quickness, and Linda stood up, overturning her chair.

"What are you trying to prove?" she demanded wildly. "You still don't believe in it, do you? You think it's real."

Michael stroked the cat, a round orange creature, which was investigating his half-empty plate.

"That shouldn't be the main point, for you," he said mildly.

"I'm grateful, don't think I'm not. Whether it's real or just a plain apparition, it isn't a figment of my imagination, or you wouldn't have seen it too. You aren't the suggestible type. You've come a long way to bolster me up, to support me. But you'd stop—you couldn't go on—if you knew what I really believe. . . ."

The lights flickered and faded, leaving the room in brown obscurity; and a violent clap of thunder seemed to rock the foundations of the house. Linda covered her face with her hands. On the roof, a thousand minuscule feet began dancing. The rain had started.

Michael stood up. He had scooped up

the cat, to keep it out of his food; and the animal, already full, hung complacently from his hands with a full-moon smirk on its fat face. The contrast between its furry blandness and Michael's drawn features turned Linda's cry of alarm into a semihysterical gasp of laughter.

"Stop it," Michael said sharply. "You're losing your grip—no wonder, in this place. . . ."

He turned, looking helplessly around the room, which still swam in an evil dimness. The stuffed monster dangling from the ceiling seemed to grin more broadly, and the heavy beams seemed to sag. Outside the window, the night was livid with the fury of the storm. But Linda noticed how gentle his hands were, holding the unwanted bundle of cat. Finally he put it back on the table, with the air of a man who is abandoning lesser niceties, and sat down firmly on his chair. The cat started licking his plate. Michael regarded it curiously.

"The cats are calm enough now," he said. "They blew their stacks when it was outside."

Linda dropped back into her chair.

“Cats are traditionally sensitive to influences from the other side,” she said dully.

Michael’s head turned sharply; on the verge of speaking, he caught himself, and she knew that his comment, when he did speak, was not the one he had meant to make.

“It only appears at dusk, or in a dim light?”

“Yes. Michael, I know what you’re trying to do. But it won’t work. The fact that the thing only comes at night is just as much confirmation of my theory as of yours.”

“You think it’s supernatural, then,” he said calmly. “Something from—the dark on the other side.”

“Don’t! Why did you say that?”

“Never mind, I’ll get to that later. All right, so it’s supernatural. The supernatural has many forms. What precisely is this thing? A hound of hell, *à la* Conan Doyle? A manifestation of hate and ill will? The old Nick in one of his standard transformations? A werewolf, or a . . .”

His voice trailed off and his eyes widened. Linda nodded. She felt quite numb now that the moment of truth was upon her, but she felt no impulse to conceal that truth. Even if he stood up and walked out of the house, leaving her more alone than she had ever been, she had to be honest with him.

"The word is too simple," she said. "But—yes. That's what it is. It's Gordon."

II

The lights had returned to normal. The storm muttered more softly, held in abeyance. Linda sat with her hands folded in her lap, watching Michael as he paced up and down. He was followed by an entourage of interested cats; but the sight of Michael as a feline Pied Piper did not seem amusing. His distress was too great.

"I can't buy it," he said, swinging around to face her. "I've believed in enough mad things in the last few hours so that you'd think a little detail like that wouldn't stick in my craw. But it does."

"I didn't expect you to believe it," she said.

His face twisted, as if a sudden pain had struck him. She watched the spasm with dull disinterest, wondering why he felt such distress. The lethargy that gripped her was pleasant, compared to what she had endured; she knew how a patient must feel after a critical session with his analyst, or a penitent after a bad session in the confessional—drained, empty, oddly at peace.

"How about settling for an abstract manifestation of evil?" Michael suggested hopefully, and won a wan smile in response. "I'm serious," he insisted. "Half serious, anyhow . . . Linda, you've been through a terrible strain, it would be a miracle if your nerves were normal. I'm not suggesting that you're insane, I wouldn't be talking to you like this if I thought so. But isn't it possible that you've concocted this—this fantastic theory out of a very real, legitimate fear of Gordon?"

She looked up, a faint spark of interest in her face.

"You're willing to admit that I might have a legitimate fear of a paragon like Gordon?"

"He's no paragon," Michael said slowly. "Not of virtue, anyhow. I don't know what he is. But I'm ready to concede that there's something seriously amiss with him. I'm all the more willing to admit it because it cost me such a struggle to admit it. Linda, do you remember a boy named Joe Schwartz? He was a student of Gordon's when you were in that class."

"Joe? Of course I remember him. He wrote some of the funniest, most scurrilous verses I've ever heard."

"Scurrilous?"

"About the professors, and the other students, and human foibles in general. Some topical, some more basic. He had a gift for hitting people's weaknesses, but he was never cruel; he could sting, delicately, without really burning. None of the parties that year were a success unless Joe performed. He'd sit there on the floor whanging out chords on his guitar and bellowing out his infamous comments in a raucous voice, grinning from ear to ear. . . . Why are you looking like that?"

"It doesn't sound like the Joe Schwartz I know," Michael said grimly.

"He did get a little peculiar toward the end of the year. People said he'd changed. I'm afraid I wasn't much aware of others just then. Love's young dream, you know."

Michael looked uncomfortable, but he went on doggedly.

"What about Tommy Scarinski?"

"You've been busy, haven't you? Yes, he was one of Gordon's acolytes. Always unstable, of course . . . At the time, I thought he was preying on Gordon, instead of . . ."

"The reverse?"

"You don't understand a process, sometimes, until it happens to you personally."

"We're getting there," Michael said. He spoke slowly, without looking at her. "We try to talk around it, but we'll have to discuss it sooner or later. Why, Linda? Why is he doing this?"

"I don't think I could explain it to you—or to any other man."

She hadn't meant it to hurt, but it did; she could tell from the change in his face. She went on quickly,

"You see? I can't talk about it without sounding like one of the militant feminists you men despise—like an embittered woman whose marriage has gone sour and who rants about the whole male sex instead of facing facts. But it wasn't like that. I'm not a romantic adolescent, I know that few relationships, marital or otherwise, are based on true equality and respect. As a rule, one partner dominates the other; and in human society there's a long tradition of masculine superiority. So —all right, I could have accepted that, I'm conditioned to it. Maybe I even wanted it. But Gordon doesn't want to dominate people; he wants to absorb them, body and soul and spirit. Living with him was—indescribable. I felt as if he were fastened to me, like a gigantic leech, pulling out every ounce of will, every thought. . . . I can see myself making that speech in a divorce court, can't you? It might come straight out of some ghastly day-time serial."

"Why didn't you leave him?"

"I did leave him. He brought me back." She laughed bitterly. "That sounds ridiculous, doesn't it? In this day and age . . . But it was so easy, really. I had to get a job, I didn't have much money. I never did. Credit cards, charge accounts, but no cash. I couldn't very well go to one of the big hotels and charge my escapade to Gordon's account. Even if I'd had the gall, I knew it would make it easier to him to find me. So I had to get a job—and quickly; I couldn't pick and choose.

I have a B.A. degree, no special training; you'd be surprised how few jobs there are for women with no special skills and no experience. Even my typing was rusty, after all those years. I turned down a couple of offers because there were special conditions of employment involved, and I was in no mood for another man who wanted to own even that small part of me. I don't know . . . I've never known . . . how many jobs I lost because of Gordon's quiet influence—he must have located me immediately—and how many because of the ordinary handicaps of my situation. There were a few things I didn't try: washing dishes, ushering at movie theaters. . . . It wasn't false pride; I was afraid of places like that."

The look in Michael's eyes hurt her, and yet she found a perverse pleasure in seeing how deeply she could move him.

"I finally got a job as live-in maid and baby-sitter for a family in the suburbs," she went on. "I held it for three days before the woman told me she didn't need me. I'm pretty sure that was Gordon's pressure; household help is darned hard to get these days. Maybe he told the woman I was mentally disturbed.

"I was pretty desperate by then. When Gordon popped into my slummy little hotel room, with his tame psychiatrist in tow, I was in no condition to put up a fight. It probably wouldn't have mattered, even if I could have kept my cool; the doctor was under Gordon's famous spell. But of course I didn't stay calm, I started yelling and screaming, and got an injection for my pains. When I woke up, I was back—home. And all the servants walked around shaking their heads and sighing. I thought at first that I'd try again, plan more carefully—scrape together enough money to get away, a long way away. But it is not easy to fool Gordon. And—I just didn't have the strength. It took all the energy I had to keep myself from giving in, from admitting that I was losing my mind."

Michael stooped and picked up a tiger kitten, which had gone to sleep on his foot. The motion of bending brought a little color back to his face.

"I still don't understand why," he said.

"Why Gordon wants to have me declared insane? I wouldn't be sent to a sanatorium, you know; he'd keep me at home, in a nice quiet padded cell, with nice quiet attendants watching me every second. Gordon doesn't give things away, or let go of the things he owns. He discards them; they don't leave him. Does that degree of vanity seem monstrous to you? It does to me, too; but that's Gordon, he's always been that way, he cannot endure rejection. Especially from me. I gave him love, devotion, admiration—but they weren't enough. When he demanded more, I started to fight back. But that's the insidious thing about a plan like his. How do you prove you're sane? It's a vicious circle; the more desperate and frightened you become, the more erratically you behave; before long you begin to wonder yourself, and then the progression downhill is rapid. I started drinking. But not until after I tried—"

"I know about that," Michael said quickly.

"You do? Oh, of course, he'd tell you that. And you—you came here?"

Michael shook his head, dismissing irrelevancies.

"I don't know what made you do it," he said. "But the end result is clear."

"Oh, yes, it was the final bar on the prison door. If I tried to escape again, he had the ultimate weapon. I was dangerous—homicidal—and he had witnesses to prove it."

"Good Lord," Michael muttered. His fingers continued their automatic caress of the kitten, which was curled in the crook of his arm, purring loudly. Linda watched the animal, using it, illogically perhaps, as a kind of live barometer. So long as the cats were quiet . . .

"But I did it," Linda went on. "I don't remember anything that preceded it, but I remember lying there on the floor, with the knife beside me, where it had fallen from my hand. There was blood on the knife. . . . He'd knocked me down; you can't blame him for that. He wasn't even particularly rough about it. The lights were blazing and the room seemed to be filled with people, and Gordon stood there with blood running down the sleeve of his shirt. . . ."

"Shirt? Wasn't he in pajamas?"

"I don't think so. . . . No. Does it matter?"

"Not really. But it stimulates my nasty suspicious mind. You don't remember actually striking the blow?"

Suddenly it was difficult for her to

speak, or to look at him.

"You do go all the way when you take up a cause," she whispered. "Michael, it's no use. I wouldn't remember that, it's the one thing my mind would utterly reject, would blot out. But I . . . had thought about it. Sometimes it seemed to me that I could hear the words, they were so loud in my mind: *Kill him. It's the only way you can ever get away*. You can twist and evade all you like, but you can't free me of that act—or excuse it. There's no excuse for killing, unless it's the only means of defense left to you. And he was not threatening my life."

"What about your soul?"

"Don't," she said breathlessly. "Don't talk about that. It's the excuse I've used . . . but I'm not sure I believe in the soul."

"Maybe that's not the right name. But it exists—some entity other than the body. It brought me here—your call."

"My call?"

"That's not a good word either, but I can't describe it because I've never felt anything I can compare it with. It hit me last night—a sudden, peremptory mental calling. You wanted me, you needed me, and I had to find you.''

"But I didn't call you,'' she said slowly. "Not that way or any other way.''

Michael stared.

"You must have. I couldn't have been so sure without . . . Last night, near midnight—didn't you ask for help? Not necessarily of me—a prayer, a mental plea . . .''

"No. Nothing.''

"Then who . . .''

In his surprise, Michael almost dropped the kitten. It eluded his fumbling hands, jumped down, and streaked for the door. In the silence they both heard the sounds. There was someone, or something, at the front door.

They moved closer together, like children afraid of the dark; their hands groped and clasped. Linda's first impulse, to hide, was canceled by Michael's behavior. He stood rock-still, facing the darkened doorway; and Linda accepted his decision. Whatever it was, running away wouldn't help.

But when the opening door was followed by the sound of footsteps coming slowly down the hall, she went limp with relief. She recognized those footsteps.

Andrea stood in the doorway like a

figure straight out of Grimm. The black, hooded cloak she wore, even while grocery shopping in the village, blended with the darkness of the hallway behind her, so that her wrinkled face stood out with uncanny distinctness. Over her arm was the basket she carried in lieu of a purse. She paid no attention to the cats, who were weaving patterns around her feet, but surveyed her unexpected visitors without surprise.

"I thought you'd be here," she said.

Linda would have accepted that statement as an example of the old woman's boasted ESP, but when Andrea raised a hand to push back her hood, she realized that there might be another explanation. Andrea was trembling. Terror and a strange exultation blended in her face.

"It's out there," she said. "Waiting for you. I saw it. Heavenly saints—I saw it!"

"It can't be," Linda gasped. "The cats didn't notice."

"There is a circle of protection woven about this house," Andrea chanted. The effect was only slightly marred by her stagger as she crossed the room to put down her basket and lay her cloak aside.

"Where was it?" Michael asked.

"Under the white lilac bush at the side of the house." Fumbling in a cupboard, Andrea accepted his presence without question. She straightened up with a bottle in her hand, jerked out the cork, and put the bottle to her lips. She drank deeply, her prominent Adam's apple bobbing up and down. When she lowered the bottle she shuddered, and wiped her mouth with the back of her hand.

"I needed that," she said. "Have some?"

"No, thanks," Michael said.

"Suit yourself."

Andrea put the bottle down on the table. Michael's eyes moved from it to Andrea, to Linda, and then off into space; and Linda knew that he had deduced the source of her private liquor supply. He must have wondered about that. . . .

Andrea got a glass from the cupboard and poured herself a stiff drink. Michael moved, as if in protest; and Andrea gave him a hostile glance.

"Need this," she muttered. "Had a bad shock."

"Why a shock?" Michael asked coldly. "You're the one who believes in demons."

Andrea collapsed onto the nearest chair. A cat left it, in the nick of time.

"Poor Tommy," Andrea crooned, reaching out an unsteady hand. "Did Mama hurt the baby?"

Michael's mouth curled expressively, and Linda turned on him.

"Leave her alone! She's not young, and her heart isn't too good."

"Nothing wrong with my heart," Andrea said decisively. She shoved the bottle away and set her empty glass down with a thud. "I said I needed that, and I did. As for you, Mr. Collins, if you're such a pretty little skeptic, what the hell are you doing here? Stooging for the great Gordon Randolph? The delectable decoy, to lead her out into his waiting—claws?"

Michael took a step toward her and stopped himself with an effort that left him shaking.

"Sit down," Andrea said gruffly. "I take it back. If you are a decoy, you're an unwitting one. I know what you're thinking—this crazy old bat has corrupted the innocent girl with her weird ideas of witchcraft. Baby, I didn't give Linda the idea. She gave it to me. And, God help me, I didn't believe her until tonight. I saw him. I knew him. He's waiting out there, waiting for her. He can't get in. Not yet. But he's summoning his powers. Can't you feel them, growing, feeding on evil? Soon he'll be strong enough. Soon he'll come."

The high, crooning voice was semihypnotic. Crouched in her chair, monotonously stroking the black cat that had sprung to her lap, Andrea cast a spell of conviction. Michael shook himself.

"I thought you said you had a protective spell around the house," he said.

"Ordinary white magic, against ordinary intruders. This isn't ordinary. He's strong. Very strong. But it takes time to build up the power. It's building now. Can't you feel it? I can feel it. Like electricity in the air. When it's strong enough—then he'll come for her."

The cat's fur crackled under her moving hand.

"What does he want?" Michael demanded. "Damn it, there has to be a reason, even if it's a crazy reason. What is he after?"

Linda felt like a spectator, or a piece of meat over which two merchants were haggling. She hated the feeling, but she could not fight it; the force of the other personalities was too strong. They faced one another like duelists. Michael's fists were clenched. Andrea's weapons were more subtle—the crooning voice, the air of conviction.

"He's after her soul," she said softly. "Her immortal soul. His own is already in pawn to the powers of darkness. He wants hers, not to redeem his own, but to suffer with him, in flames, through eternity."

Michael turned away.

"That's insane."

"Why should you stop at that, when you've accepted so much?" Andrea asked, in the same insidious whine. "You came here to save her, didn't you? Oh, you don't need to answer; I know, I know it all. I've seen the thread, the silver thread that binds the two of you. It's knotted and tarnished now, but there's no break in it. It will bind you forever, into death and beyond. It drew you here, to her side, when she needed you."

Andrea stood up. The cat slid down like a pool of viscous ink. There was a power in the old woman, if only the power of her belief. It forced Michael to face her.

"But you can't save her," she said.

"Love is a strong force, the purity of the soul is stronger; but nothing can avail against the powers of darkness except the concentrated power of good. And only I can control that power. I can save her. And I will! All my life, all my studies, have led me toward this moment."

Michael spoke to Linda. He had himself under control now; there was even a certain compassion in his face as he glanced at the old woman.

"Will you stay here, with her?" he asked. "Or will you come with me, now? The choice is yours, Linda. It has to be yours."

Linda hesitated. The tone of his appeal reached her, drawing on some core of sanity and strength. The appeal of being allowed—no, forced—to decide her own fate was something only she could fully appreciate, after years of life with Gordon. Michael waited patiently for her to answer, but Andrea did not.

"No, no," she shrieked. Rushing toward Linda, she caught at the girl's shoulders with both hands. They felt like bird's claws, fragile and fleshless.

"You can't go out there," she whimpered. "Don't think it, don't dream it.

He doesn't understand. He wants you, he wants you for himself, to save you for himself and keep you. Make him stay. He can help. He can help if he will, he's strong and young. . . . But if he will go, don't go with him. Stay. I'll save you. Andrea will save you, she knows. . . ."

"All right," Linda said. "All right, Andrea."

She turned to Michael.

"I can't go," she said. "It isn't only because of Andrea. I'm afraid, Michael. I'm afraid to go out into the dark—even with you."

She knew that Andrea's hysteria had convinced Michael, but not in the way she had hoped. The very wildness of Andrea's appeal had swayed his mind back toward rational rejection. If there ever was an obvious picture, this is it, Linda thought dully—a crazy old woman and a weak-minded young one. She wondered how much of her decision to stay was due to her pity for Andrea rather than fear—and how much to her instinctive recoil from one of Andrea's statements: "He wants you for himself."

"We'll stay, then," Michael said. "If that's what you want. I guess it can't do any harm."

Her purpose achieved, Andrea turned brisk and businesslike. The volte-face was so sudden that Linda was left wondering, futilely, how much of Andrea was real and how much was calculated theatricalism.

"We must begin," Andrea said, rubbing her hands together. "At once. The time is short. Purification. It must be symbolic. I daren't let you out of my sight. Come along, both of you."

Andrea's workroom, as she called it, was a small separate building, once a shed or outdoor kitchen, now connected to the house by a low-ceilinged passageway. Linda heard Michael's gasp, and sympathized; if the kitchen had been picturesque, this room came straight out of the pages of alchemy.

Its single window was heavily draped. There were no electric lights. Andrea moved about lighting candles—candles in bottles, candles in tall brass candlesticks, candles stuck onto saucers in puddles of grease, candles in glass-covered brackets on the wall. In their eerie, moving light, the room looked even more uncanny than it did by daylight.

A long, rough table was completely covered with a fantastic collection of miscellany, from papers of all sizes, shapes, and colors, to samples of dried vegetation. Small baskets, boxes, and ordinary brown paper bags were stewn about. One pile of papers, whose vivid colors and angular shapes suggested Japanese origami creations, was held down by a human skull. Another, narrower, table had oddly shaped glass bottles and beakers, filled with colored liquids, like those in an old-fashioned pharmacist's window. The contents of the flasks glowed, lambent in the mellow candlelight—sea blue, crimson, gold, and green. Rough wooden shelves along one wall held a collection of crumbling leather books. The walls, of white-washed, unfinished planks, were hung with drawings and diagrams. Dominating the room, on the wall opposite the door, was a huge medieval crucifix with its tormented Image, flanked by glass-covered candle sconces. The center of the floor was empty and uncarpeted and almost without varnish after centuries of traffic. The air in the room was close and stale, permeated by a cloyingly sweet smell.

As soon as the candles were lighted,

Andrea fumbled in the basket she had brought with her. Another scent, pungently different but equally unpleasant, wafted forth to war with the stench of stale incense. Linda recognized it; her guess was confirmed when Andrea scooped up a double handful of small whitish-gray bulbs. She opened her hands and the bulbs separated, like the Dutch chocolate apples which are made up of pre-formed slices; but instead of dropping to the floor, the segments of garlic hung from her hands, suspended on long pieces of twine.

Michael sneezed.

"God bless you," Andrea said, with the force of an incantation.

She draped the threaded cloves of garlic over the window and the threshold of the closed door. Michael watched silently. Linda watched Michael. She saw, with growing despair, that the pendulum of his thinking had swung back, toward the rational world and away from her. Andrea's mumbo jumbo had destroyed his sensitivities; his hostility and distaste for her were so strong that he couldn't feel that dreadful reality behind the ritual. Linda felt it even more strongly here, in this frail wooden box that was exposed to the night on all four sides. No. Not four sides—five. On the roof, the rain drummed with importunate demand; but above the normal pressure of the storm, Linda was conscious of other forces gathering, closing in.

When the garlic was in place, Andrea went to a cupboard and took out a flask, crossing herself as she did so.

"Sit over there," she ordered brusquely, indicating the spot with a jerk of her head. "In the middle of the floor. Take some cushions from that corner. We'll be here for a good long time."

Michael muttered something under his breath, but obeyed. As he and Linda seated themselves, Andrea anointed the doors and windows with liquid from the flask and then, walking backward, dribbled the contents of the flask in a wide circle around the seated pair. She was careful to stay within the circle. When it was closed, a dark, unbroken wetness on the worn boards of the floor, she came to Linda.

"Hold out your hands," she ordered, and poured a few drops of the remaining liquid into Linda's cupped palms. As she directed, Linda touched the water to her forehead. Michael followed the same procedure, reluctance slowing his movements.

Andrea scrambled to her feet. She seemed to have regressed, both mentally and in time; hobbling, mumbling, she might have stepped out of a sixteenth-century village street—the wise woman, the white witch, Old Mother Demdike. She took a piece of chalk from one of the pockets concealed in her ample skirts and crawled around the interior circumference of the circle of holy water, scribbling designs and symbols onto the floorboards, taking care not to touch the dark dribble of wetness. When she had finished, she crouched down on the floor facing the other two, and poured the last few drops of water into her right hand, crossing herself repeatedly. Her scarlet skirts made a puddle of bright color in the candlelight; her back was curved. The drone of her voice was unbroken except for quick, shallow breaths that came faster and faster and reminded Linda unpleasantly of an animal panting.

Gradually, as Linda watched the old woman's intent face and glazing eyes, the drone of her voice and the monotonous drumming of the rain blended into a single soft whine, like the buzz of a giant insect. Linda's cramped legs grew numb. She tried to move her hand and found it would not respond to her will. The man beside her, the other objects in the room, drew back and lost reality. There was nothing else in the universe except the mingled drone of voice and rain, and the steadily mounting pressure of an invisible force.

The room seemed darker—or were her eyes failing? The low sound was inside her head now, reverberating against the bony dome of her skull. She could hardly feel the wooden floor under her bent legs, but every inch of her skin tingled with the force. It was as if the encompassing air had grown heavier, or as if she were newly sensitized to its constant, unfelt pressure. A picture began to form behind her eyes. She saw the room in miniature, like a small cube of light in the midst of towering, indistinct shapes of darkness, which surrounded it like storm clouds. Featureless and black, yet living, they leaned in over the frail walls; but within, another force moved and grew, holding back the dark. She saw it all, in that moment, as a cosmic manifestation—the struggle of light against darkness. Across the world and the ages the battle raged, unseen, with the balance swaying now to one side and now to the other. In their small microcosm of the universe, the scales were balanced; but the struggle was not static. The pans dipped and swayed as the opposing strengths changed to counter each other's weight. She could not see beyond the darkness; but within the light, the power emanated from one hunched figure. She herself was not part of that cosmic struggle; she was only a pawn, a fly trapped by two great winds, an animal caught between two armies massed for battle. . . .

Deep down inside her dazed consciousness, a small spark of outrage flared. True or false, a cosmic vision or a fancy of hysteria, that view of the universe was not to her liking. She would not surrender her will, even to good, without a voice in the decision. Linda made the greatest effort of her life—an effort all the harder because it was without a physical counterpart. It was like pushing, with her mind, against a barred and bolted door. Then something gave way, with an almost audible snap, and the room flashed back into focus.

Michael's hand clasped hers; she felt the pain of his grasp now. He was not looking at her, but at Andrea; his face was as white as paper. As Linda turned dazed eyes on the old woman, Andrea's voice faltered, caught, and stopped. The rain pounded on the roof in a roar of water. Linda saw the candle flames swaying like live things trying to escape from an attacker. The gritty boards of the floor were harsh against her bare legs. Only one residue of her vanished vision remained; the consciouisness of pressures mounting, building up to a tension that could not hold. Like an overload on an electrical system . . . Sooner or later something would blow.

Andrea raised clawed hands to her throat. Her mouth gaped open. She made hoarse sounds, her eyes bulged. Then her hands fell, and for a dreadful moment she balanced on hands and knees, head dangling, like a sick animal. Knees and elbows gave way; she rolled over onto her side and lay still.

The storm rose up, howling with wild winds around the eaves, battering at the walls. As Linda sat frozen, staring at the old woman's empty eyes and still face, Michael got to his feet. He staggered as his numb legs took his weight, and then leaned forward over Andrea's body. When he turned, Linda knew what he was going to say.

"She's dead. We must—good God Almighty!"

The impact of the mighty wind was strong enough to break the window; but it was not wet air that came through the shattered pane in one great leap. Michael's left arm swept out, catching Linda as she stood up, and throwing her back against the wall. Most of the candles died in the gust of rain and wind. The pair that flanked the crucifix wavered and held. Pressed against the same wall, her body aching with the violence of the impact, Linda saw him go down buried under the solid black mass of the thing that had come through the window. It made no sound, none that she could hear over the agonized wail of the storm, which was whistling through some crevice in the broken glass with a noise like that of a pipe or whistle. And there was another sound—the sound of Michael's gasps, as he fought for his life.

Nine

Linda's outflung hand touched an object, and she seized it without looking to see what it was. She felt only its weight and convenience of shape, fit for grasping; she wanted a weapon, and that was how she used it, swinging it high and bringing it down with all her strength. If it struck home, she never felt the impact; at the same moment the air erupted like a volcano, deafening her with sound, blinding her eyes, shaking the floor under her feet. Swaying, her hands over her dazzled eyes, she heard the echoes roll and die. Echoes of thunder . . . The lightning bolt must have struck the roof, or something just outside.

Linda opened her eyes. Through the chaos of wind and rain, the two small lights on the wall burned steadily.

Andrea's body lay huddled on the floor, grotesquely tumbled by the struggle that had gone on over it. Michael was on the floor too, flat on his back, his arm thrown up across his face. The curtains billowed at the broken window; a branch protruded like a bony arm through the gap between the torn curtains. The big oak tree outside the window had been the lightning's target. There was nothing else. Whatever else had been in the room, it was gone.

On the floor beside Michael lay the crucifix, which she had used as a club. It was cracked, straight across the stem.

She went to Michael and bent over him. His eyes were closed. His sleeve, and the arm under it, were shredded. Blood dripped down and formed in a dreadful pool beside his head. But the gesture had saved his life. The dog had gone for his throat.

He opened his eyes when she touched him.

"It's gone," she said quickly, feeling him stiffen under her hands as memory returned.

"Gone? How?"

"I don't know. I hit it—with that." She touched the crucifix. "But the last lightning flash was so violent that it stunned me for a few seconds. It hit the tree outside the window, and—" She broke off, he eyes widening with a new fear. "Michael, there's fire out there. I can see the light. The rain is stopping, too."

The light was only a flickering redness, but as she spoke the curtains at the window caught in a flare of flame.

"That does it," Michael muttered, struggling to stand. "The outside of the house is soaked, but inside it's as dry as sawdust. It will go up in a second. We've got to get out of here."

"Get out!" She caught at his injured arm, heard him groan, and transferred her weight to support him as he swayed. "We can't just walk out and leave the house to burn!"

"How can we stop it? The wood is dry with rot, and there are these papers and books. Someone will see the flames and call the fire department. We must be away from here before anyone comes."

"I can't leave."

"You aren't afraid of—what's out there, are you? It, or its master, will be too canny to stick around. The place will be swarming with people in five minutes.

There couldn't be a safer time for us."

"It's not that. I can't leave . . . her."

She was surprised to feel wetness on her face. Michael's own face, bloodless with pain and shock, softened. They looked at the huddled body, roused to a terrible imitation of movement by the flickering light of the fire, which had seized avidly on the wooden walls.

"She's dead," Michael said. "There's no doubt of that, Linda—I know. What else can you do for her? It's purifying—fire." He added, with a glance around the strange little room, "I know, she thought she was doing good. All the same, it seems fitting, somehow, that this should burn. . . . Linda, please."

His weight was heavy against her; the fact that he made no mention of his own need was the strongest appeal of all. With one last look at the still body, she turned, bracing him; as they passed through the door, the flames leaped from walls to floor. Half the room was ablaze. As they went down the passageway, Linda wondered why Andrea's body had looked so small. Shrunken, almost as if part of its substance had been sucked out.

One good look at Michael's arm made

Linda forget her other concerns, but he wouldn't let her do much, except apply a bandage to stop the bleeding, and arrange a rough sling. A swig of brandy from the bottle on the table brought some of the color back to his face. It also brought him to his feet.

"Take the bottle," he said, thrusting it at her. "Hurry. God, I can hear the fire now, it's not raining hard enough to stop it. Let's go, Linda."

She lingered, looking affectionately at the old kitchen.

"I hate to see it go without making a fight to save it. The house is two hundred years old."

"Yes, you're a fighter, aren't you. But pick your causes, for God's sake. Do you want to be found here, with the house ablaze, a dead body, and signs of what the newspapers will be delighted to refer to as unholy practices? The least that can happen is that I'll go to jail and Gordon will lock you up for the rest of your life. I can just see what his tame psychiatrists could do with this mess."

It was brutal but effective. She turned, without another word, and started toward the door.

"Wait a minute," Michael said. "The cats. We can't leave them inside."

"They can get out, through the cellar."

"Just in case . . ."

Michael drew the bolts on the back door and threw it open. The rain was falling gently now, as if spent by its effort.

"Come on," he said, and led the way to the front of the house.

II

They made it, but with only seconds to spare. As the car skidded onto the paved road and turned, they heard sirens and saw the flashing red lights of fire engines coming the other way.

Linda was driving. Michael had tried to, but the effort of turning the car in the narrow lane, which was now a bog of mud, was too much for him; he blacked out, over the wheel, with the first movement.

"Stupid," he said hazily, as she took his place. "Too dangerous, on the highway . . . I hope you can drive. I forgot to ask."

"I hope so too. It's funny, though," she added, nursing the wheel and the brake as the car curtsied coyly into a rut, "how it comes back to you. I drove one of my boyfriends' jalopies through an entire Cleveland winter. Ice and snow and mud and . . . woops."

He didn't answer, either to commend her skill or to make suggestions; she knew he was fighting to stay conscious, and she did her best to avoid jolting him. When she swung onto the highway, she was conscious of an absurdly warming glow of pride. It was a long time since she had done anything for herself. Some of the dependence was inevitable when you were married to a man as wealthy as Gordon; you didn't mend your own socks or scrub scorched pans. Even so—hadn't Gordon overdone the servant bit? He didn't do anything himself, except for the exercise necessary to preserve his splendid physical condition. He didn't even drive a car; he hired the best chauffeurs that were to be had. He didn't build a fire in the fireplace, or plant a bulb, or groom a horse. The moral value of work was a myth, of course; or was it? Surely there was a healthy feeling of satisfaction in doing some small, needed job and doing it well; cleaning a dirty kitchen, mending a piece of broken furniture—getting a car out of a muddy back lane.

She thought Michael had lost consciousness, he was so still; but once they were on the paved road, he spoke.

"You've got a good, efficient fire department. There they come now. Maybe they can save the house after all."

"I hope so. Don't think I'm sentimental—"

"What's wrong with being sentimental?"

"Well, this is no time for it," she admitted. "I don't know what you want to do now; I didn't think about anything except getting away from there. But you've got to see a doctor, Michael, right away."

"Sounds good," Michael said.

"Doctor Gold lives down the next street," she said, her eyes on the road.

"Isn't he your little pal? The one I met?"

"Yes."

"I think we'll pass him up."

"But, Michael, he's the closest."

"Too close. He'd be on the phone to Gordon before he did anything else."

"I could stay in the car."

"Alone? No."

"I can't stand knowing how much it hurts you," she said unsteadily. The car swerved.

"Keep your eyes on the road. . . . Don't waste your sympathy. I am just about to pass out. . . . Thank God."

"There must be a doctor in the next town," Linda said, putting her foot down.

"No, wait. . . ." Michael roused himself; his voice sounded miles away. "What ever you do, don't panic. Keep at the speed limit, we can't risk . . . a wreck, or a cop. One thing to do . . . obvious . . ."

"Michael . . . Michael!"

"Don't wreck the car," he said; weak as it was, his voice was amused, and Linda was conscious of a strange constriction somewhere in the region of her diaphragm. "Don't stop . . . Put a couple of dozen miles between us and the house. . . ."

She heard his sigh of exhaled breath as his head fell back against the seat.

The drive was almost too much of a challenge; it was one of the worst jobs she had ever undertaken. Terror is strong and breath-stopping, but it is usually brief;

it passes quickly. Fear, the kind that had haunted her for months, has its own built-in anesthesia. And when despair is deepest there is no need to struggle, only to endure. What made the drive so bad was the need to keep constantly on the alert, to anticipate, not only the normal hazards of the road, but any unexpected, almost unimagined supranormal danger. She realized that the worst kind of fear is fear for someone else. She damned herself for involving Michael in her danger, and speculated wildly to how she could extricate him—if it wasn't already too late.

Through it all she drove steadily, surely, never taking her eyes from the road. The torrential rains had flooded out many sections, and she drove through shallow sheets of water at a crawl, her throat tight with fear of flooding the engine. But the worst moment was the roadblock.

A tree was down on the road ahead; but she didn't know that, not at first, she saw only the barriers and the flashing lights of the police car.

Her foot hit the brake and her hand fumbled for the gear lever. There was a side road, a block or two back. . . . She realized the stupidity of that move, just in time, and brought the car to a sedate stop. She had barely time to reach over and pull Michael's jacket across his slung arm as the police officer came up to the side of the car.

She rolled down the window.

"What's the trouble?" she demanded, with the ordinary annoyance of an innocent motorist who is delayed.

"Tree across the road. The crew is working on it, but you'll be better off going around; it'll take some time." The man's eyes moved past her, to the silent figure sprawled across the other seat. "Something wrong, miss? Need any help?"

He was very young, the policeman; his voice was kind. Momentarily Linda fought the urge to break down and tell him the truth. A doctor, a nice safe hospital for Michael . . . Then she saw the boy's nostril's quiver, and she realized that the brandy bottle must be leaking. Either that, or Michael had taken more than she thought.

"That must have been quite a party," the policeman said. "Your husband, ma'am?"

"What makes you so sure we're married?'' Linda asked, with an attempt at a smile.

He was young, but he wasn't stupid. Pushing his cap back, he smiled at her.

"I didn't see your ring at first," he explained, indicating her left hand, which was taut on the wheel. "But, you know, it's a funny thing; we see a lot of drunks, you can imagine. Sometimes a girl's date passes out, but usually it's a married guy."

"That must give you rather a jaundiced view of marriage."

"No, not really. Oh—oh, I get it. You mean the husbands are driven to drink?" The young man laughed. He had pink cheeks and even, white teeth, and he was obviously bored with his dull post. "Well, maybe. But what I always figured was, I figured the boyfriends were more anxious to look good. It's not a very nice thing to do, pass out on a date and make her drive you home."

"I'm sure you'd never do a thing like that, whether you were married to the girl or not," Linda said. Every nerve in her body was screaming for haste, but she couldn't show it. If she gave him any cause to ask for her driver's license, they were finished.

"Well, I'll tell you, ma'am, you pull a few bodies out of the wrecks and you get to realize it isn't worth it. Well, I guess you don't need a lecture; you look like you'd never had a drink in your life."

"Thank you," Linda said sweetly. She battered her lashes at him. "I certainly haven't had one tonight."

"No, I could tell that. If you had—well, I'd have wanted to stop you from driving. It's even more dangerous on a bad night like this. You sure you don't need any help with your husband?"

"Thank you, but I can manage." Michael stirred and muttered; and Linda said quickly, "I'd better get him home to bed. You say there's a detour?"

"Yes, ma'am. Two blocks back, you turn right, then left at the next corner, and you're on Main Street. . . ."

She didn't need the directions, but she nodded her thanks and pretended to listen intently. She turned the car carefully under his benevolent but critical eyes, and started back; wondering, as she did so, why she had the urge to hide their tracks. She was acting as if they might be objects of an ordinary search, instead of a quest by something not limited by human senses. Was that her intelligence, struggling against superstition, or simply overcaution? She gave it up, with a shrug that was a little desperate. Rational or not, the purpose was achieved; that nice boy would not think of her and her drunken bum of a husband if anyone came looking for a crazy girl fleeing with her lover.

Her lover. She drove on, automatically, through the night. Once, at her worst, she had prayed that she would never love anyone again. Love had betrayed her too often. With her father, who had died and left her, and her mother, who had never given a damn about her because she was a girl, and had "all these funny ideas." And, after she had gone to him for the security her childhood had lacked, with Gordon. He had not only failed, he had used love as a weapon against her, a blindfold to hide his true nature, a spy that betrayed her own weaknesses. Love? It was a chameleon word with a thousand meanings. There were as many kinds of love as there were human beings—a hundred times more, because every human being had that many different feelings which he called by the same name.

Beside her, Michael moaned and shifted. His head dropped onto her shoulder. She adjusted her weight and kept on driving, eyes steady on the road.

When she first saw him, she regarded him not as a man but as a ladder by means of which she might climb out of the pit where Gordon held her prisoner. She had meant to ensnare his senses so that his reasoning faculties would be blinded, and he would obey her demands with the uncritical partisanship which that kind of "love" induced in the victim. It was a blindness with which she was only too familiar.

Not that she had meant to tell the truth. Some tale of conventional "mental cruelty" would have done the trick—or so she thought. She knew now that she would never have caught this man with anything so crude. She might more safely have appealed to his sense of compassion. But that was a double-edged weapon, too easily turned against her—"poor girl, she needs help but doesn't know it; we must hurt her for her own good." Gordon had already used that, and it had almost worked. But that was Michael's strength; no appeal that was purely emotional could convince him completely. He had a critical brain, critical even of himself, and it functioned. Even now, though he "loved" her—whatever he might mean by that word—he was still asking questions. He had come to her defense not because of "love" but because the tireless critical brain had produced facts that cracked his first predilection in favor of Gordon and Gordon's explanations.

With that kind of intelligence she had no quarrel; in fact, it might be the only solid thing in a shifting universe, and the one quality above all others that had made her turn to him. But love, whatever else it was, was not a sterile agreement of similar minds. And, after the last agonizing months, she was no longer sure of her capacity to give anything beyond that.

The inert mass beside her stirred again, and she started.

"Are you awake?"

"I'm not sure. . . . Where are we?"

"About halfway to the city. I haven't been planning; I've just been driving."

"Pull over as soon as you can find a place."

They were approaching a town, and she found the parking lot of an all-night diner. She left the engine idling, pushed down the parking brake, and turned to Michael.

He was upright and aware, but the dull look in his eyes alarmed her.

"You've got to have a doctor. I'll ask, at the diner."

"Wait a minute. I've got to think. . . . What sort of story are we going to tell a doctor?"

"But it's nothing the police need to . . . Oh, I see. He'll know it was an animal, won't he? He'll start fussing about rabies. He'll want us to report it, describe where it happened, so the police can check. If we said the dog belonged to a friend of ours—"

"He may wonder what kind of friends we have, that they didn't call in their family doctor. Lying is complicated, isn't it?"

"Sometimes telling the truth is more complicated. Michael, we'll have to risk it. Maybe he'll be sleepy and bored and won't care."

"Yes, we'll have to risk it."

"Does it hurt terribly?"

"Yes, damn it, it hurts. But that's not what's bothering me. I can't risk being incapacitated. Don't you understand? What happened tonight was the first round. And we lost. You don't think he'll give up now, do you?''

"No. But I wouldn't say we lost. We got away."

"Leaving one dead on the field of battle. She lost. She's dead because she lost. Whatever she was doing, or thought she was doing, it failed."

"That couldn't have been part of his plan. He didn't know she'd be there."

"I don't know what his plan is, that's why I feel so helpless. But I'm beginning to suspect that my involvement isn't coincidental. Why he's got it in for me I don't know, but he asked for me; he did everything he could to throw us together. He has something in mind. And until we figure out what, we're fighting blind. Let's locate that doctor. You go and ask while I try to think of some disarming lie."

The doctor was suspicious and hard to soothe. Groggy and querulous at first, he woke up completely after a look at Michael's injuries, and only the latter's quick imagination kept him from calling the police. Michael managed to suggest a drunken party and considerable provocation; the smell of brandy on his breath went a long way toward convincing the doctor that the affair had been an ordinary middle-class brawl, with possibilities of scandal, in which he was better not involved. They left as soon as they could get away.

"Well," Linda said, when they were back in the car, "if the police made any inquiries, we won't be hard to trace this far."

Michael shook his head. The pills the doctor had given him were working. He looked much better.

"I don't think we need to worry about the police. Not that we can go to them for help; our story is too wild. And if we'd been found there, with Andrea dead and the house blazing, we'd have some embarrassing questions to answer. But a common garden-variety scandal can't be Gordon's aim. He won't turn us in, and nobody else knows we were at Andrea's."

"I'll bet the police would love to have some witnesses as to what happened there."

"Not even that. Even if they find the—evidence intact, the logical conclusion will be that Andrea was carried away by her histrionics and had a heart attack. There wasn't a mark on her. In fact—that may have been just what did happen."

"You don't believe—"

"I don't know what to believe."

"The dog. It was real enough."

"Too real. I felt it, all hundred pounds of it. It felt like a dog; it even smelled like a dog."

"But the others—the supernatural animals—"

"Werewolves," Michael said roughly. "Say it. My God, are we going to cringe away from words?"

"Werewolves are real; they take material form."

"I know, I've read all the horror stories. Everything works two ways, doesn't it? Do you realize that nothing that has happened couldn't be explained in rational terms?"

"But Andrea . . . I see. Self-induced?"

"She had a bad heart. And a firm belief. Linda, the phenomenon is known, documented—not only in the jungles of Haiti and Africa but in American hospitals."

Linda's eyes were straight ahead, watching the dark ribbon of road unwind.

"You know what your rationalist interpretation means, don't you? You're sitting next to an attempted murderess."

"Forget that!"

"I can't forget it. I'll try not to think about it, but . . . Where are we going, Michael? We'll be in the city soon. I'd suggest some place brightly lit, with lots of people around you. . . ."

"'All right, then." Michael turned, his arm over the back of the seat. "We may as well drag all the dirt out into the open. Those other times, when you ran away to other men—what happened? What did you do?"

Linda didn't answer at first. She had to fight to keep her voice steady.

"I ran away once. I told you about that. There was no other man, then or ever."

"Then Gordon lied?"

"He's a very convincing liar. It's his word against mine, of course, and I'd have a hard time proving I was telling the truth. What difference does it make? How many times do I have to try to kill someone before you'll admit—"

"Stop it! Under any circumstances, by any possible interpretation, that kind of thinking is dangerous. Don't . . . open your mind to it."

"I'm afraid!"

"I'm not. Not of you. Remember that. We do have to decide where we're going, though. I know where I'd like to go."

"To your friend—Galen. I've forgotten his last name. The doctor."

"Reading my mind? How much of that conversation with Galen did you overhear?"

"All of it. Except when you went downstairs with him."

"I hate women who are smarter than I am," Michael said, amusement coloring his voice.

"Do you know, I almost ran out and tried to catch him. He sounded . . . wise. Wise and stable."

"He's the wisest man I know, and the sanest. That's why I want to consult him. Not because—"

"You don't have to reassure me. Not any longer."

"Furthermore," Michael muttered, "he knows something. Something about Gordon."

"I wondered, when I heard the way his voice changed when you mentioned

Gordon's name. Do you think Gordon was ever a patient of his?"

"No, it was something else." Michael told her about the letters. "I don't know what they mean, though," he ended. "There's some hint there. . . . But it slipped past me."

"I'd like to see them."

"Yes, I think you'd better. But they date to a period some years back, before you met him. When I get my hands on that cautious psychiatrist, I'll interrogate him. The son of a gun must know more than what is in the letters. My dad may have talked to him."

"Then let's go to his place."

"Can't. He's not back yet."

"When will he be back?"

"The weekend, he said. Not before tomorrow."

"Then where do we go? There's the bridge, up ahead."

"My place, I guess."

"He'll know. . . ."

"What can he do there that he couldn't do anywhere else?" Michael asked reasonably. "I thought of a hotel, but I don't like the idea, I'd feel more insecure in an unfamiliar place. It isn't physical attack we're worried about, is it?"

"No, but . . ."

"Any other ideas?"

His voice was calm and patient, but Linda sensed his utter exhaustion. They were both exhausted, not only by long hours of wakefulness, but by mental strain. She couldn't think clearly. Certainly she couldn't think of any rational objection to his idea.

"I guess you're right," she said slowly. "Give me directions, then. I wasn't paying attention the last time I came to your apartment."

The streets were not crowded; it was well after midnight. Linda drove slowly, nursing her growing fatigue. The rain had stopped, but the streets were shiny with water, and clouds bumped the tops of the tallest buildings. They left the car in the garage, for which Michael paid, he informed her, a rent equal to that of his apartment, and walked the short distance in exhausted silence. There were no pedestrians on the street. The city might have been struck by some silent science-fictional weapon, and all life destroyed except their own.

The presence of Napoleon, squatting

like a leopard by the door, should have been reassuring, for he was obviously glad to see them. But as she bent to fondle the scarred head that was banging against her ankles, Linda was conscious of an increase in her dark forebodings.

"He must have eaten up all the food," Michael said, watching Napoleon's activities cynically.

"I'll get him something. You sit down."

"There's some of the canned cat tuna on one of the shelves," Michael said as she went into the kitchen.

The sight of the littered sink and empty refrigerator made Linda wrinkle her nose in disgust.

"It's a wonder you don't both have rickets and scurvy," she said, searching the drawers for a can opener. "There isn't a drop of milk. I should think you could at least feed that poor cat milk."

"He hates milk," Michael said. "Whiskey, gin, beer, Coke—he loves Coke, but he'll drink anything. Anything but milk."

Linda found the can opener in the sink, and went to call Napoleon. The cat was sitting on Michael's stomach, glowering.

"He knows I've been in a fight," Michael said. "And he has a pretty good idea as to who lost."

The cat sneezed and walked back down the length of Michael's semirecumbent form, planting his feet heavily. He went into the kitchen, contempt radiating from every hair.

"I've lost face," Michael said.

Linda was unable to be amused. Michael didn't seem to feel anything wrong. What was the matter with her, that she couldn't give way to the fatigue that dragged at every muscle? Unable to relax, she began to walk up and down the room. Her eyes felt hot and her skin had begun to prickle. Not for the first time, she speculated about drugs. Gordon had every opportunity to administer anything he chose. Coffee, wine, even the aspirin in her bathroom . . . What a nice, neat satisfying solution that would be. It explained so much. . . . But not, unfortunately, quite enough. She turned.

"Where are those letters you mentioned?"

"What?" Michael started; he had fallen into a doze, slumped in the big chair. Linda's heart—or whatever internal organ it is that behaves so peculiarly in moments of emotion—twisted as she watched him blink and brush at his ruffled hair. "They're in that envelope I brought up from the car," he said, yawning. "Why don't we wait till morning? We can think better after we get some sleep."

"I'm too keyed up to sleep yet," she said. "What about a nice soothing cup of tea?"

"Okay."

Linda went into the kitchen. She couldn't tell him of her feelings; he was too tired to cope with anything else tonight. But her panic was real, and it was steadily growing. She had to see the letters now, without delay, as a hunted man, feeling the approach of the hunters, might desperately try to fashion the smallest scrap of wood or metal into a weapon.

The letters were too small a scrap. They told her nothing she didn't already know. But the warm drink and the forced concentration helped her nerves. Lethargy replaced her earlier anxiety. Even the sudden movement of the cat did not startle her; but Michael started and swore as the long, lean body streaked for the kitchen.

"That's funny," he said.

"What?"

"There goes a plate. . . . Oh, nothing. But he usually doesn't move that fast unless he hears someone coming."

He was sitting upright, frowning. Funny, Linda thought. Now he's getting nervy, and I'm falling asleep. She put the last letter down.

"Your father didn't like Gordon," she said.

"No. I wonder why."

"Antipathy, he says."

"That's just a word people use to explain reasoning they aren't consciously aware of. What I don't understand is that letter about the Hellfire Club."

"Oh, that was Gordon," she said vaguely. She yawned.

"What do you mean?"

"He's been dabbling with demonology for years. Good God," she said, roused by anger, "you still think I invented all this, don't you? Where do you think I got my ideas? Why did you think Gordon and Andrea were at swords' points? Why do you think she hated him?"

"I never imagined . . ." Michael looked dazed. "He's such a fastidious person. . . ."

"You're thinking of Satanism in terms

of Aleister Crowley, and the Great Beast, and sexual orgies. That's only a perversion added by some psychotics. It was never like that with Gordon. If anything, he's too puritanical, too cold. It's power he wants, power and control. Isn't that the ultimate control—over the minds and the will of others? He tried teaching and he tried politics, but they weren't enough. Through them he could partially dominate certain types, but there were always a few who were immune, and they were the ones he wanted most to dominate."

Another wide yawn interrupted her. It was a pity, she thought sleepily, that she should be so tired. This was an important point, something Michael hadn't realized, something he had to know.

"The clue to Gordon Randolph," Michael muttered. "Is this what I've been groping for? Hey—you're going to fall apart, you're yawning so. We'll talk more in the morning. Bed for you."

Linda let him lead her toward the bedroom, knowing that she ought to be reading to him, but too sleepy to care, too sleepy to pay attention to his explanations and his arrangements. He said something about sleeping on the couch. Linda looked up at him, blinking; her eyelids were so heavy.

"All right," she said obediently.

She might have been able to prevent it if she had seen it coming; but she was too sleepy and he was too strong. His arms went around her; even the arm that was bandaged from wrist to elbow held her close. His mouth was warm and hard and insistent on hers. For a few sleep-dazed moments she was lax in his embrace, not responding, but not resisting. Then a frenzy of revulsion filled her, and she struggled.

He let her go at once.

"I'm sorry," he said. "I didn't mean to do that. But you looked so . . ."

He was pale; whether with pain or anger, she could not tell. Linda swayed, gasping for breath; and the words that came out of her mouth were not the words she had meant to say.

"Michael. Lock me in!"

"No," he said violently.

"Please."

"No." His voice was gentler but inexorable. "I won't, even if I could. Hell, I don't know where the key is, if there is a key. There is no need for me to lock you in. Now go to sleep. Sleep well."

With a whimper she turned away, stumbling, and threw herself down on the bed. The movement took the last of her strength; a great weight seemed to be pressing down on her, on mind as well as body. But her mind fought off the pressure for several seconds, after her body had succumbed; she knew what was coming. And knew also that those few seconds of awareness were part of Gordon's plan—the realization of danger coupled with the inability to avoid it is the highest refinement of cruelty. Then, finally, the weight closed in, and her last spark of will flickered out.

III

Michael watched until her breathing slowed and she lay quiet. His hand went to the light switch, and then withdrew. If she woke, in the dark . . .

Was it only an irrational symbol, this concept of darkness versus light? Darkness concealed; but why need the objects it hid be objects of fear? They might be friendly things, things of beauty. Perhaps they only feared the dark who had seen some frightful thing come at them out of the veils of darkness. From the dark, the dark on the other side . . .

Turning away from the door, Michael wished fervently that he had never met Kwame nor heard that enigmatically threatening phrase. What did it really mean? It meant something to Kwame, something he felt so strongly that he could transfer the impression to other people. Michael remembered the horrifying vision he had had when Kwame first spoke the words. That had to have been some kind of ESP; he couldn't have thought of it by himself.

And it was a hell of a picture to have in the back of his mind, especially after a night like this one. Michael found himself reluctant to turn out the lights in the living room, though the glow from the open bedroom door was brighter than his sleeping room usually was.

He threw himself down on the couch, too tired to look for blanket or pillow. His feet were propped up on one arm of the couch. It was too short for comfort, but tonight he didn't care; he could have slept on a stone. He was too tired to think—and that was just as well, because the thoughts foremost in his mind were ugly thoughts. Satanism, possession, werewolves, the dark on the other side . . . His arm was throbbing. The pain killer was wearing off. He thought about getting up and taking another pill. But the bottle was in his coat pocket and his coat was in the closet and the closet was ten feet away, and that was just too damned far for a man who had been up all night, battling werewolves and witches and . . . Heavily, Michael slept.

And woke, with one of the wenching starts that sometimes rouses a sleeper from a dream of falling. He had only been asleep for a few minutes; his muscles still ached with fatigue. Something had wakened him.

Mind and body drugged by the short, annihilating nap, Michael lay quiescent and listened. There were sounds, out in the kitchen. That was what had roused him. Someone was in the kitchen, moving around.

The most logical source of noise was Napoleon. But his sleeping mind was accustomed to the cat's comings and goings, it would have noted the sounds, classified them, and let him sleep. These were not the noises the cat made when it thudded down into the sink or lapped water or chewed the hard, crunchy bits of food. These were small, metallic sounds, like coins chinking in someone's pocket . . . a loose metal strip blown by the wind against another piece of metal . . . knives and forks in a drawer, being shifted. . . .

When he recognized the sounds and identified the key word, his brain refused to accept the conclusion. Maybe Linda had been unable to sleep. Looking for the wherewithal to make coffee or food, she would naturally move quietly, so as not to disturb him.

Then he saw her. The kitchen, out of the direct beam of light from the bedroom door, was very dark. As she moved out into the diffused dimness of the living room, her slim body seemed to be forming out of shadows like a dark ectoplasmic ghost. She stood still for several seconds, as if listening; and Michael remained quiet, not from design, but because his paralyzed body was incapable of movement. There was just enough light to reflect, with a pale glitter, from the long shiny object in her right hand.

Ten

She moved very slowly. When she reached the couch, she stood motionless for several long moments. He could see the knife distinctly now, it was only inches from his face. It hung from fingers so lax that they seemed about to lose their grip altogether. He could hear her breathing. It was quick and deep, long gasps of effort.

Her fingers tightened and her arm began to move. Up—slowly, in abrupt jerks and starts, as if struggling against a force that tried to hold it. Michael watched in an unholy fascination; the whole bizarre episode might have been happening to someone else, with himself an unwilling and helpless spectator. Now her arm was high above her head. A strained, impractical position for a downward blow . . . The arm started down.

Michael moved. To his outraged nerves it seemed as if the whole thing were taking place in slow motion, that he had an infinite amount of time in which to act before the knife struck. In an almost leisurely movement his right arm lifted and his fingers clamped around the wrist of the hand that held the knife.

His touch affected her like a jolt of electric current; every muscle in her body stiffened, her wrist twisted frantically in his grasp. She screamed, a thin, high sound that was more like the voice of an animal in agony than anything human. It was the scream as much as anything else that made Michael take more than defensive action. A few more moments of that, and someone would call a cop.

He tried not to hurt her. Rolling sideways off the couch, he pulled her down with him, pinning her kicking legs with his body, his right hand still tight around her wrist, his left fumbling for her mouth. They struggled in darkness; the back of the couch cut off the feeble light from the bedroom. He could feel her struggling, feel the writhing of her lips against his palm. He had half expected the maniacal strength he had read about, but he encountered very little difficulty; she was a small woman, and it took only seconds to immobilize and quiet her. Flaccid and cold under his hands, she lay still. He couldn't even feel her breathing.

It never occurred to him that her collapse might have been a ruse. He scrambled up. His need for light was more than a need to see, it was a craving for the power that opposed the dark.

She looked like a sick child in a sleep troubled by pain—tumbled hair, pale face, mouth drawn down in a pathetic grimace. She was wearing his old bathrobe, which had helped to hamper her movements; the struggle had torn it open, but she was still wearing her slip and underclothing. Michael revised his comparison. Not a child, no. But she looked pitifully young. The wrist he had twisted seemed too fragile to resist the lightest touch. By her right hand lay his big carving knife.

Michael kicked it out of the way. He knelt down and put his ear to her breast. Faint and abnormally slow, but it was there—the pounding of her heart. He straightened, studying the pale face with a mixture of different terrors. The closed lids veiled the eyes; he wondered what he would see in those eyes when the lids lifted.

After a moment he stood up and went into the bedroom. When he came back, she hadn't moved. Carefully he wrapped the bathrobe around her; the coldness of her skin and the sluggish pulse suggested shock. Then he set about the rest of the job. His mouth was set in a tight, twisted line as, using the neckties he had brought from the bedroom, he tied her wrists and ankles together.

A pale, ugly dawn was breaking before she came to. Michael had tried everything he could think of to bring her out of her faint—wondering, all the while, whether he really wanted her to wake up. Faces in sleep or unconsciousness were like blank pages; waking intelligence, the expression of eyes and mouth, are what give individuality and character. What would he see when her eyes opened? The face, now familiar and beloved, of the girl he wanted; or the Medea figure who had stood over him with a knife?

He had carried her back into the bedroom and piled every blanket he owned over the waxen body. He had bathed her face and rubbed her wrists. The slow, mechanical breathing did not change; the muscles of face and body remained flaccid. And the night wore on. It seemed to Michael at times as if the sun would never rise, as if some astronomical miscalculation had stopped the earth on its axis. Then the first sullen streaks stained the clouds; and her eyes opened.

Michael saw what he had hoped, but not really expected, to see. His relief was so great that he dropped with a thud onto the edge of the bed. But the realization that dawned in her face, as memory returned, was almost worse than the madness he had feared. Her horror and consternation were genuine; if he had had any lingering doubts of her honesty, they vanished then. Her eyes moved from his face, downward, toward her bound wrists and ankles. They were hidden under the piles of blankets, but he knew she could feel the bonds.

"I'll take them off," he said quickly. "I just wasn't sure . . . It's all right now, I'll get them off. . . ."

He turned the covers back, and she twisted frantically away from his hands.

"No—no! Leave them on, don't let me—"

"It's gone," Michael said, hardly knowing what he was saying. "It's all right."

"How do you know?" Her voice was quieter, under a fierce control, but she still held herself away from him. Michael's hands dropped back onto the blankets.

"Don't you see," she went on, "that we can't take the chance? I can't take it, even if you will. Call your friend. Call Bellevue, some hospital. And leave me tied until they come for me."

Michael shook his head dumbly. He was incapable of speech, but she read his face, and her own expression changed. Her eyes flickered and then dropped away from his.

"All right," she said. "I'm sorry, I was upset. Untie me."

She held her bound wrists toward him. The cloth was soft, and he had not tied the knots tightly; but he saw the red marks on her wrists, and his first impulse was to do as she asked. Yet he hesitated—noting her reluctance to meet his eyes, remembering the quick, cunning expression that had flickered across her face.

"What will you do if I untie you?" he asked.

Her silence was all the answer he needed. The minute his back was turned, she would run, and not stop running until she had found a safe padded cell in which to hide. She might even go back to Gordon, she was desperate enough for that. . . . And through the black despair that enveloped him he felt an incongruous flash of something like triumph. She hadn't reacted this way after her attempt on Gordon. Rather than risk hurting him, she would run to meet the fate she had been fleeing.

"No," he said decisively. "Not that way, Linda."

Her eyes blazed up at him, and she started to speak. The words caught in her throat as they heard the sound of a knock at the front door.

The same idea came to both their minds simultaneously: Gordon. Michael moved just in time to stop the scream that had gathered in her throat. He knew what she meant to do, and he knew what his course of action must be. The struggle was short but ugly, because now he was not fighting some sick manifestation of hate, but Linda herself. When he stood up, he was wet with perspiration. His stomach contracted in a spasm of sickness as he looked down at the writhing figure on the bed—gagged with a towel, its wrists and ankles tied firmly to the bedposts. The knock was repeated. It had come again twice while he was . . . Whoever it was must know he was there.

Michael turned on his heel and went out, closing the bedroom door tightly behind him. As he reached the front door the knock was repeated. He wrenched the door open with a violence that did little to relieve his fury and frustration. He was almost hoping that his surmise was correct. It would have been a pleasure to get his hands on Randolph.

But it was not Randolph. It was his secretary.

"Good morning," Briggs said politely.

Michael stared back at him, deflated and uncertain. He was not sure of Briggs's role. Involved he must be, but perhaps only as one of Gordon's blinded disciples. If that was the case . . . Michael's stomach contracted as he remembered what lay on the bed in the next room. Linda wouldn't be the only one locked up if Briggs happened to see that pretty picture.

"Good morning," he answered, wondering how his voice could sound so normal. "Looking for something?"

Briggs blinked; a sly, appreciative smile moved his mouth. The expression was so ugly that Michael fell back a step. Briggs took advantage of his movement to enter.

The man was dressed in an imitation of Gordon's impeccable taste. The suit had been well fitted; but not even Savile Row could have done much with Briggs's figure. The expensive leather belt had slid down below the equator of his round belly, and the Italian silk tie curved out to follow the hump. In his hand Briggs held a hat. He put it down on a table and glanced around the room.

"Nice place you have here," he said.

There was no sound from the bedroom. Michael wondered whether Linda had recognized Briggs's voice and found him too much even for her new resolution. He couldn't risk it, though. He had to get the man out of here.

"I don't like to seem inhospitable," he said, "but I'm just about to go out."

It was such a glaring lie, considering the hour and the state of Michael's apparel, that Briggs didn't bother to comment. But another of those faint, unpleasant smiles touched his pale mouth.

"Oh, I shan't stay. I just came by at

Mr. Randolph's request. You haven't seen anything of Mrs. Randolph, I suppose?"

A series of soft thuds came from behind the closed door. Michael glanced at it.

"That damned cat," he said.

"Your cat? How nice that you have a pet."

"If you don't mind . . ." Michael felt he couldn't control himself much longer. In about thirty seconds he was going to grab Briggs by the collar of his pretty suit and heave him out the door.

"Yes . . . You see, there was a sad occurrence last night. You remember our local witch, I'm sure. Apparently she got carried away by one of her experiments and set her house on fire."

"Really?" His tone didn't even convince Michael himself, but suddenly he no longer cared. Briggs knew. He knew all about everything.

"Yes," Briggs cooed. "Very sad. Burned to a crisp, the poor old lady was. Well, naturally Mr. Randolph thought Linda might have been involved."

"Linda," Michael repeated.

"I think of her that way," Briggs said, with an indescribable smirk. "I wish we could find her, help her. . . . She's a beautiful young lady. A shame to have all that go to waste in some asylum."

Two things kept Michael from planting his fist right in the center of Briggs's leer. One was the thought that it would be like hitting a fat woman. The other was the knowledge that Briggs was trying to anger him into an indiscreet act.

"How is Mr. Randolph?" he asked.

"Not well." Briggs shook his head sadly. "He's very upset, naturally. Knowing Linda's sad history as he does, he wondered about what happened to Andrea. Luckily the evidence was destroyed. The body, I mean."

"I'm late now," Michael said.

"How thoughtless of me to keep you, then." Briggs turned toward the door. Then he made a sudden dart to the side, his pudgy hand shooting out.

"Here it is," he exclaimed guilelessly, holding up a small black notebook. "Mr. Randolph thought he might have misplaced it here."

Michael looked at it.

"Randolph's? But it must have been here for days. I never saw it."

"Somehow it seems to have worked its way under a heap of magazines," Briggs said blandly. "You busy writers aren't the neatest housekeepers in the world, are you? He'll be glad to have this back. And to think this was the reason why he asked me to stop by. I declare I'd have forgotten to ask if I hadn't seen it, peeping out. Well, then . . ."

"Wait a minute," Michael said. An insane suspicion had entered his mind. "Let me see that."

Briggs surrendered the notebook without comment. Only his raised eyebrows indicated courteous surprise.

Michael flipped through the pages of the notebook. It was an ordinary little looseleaf pad, except that its cover was of tooled leather instead of plastic. It was certainly not Michael's property, and the handwriting on the pages resembled what he remembered of Gordon's script. The entries were cryptic and abbreviated; they might have been written in the sort of personal shorthand a busy man had developed in order to jot down appointments and reminders. A few of the signs reminded Michael of chemical or mathematical symbols.

With some reluctance he returned the notebook to Briggs. He had an odd feeling that if he could study those entries at leisure, he might learn something important. But he couldn't refuse to let the man have it, and the need to get Briggs out was stronger than any possible gain from the book.

"Well, I must be running along," Briggs said affably. "I hope you'll excuse the intrusion, at this hour. I have a busy day ahead of me. Oh, and by the way . . ."

Already in the doorway, he turned.

"If Linda should turn up, do be kind to the poor girl."

"Naturally."

"But don't forget . . ."

"Forget what?" Michael snapped.

"She might be dangerous," Briggs said softly. "Be careful."

He went out, and just in time; the itching in Michael's fingers was almost intolerable. He slammed the door and leaned against it, twisting his hands together. When he was able to speak without stammering, he went back to the bedroom.

She lay quiet, staring at him over the gag, her eyes liquid and enormous. Michael took the gag off and untied the cords that held her down. Neither spoke. He sat down on the edge of the bed, knowing he dared not touch her, and watched the tears slide down her cheeks and soak into the pillow on either side of her face.

II

Michael put down the telephone.

"They expect him tonight or early tomorrow," he said.

Sun streamed in the window. It was midmorning, and a beautiful spring day. Outside. The room had another atmosphere. They had both fought their way back to some kind of calm, but the air was cold with tension.

"Tonight," Linda repeated thoughtfully.

"Or tomorrow. He never knows till the last minute what plane he'll be catching. Usually he wires to let them know, but not always; he drives himself, so he doesn't have to be met."

Michael knew he must sound like a host trying to entertain an unwanted guest. He couldn't help it; something had happened to his brain. Up to this point he had been able to consider and discuss everything that had happened; he had even been able to apply logic to a concept that was considered to be beyond logic. But last night . . . His mind balked at that, he couldn't even think about it, much less discuss it. He was behaving as if it hadn't happened. Which was not only stupid; it was potentially dangerous.

He looked at Linda. Sitting upright on the bed, she sipped her coffee. Her hands were free, but her ankles were still bound; at her insistence, he had again fastened them to the footboard of the bed. He had felt sick while doing it, and he felt sick every time he looked. But it was a small price to pay for the composure of her face. She had fought this latest catastrophe, and come through it, as she had come through all the others; but he thought that she must be like someone clinging to a single strand of rope, over an abyss, slipping inexorably down each time her grasp on reality failed. The frantic hands might tighten, temporarily stopping the descent, or even claw their way back up the rope, a few precious inches toward safety. But inevitably the grasp would weaken again, and each time the fall would be arrested a little farther down, toward the end of the rope and the final plunge.

"I left a message," he said. "Asking him to call the minute he gets in."

"We're acting like children," Linda said. "Waiting for this man as if he were God, or . . . Why do you think he can help us?"

"I don't. I just don't know what else to do."

"How is your arm?"

"Hurts. It's not that, not the fact that I'm bushed. Something's happened to what passes for my brain. I can't . . . I can't think."

"Physical exhaustion doesn't help," she said, with a briskness that was contradicted by the tenderness of her mouth. They both knew that they could not afford an exchange of sympathies. In a battle, minor wounds must go untended.

"My own brain isn't working very well either," she went on. "But one thing is clear, Michael. I can't spend another night with you."

"It's a good thing nobody is listening to this conversation," Michael said wryly.

She gave him a strained smile.

"I mean it, though."

"Why is it night you're afraid of? Isn't that childish too?"

"Fear of the dark . . . Maybe. But everything that has happened so far happened at night."

"When the powers of evil walk abroad . . ."

"You see? It means something to you. What was it you said, last night—about the dark on the other side?"

Michael twitched uncomfortably.

"Kwame—Joe Schwartz—said that. About Gordon. He was talking about the old Platonic image of the shadows on the wall of the cave, but it turned me cold to hear him, I can tell you. Not the shadows, but the Things that cast the shadows, the Things that prowl the dark, on the other side of the fire. Gordon knows about them, he said. It was pretty obvious that he did, too."

"Poor Joe."

"He takes dope," Michael said. "Some kind of hallucinogenic."

"But you don't. Why does the phrase make you so uncomfortable?"

"Racial memory?" Michael offered wildly. "Some hairy, beetle-browed ancestor of mine, squatting in his cave, with his puny fire and his club the only defense against the things that prowled outside in the dark. Saber-toothed tigers and mastodons . . ."

There was no answering spark of amusement in her face.

"Go on," she said.

"Well . . . Too many horror stories when I was a kid. The other side of what? Eternity? The threshold of this world? The doorway that separates the living from the dead? Spiritualists talk about 'the other world,' don't they, to describe the region from which they get their communications?" He was getting interested; he went on, catching the impressions as they floated up into consciousness. "When Kwame talked of the dark on the other side of the fire, he was thinking of *The Republic,* but also of that other image. This world, narrow and circumscribed as opposed to the spiritual reality of the other side. The dark . . . That idea is not in Plato, damn it, if I remember my classics, which I probably don't. For him, the non-material, ideal world was one of light, of true consciousness. A spiritualist would see it that way, too. What do the discarnate entities keep mumbling when they are asked about their world?"

"Sunshine, light, flowers, love," Linda said promptly.

"Right. So why does this world of light and flowers seem to Kwame to be transmuted into darkness—not empty night, but a place where shadows live? Darkness and light, the primeval symbols of evil and good; the notion of a balance of forces, eternally warring, never ending. There are times, for everyone, when he feels himself the plaything of forces from somewhere outside, forces beyond his control, which strike him when he least expects it. 'Out of the night that covers me . . .' "

"Imagery, poetic," Linda said, as his voice trailed away. It's frightening, though, isn't it? 'Black as the pit from pole to pole . . .' "

"Poetic imagery is part of the picture I get. Black as the pit . . . black as Hell . . . There's a nice conventional image of fire and darkness for you."

"The familiar Calvinist Hell."

"It's funny," Michael went on thoughtfully, "how many of the pre-Christian afterworlds were dark. That terrible twilight place the classical poets describe, where the dead speak with faint voices like the piping of birds . . . Didn't the Egyptians go down under the earth into darkness where the sun-god never came?''

''You're out of my field,'' Linda said.

''Darkness and light, black and white; even the colors have symbolism. White is the color of purity, the garments of the Virgin and the priest. . . . What's the matter?''

''Sorry. It reminded me of Briggs, and every time I think of him I get a chill.''

''Why Briggs?'' Michael grinned. ''Not the color of purity, surely.''

''Didn't you know? No, I suppose you wouldn't. Gordon must have told you about Briggs's being unfairly dismissed from his job, and all that? He never told you what the job was, though. . . . Briggs is an unfrocked priest.''

''What?''

''I guess that sounds melodramatic. Actually, he was a student for the priesthood. They threw him out. Very politely, I imagine. I can also imagine why.''

''My God . . . Linda, what is Briggs? I mean, what role does he play in relation to Gordon?''

"I've wondered so often myself. Sometimes I think he's just another victim, but a willing one. Sometimes I see him as the *éminence grise* behind Gordon's latest activities. They're hand in glove, anyway, never doubt that."

Her face was averted, her voice rapid. She could hardly speak of the man, her loathing was so great. Michael realized that the basis for her aversion was more than a spiritual rejection. Perhaps it had not been Briggs's dabbling in questionable theology that had caused his expulsion, but rather his inability to conform to the basic tenets of the priestly orders. He wondered whether Gordon was aware of his colleague's attitude toward his wife; and knew that, if Gordon was what they had conjectured him to be, this would only be another weapon in his hands.

In the middle of the afternoon, Napoleon returned.

Michael hadn't noticed his long absence; he had too many other things to worry about. He was in the kitchen making another pot of coffee when the heavy body thudded down onto the counter; and then he remembered that Napoleon never missed coming home for breakfast.

He reached out for the animal, expecting the usual snarl and rebuff. But Napoleon's lackluster stare remained fixed on thin air and he did not move. Michael passed his hands over the cat's body. He found no new wounds. Whatever else he had been doing, Napoleon had not been fighting. Which was in itself a sign of something wrong.

Lifting the unresponsive bulk, he carried it into the bedroom.

"He's sick," he said, sounding like a nervous parent.

Linda looked up from the book she was not reading.

"Let me see."

Michael dumped the cat onto her lap and Linda investigated.

"I don't know," she said doubtfully. "He's a mess—why don't you chaperone him better?—but what's left of his fur feels sleek enough. And his eyes look okay. . . ."

Returning her look owlishly, Napoleon made the rusty grinding noise that passed for a purr. When Michael reached out for him, he eluded his master's hand with the old agility, and leaped down off the bed. Michael trailed along after him while

Napoleon made a thorough inspection of the apartment, from bathroom to kitchen. Having arrived at his food dish, he squatted down in front of it and began to gulp with a ravenous intensity that relieved much of Michael's worry.

He wandered back into the bedroom.

"He's eating."

"I expect he's all right, then. Michael . . . Would you think me ridiculous if I found his return reassuring?"

"I never thought of that. Hell, honey, it's illogical. Cats are supposed to fawn on demons."

She didn't answer. Michael sat down wearily on the edge of the bed and put his hand on her ankles. He ran his finger under the thick silk, making sure it was not too tight.

"Don't," she said.

"It's stupid," Michael burst out. "You can untie yourself any time you want to."

"But it would take time. You'd have some warning."

"For God's sake—"

"What time is it?"

"About two."

"Don't lie."

"All right! Three. Well, maybe

three thirty . . ."

"Another hour," she said. "We must leave a wide margin."

"I'll call Galen again."

"You've called twice in the last hour. They'll give him your message."

"And if he doesn't come by the time your deadline is up?"

"I won't stay here tonight."

"A hotel room won't be any safer," Michael said, deliberately misunderstanding her.

"It's not a hotel room I'm contemplating."

"Linda, you can't do that! If you get yourself committed to some hospital, the only one who could possibly get you out is Gordon himself. I don't even have the legal right to ask questions. You can't lock yourself into a room and throw away the key."

"I will not stay here tonight."

"You'll have to," Michael said. "I won't let you go."

She looked up at him, a pale ghost of humor in her face.

"Funny. You're driven to the same extremity I tried to force you to earlier. Yes, you can keep me here. Bound and gagged

. . . Have you thought about how it would look, if someone forced his way in and found me like that?"

"Constantly," Michael said with a groan.

"And you'd risk that?"

Michael reached out for her, compulsively, but she fended him off with a strength that had panic behind it.

"Don't, don't ever do that! You kissed me last night, before—"

"You don't mean . . ." Michael hesitated. He was surprised, and disgusted, to realize that his predominant emotion was jealousy.

"There may be a connection," she said. Her eyes refused to meet his. "I won't . . . go into details. But there may be."

"I see."

"That would have to be one of the conditions we must agree to, if I do stay."

"I'm not that big a fool," Michael said roughly. "Even if I do act like it most of the time. What other conditions?"

"Have you got any sleeping pills?"

"Never use the things. What makes you think they would help? I'd be inclined to suspect the reverse. The less control you have over your conscious mind . . ."

"Since you don't have any, there's not much point in debating that."

"How true. Anything else?"

"Find a key for that door. And barricade it."

"Honey, for the love of Mike—what if there's a fire, or a burglar, or—something else? We can't anticipate his moves; he might do anything. If I couldn't get to you—"

"It's a risk we must take." Her eyes were hard as stone; the eyes of a fanatic. "Another thing, I want you to search this place from top to bottom. Make sure Gordon hasn't left any other little souvenirs, like the notebook."

"You think . . .?" Michael cogitated. "I wonder."

"I'm not thinking, I'm just grasping at straws. But according to some occult theories, there must be a physical connection between the spell and the person whom it is meant to affect—like the doll, which uses the victim's own hair or nail clippings. Why not a physical connection, a focus, for the warlock's spells? Gordon isn't careless about his belongings. That notebook was left here deliberately.''

"I agree. I'm sloppy, but not unconscious; the book was planted under a pile of material I wouldn't ordinarily refer to. Wait a minute. If your theory is right, he must have planted something at Andrea's house.''

"He's been there any number of times.''

"He went there looking for you, before you came here the first time,'' Michael said. "He admitted entering the house.''

"So it's possible. I'm not sure of this, Michael. I think it's worth checking, though.''

"I'm trying to figure out when he could have hidden the notebook.''

"Hiding it wouldn't take more than a few seconds. It must have been here for several days, Michael. Because the summoning that brought you to Andrea's didn't come from me. There's only one person who could have sent it.''

"The idea had occurred to me. But I can't think of any reason why he should do such a thing.''

"His reasons aren't comprehensible to normal people. I can think of an analogy, though: the pathologically jealous husband who keeps accusing his wife of infidelity until finally, in sheer desperation, she goes out and acquires a lover."

"Yeah. I knew a guy like that. His wife finally left him, and he took it as proof that he'd been right about her all along. All right." Michael stood up. "I'll search the place. The fact that Briggs was so ostentatious about removing the notebook might have been a bluff, to conceal the existence of something else."

He was not willing to admit, even to himself, the flaw in his reasoning; that if Briggs had removed the notebook, it might be because Gordon no longer needed it. Once the link was established . . .

When he had finished his search, the apartment was neater than it had been for months. He found nothing, but he was aware that the negative results were not conclusive. Unless he tore furniture and walls to pieces, he could not be sure that some small object was not still concealed.

He searched the bedroom last, at Linda's request; he knew that, as twilight closed in, she wanted him near by, where he could watch her. She seemed convinced of her theory of a physical link; Michael found it weaker and less convincing the longer he thought about it.

Napoleon, fully restored to health and malevolence, was still with them. Curled up on the foot of the bed, he watched Michael suspiciously.

Michael backed out of the interior of the wardrobe, carrying the pile of dirty shirts he had inspected several times before. He shook each one out, feeling in the pockets, and dropping them one by one to the floor as he finished. He viewed the untidy pile indecisively, and then shrugged and left it there.

"Can you think of any place I missed?" he asked.

"No." Linda's voice was strained. "Michael, it's almost dark."

"Not yet."

"Yes. Now." She held out her hands.

When he had done it, Michael was shaking. It got worse every time he did it. Napoleon's disapproval didn't help matters. The cat protested so violently that Michael finally had to shut him in the bathroom.

"All right," he said, straightening up after he had tied the final knot. "That's it. I'm not going to gag you, I don't see the need for it; and anyhow, it is simply too goddamn much for me to stomach.''

"Okay,'' she said submissively.

Michael had turned on the lights; the darkness outside was complete. The lamp by the bed cast a warm glow on Linda's face, and he was outraged to see that she was smiling. Maybe she felt better this way. He sure as hell didn't.

He couldn't look at her any longer. He couldn't stand the thoughts that kept worming into his mind. Abruptly, he turned and blundered out of the room; when he was out of her sight he leaned up against the wall, his head resting on his arm. It was barely seven o'clock. How in the name of God was he going to get through the rest of the night?

It was the hour of midnight he dreaded most. Superstition . . . but no more mad than any of the other things that had happened. He forced himself back to Linda and found, as people usually do, that he could stand it, and would stand it, because he had to.

They talked, but no longer of theories and interpretations. They spoke of defense, like the decimated garrison of a beleaguered fortress. But the weapons they discussed were not in any modern arsenal.

"I don't happen to have any holy water on hand," Michael said, driven to a fruitless sarcasm. "Ran out last week. . . . It didn't help Andrea, remember?"

"Could you—could you pray?" she asked diffidently.

"No." Michael looked at her. "Yes. I could pray. If I knew What to pray to."

The idea came into both minds at the same moment, or else she read his face with uncanny quickness.

"You can't do that," she said.

"Why not? If we're right—or even if we're wrong. Any kind of mental assurance, confidence—"

"Not that kind, no—there's a limit, Michael. It would be spiritual prostitution, unimaginably worse than any physical contamination. You couldn't do it—not if you really believed. And if you didn't, it would just be a dirty game."

Again Michael was reminded of the gulf between their minds. His idea of trying to fight Gordon on his own ground had been partly a counsel of desperation, partly an academic theory. There was nothing academic about Linda's attitude; she looked sick with disgust.

"Besides," she went on; her voice was

shaking. "Besides, you'd be a novice, a probationer. He's studied these things for years. All you would do is weaken yourself, don't you see? He could walk right into your mind and destroy it."

"Okay, okay. It was just an idea. Then what can we do?" Linda relaxed.

"Do you love me?" she asked.

The question was so unexpected that it caught Michael off guard.

"Someone asked me that, once," he said slowly.

"Well?"

"I said I didn't know what the word meant. I still don't. But I love you."

"Then love me. No—" His hand came toward her and she shook her head. "Don't touch me, don't think of touching me. Think of love. Not of desire; they aren't the same. I don't know what love means either. But most people confuse loving with being loved. Love isn't reciprocal. It doesn't ask, or expect, or demand. It isn't an emotion, it's a state of being. Love me, Michael."

"It sounds rather one-sided to me," Michael said; for the life of him, he could not have kept the bitterness out of his voice. "And also rather esoteric. You aren't talking to Saint Francis, you know."

"I noticed that. . . . Oh, Michael, I'm sorry! I'm sorry you're involved in this, I'm sorry for talking to you like a third-rate mystic, I'm sorriest of all for asking, demanding, and not offering you anything in return. I haven't anything to give, not any longer. I did once; I think I did. . . . But I lost it, somewhere along the way, when Gordon taught me his way of loving. He does love me, you know. He calls it that. And I'm almost as bad as he is now; the only difference is that I know that that insatiable demand is not love, but a perversion of it. That's why I can't fight him. But you can."

Without answering, Michael stood up and walked across the room. From Linda's earnest confusion of half-digested philosophy he derived only despair. Even if they fought their way out of the present crisis, there was no future for him with a woman who was literally frightened to death of loving. She was sick, incurably sick, if she could believe what she said she believed. Like most theories, hers sounded fine on the surface; but if love was not reciprocal, only the saints could derive much satisfaction from it. A normal human being had only so much to give without getting something in return. Depletion was inevitable.

And this present situation, which she had talked him into, was impossible. Linda was immobilized, defenseless. If she was wrong—and she had to be wrong!—about her idea of vulnerability through the lack of love, then he was as susceptible to mental invasion as she was. The logic of Gordon's next move came to him so strongly that it was as if he had read the other's mind. Even if Linda had not been bound, she would be no match for him; he was stronger and heavier. She could scream; and she would, as long as she had breath left with which to scream, long enough for the neighbors to call the police, who would not arrive in time. . . . They would find him standing there, over the bloody thing on the bed. Gordon would keep control over him that long. Just that long. He would release the mental bonds in time for Michael to see, and comprehend, what he had done. . . .

Just in time, Michael realized what was happening. He flung himself around, grasping at the first solid object that came within reach. Something rocked under the thrust of his body, something fell and crashed; and he found himself leaning against the big dresser, his arms grasping it as a drowning man would clutch an oar. A broken ashtray lay on the floor. His face was streaming with perspiration, and his heart pounded as if he had been running a race. Something else was pounding—an irate neighbor, from the floor below. The howls of Napoleon, imprisoned in the bathroom, were loud enough to wake the dead.

"Michael! Michael—is something wrong?"

How long had she been calling him? With an enormous effort, Michael removed his hands from the dresser and turned around.

"It's all right," he said thickly; and then said it again, because his voice had been almost inaudible.

He saw Linda staring at him. There was concern in her face, but no fear; apparently the meaning of his sudden movement had escaped her.

"What is it?" she repeated.

"Liver, or something," Michael said promptly. His voice and body were once again under his control. The mental grasp had left his mind, but he derived no comfort from his victory. This might have been only a preliminary, testing thrust. He knew that he did not dare tell Linda what had happened.

"Hadn't you better let Napoleon out?" she asked. "He's beside himself."

"Huh? Oh, yeah."

Michael opened the door warily, putting himself into a posture of defense. Napoleon's shrieks stopped abruptly, but he did not appear; looking around the corner of the door, Michael saw him crouched in the farthest corner, behind the hamper.

"It's all right," he said. "You can come out now."

The cat refused to move until Linda called him. He curled up on the foot of the bed.

"I'll make some coffee," Michael mumbled, and fled without waiting for an answer.

He got to the kitchen before his legs gave way, and collapsed into a chair, letting his head drop down onto the table. For a long time he sat and shook, while his mind raced desperately from one blank wall to another. He had thought, when he fought Linda for his life, that that was the worst thing that could happen. He knew now that he had yet to experience the worst. If he hurt Linda, Gordon wouldn't have to take any further steps; he would sit screaming in a cell for the rest of his life, until he found some means of ending it. And even this might not be the ultimate disaster. Gordon had a fertility of imagination that was far beyond his own feeble concepts of evil. . . .

And the end of it all was that there was nothing he could do. He was boxed into a corner. Whatever he did now would be dangerous. He could lock himself in one room and Linda in another; but his controlled mind would find some means of breaking through any barricade he could construct. He could go out, and smash a window, or insult a cop, and maybe get thrown in jail—if he could find a cop willing to arrest him. That would leave Linda alone, at the mercy of whatever attack Gordon planned next. He could let the police take Linda—which would be just what Gordon wanted. If he untied her, and begged her to immobilize him, she would know what had happened, and with her susceptibility to suggestion—or mental control, call it what you liked—she would then become his Nemesis, instead of the reverse. There was no way out.

The sound of knocking roused him, after a timeless interval of sheer despair; and he was, somehow, not surprised to realize that his lips were moving soundlessly in words he hadn't used since childhood. He moved like a machine to answer the door. Neither hope nor fear drove him; he was simply geared to accept, and deal with, whatever was there.

For a few seconds after he had opened the door he stood with his mouth slightly ajar, assessing the man on the threshold as he might have studied a perfect stranger. The tall, spare figure and unlined face; the odd, silvery-gray eyes and the close-cropped hair that was a matching silver . . . Galen had been gray ever since Michael had known him. He carried a light suitcase and a topcoat. No hat. Galen never wore a hat.

Michael stepped back, throwing the door wide.

"How did you know I wanted you?" he asked.

"I called from the airport," Galen said

prosaically. He threw his coat onto a chair and put his case down on the floor beside it. "Henry said you'd been phoning all day."

His gaze swept the room and returned to Michael; and the latter was conscious of his appearance, which was both haggard and unkempt. He ran his hand self-consciously over the stubble of beard on his jaw and glanced down at his unspeakable shirt—rumpled, sweat-stained, dirty—before meeting Galen's eyes.

"I'm glad you're back," he said inadequately.

"Why?"

Michael opened his mouth, and closed it again. Coherent explanation was beyond him.

"You might as well see the worst," he said. "Come into the bedroom."

He had always admired Galen's phlegm, and wondered what degree of shock it would take to startle him out of it. He found out. Galen paled visibly at the sight that met his eyes.

Flat on the bed, arms outstretched and bound, ankles tied to the footboard, Linda looked like a character out of one of the books Michael never read, much less wrote. Apparently she had recognized Galen's voice; she was not surprised to see him, but she blushed slightly as the incredulous gray eyes swept over her.

"It isn't what you think," she said.

"I'm not sure what I think." Galen sat down in the nearest chair. "Give me a minute to catch my breath. Michael . . ."

Michael talked. It was an unspeakable relief; he knew how Linda had felt all those months, bottling up her fears. He talked without critical intent or editing, mixing theory and fact, interpretation and actuality. And Galen listened. He blinked, a little more often than was normal, but his face had smoothed out into its professional mask. Michael finished with an account of the mental attack he had just experienced. Linda, who was hearing this for the first time, gasped audibly, but Galen went on nodding.

"Well, well," he said, after Michael's voice had stopped. "No wonder you look like hell."

"Is that all you can say?"

"What do you want me to say?" He glanced from one of them to the other, and smiled faintly. "If it comes to that—what do you want me to do? Put on my wizard's robes and exorcise the devil?"

Michael sat down on the bed. He grinned.

"I rather expected you to put in a call for the men in the white coats, and order rooms for two."

"I may yet," Galen said coolly. "You realize—neither of you is unintelligent—that everything you've told me can be explained in terms of pathological mental conditions?"

Michael glanced apprehensively at Linda and was reasured by what he saw. The strain, the underlying fear were still there, but Galen's comment had not shaken her. She had anticipated it. Perversely, he was moved to marshal the very arguments he had once demolished himself.

"Andrea's death?"

Galen shrugged.

"The phenomenon is sometimes called thanatomania. With the heart condition you mentioned, the result was virtually a foregone conclusion. I've seen several cases myself where there was no diagnosable organic weakness. You must have read the newspaper accounts, a few years ago, of an excellent example of thanatomania. The woman had been told, by a soothsayer, that she would die on a certain date. She died. In a modern hospital, under professional care."

"I read about it," Michael admitted unwillingly. "What about the dog, then? I saw it too."

"Then the dog is a collective hallucination, or a real dog."

"Hallucinations don't bite," Michael said.

Galen glanced at the dirty bandage on his arm.

"I'll have a look at that later," he said calmly. "Aside from my concern, personal and professional, for your physical health, I'd like to examine the marks."

Bemused by fatigue and relief Michael grappled with that one for several seconds before he understood enough to get angry.

"Another example of thanatomania?" he said sarcastically.

Galen's tone of annoyance was indicative; he usually had better control of himself.

"Good God Almighty, Michael, do I have to synopsize the professional journals? You've read enough of the popular literature to know that patients have inflicted everything from fake stigmata to signs of rape on themselves, in order to prove whatever point they feel they must make. And don't try to tell me you aren't deeply enough involved, emotionally, with Mrs. Randolph, to be suggestible."

Linda spoke for the first time.

"So involved that he would be forced to concoct a crazy theory in order to excuse my attempt to kill him." It was a statement, not a question. Galen nodded, watching her. She went on calmly, "Yes, I can understand that kind of reasoning. But I do have one question, Doctor. Why did you give Michael his father's letters?"

Galen's slow, close-lipped smile spread across his face.

"The first sensible question anyone has asked yet," he said. "The answer is complex, however. I suggest we adjourn."

"Where?" Michael asked.

"My house, naturally. I want to have a look at that arm. And I agree that, for whatever reason, this atmosphere is unhealthy for both of you. Pack a bag, Michael, while I untie Mrs. Randolph."

Michael turned to obey, but he was diverted by the spectacle of Galen, every professional hair in place, calmly untying the knots that bound Linda to the bed. Glancing up, Galen met his eyes and smiled affably.

"This is not, by any means, my most unusual experience," he said, and turned his attention back to his work.

Eleven

"Not self-inflicted," Galen said.

"Thanks a lot."

Michael rolled down his sleeve. Linda knew he had been trying not to wince; Galen's poking and probing, which appeared to be prompted more by a spirit of scientific inquiry than concern for his patient's pains, must have hurt more than the original dressing of the wound.

Galen leaned back in his chair.

"Unless you found a cooperative dog," he qualified.

Linda bit back the comment that was on the tip of her tongue. She did not have Michael's lifelong experience with the older man, which had apparently given him a childlike faith in the great father figure. She had welcomed Galen's appearance for two reasons: first as an ally, who would help guard Michael from herself, and, second, as the key to the final door through which she meant to pass when all other means were exhausted. But although she herself had anticipated and considered every one of Galen's rational objections, she found them irritating coming from him.

Glancing around the doctor's study, she thought she would like the man if she weren't prejudiced against his profession. The furnishings of the room were so luxurious that they were inobtrusive; every object was so exactly right, in function and design, that it blended into a perfect whole. The exquisite marble head on the bookshelf looked like one she had seen in an Athens museum, but it was not a copy. The rugs were modern Scandinavian designs; their abstract whirls of color went equally well with the classical sculpture, the Monet over the fireplace, and the geometric lines of the rosewood tables and desk. Heavy hangings, deep chairs, beautiful ornaments—they made up a room of soft lights and warm, bright coloring as soothing to the nerves as it was stimulating to the senses. Only one object—Linda's eyes went to the soft couch, piled with cushions; and Galen, who saw everything, smiled at her.

"I use it more than my patients do," he said. "Most of them prefer to confront me, face to face."

"I didn't think you ever slept," Michael said.

"Catnaps. Like all the other great men of history. Hence the couch, in here."

He had a beautiful speaking voice, as modulated and controlled as an actor's. And used for the same purpose, Linda thought. Fighting the influence of the voice and the room, she returned to the attack.

"You don't honestly believe we went looking for a dog and provoked him into attacking Michael?"

"It does seem unlikely," Galen admitted.

"But not impossible?"

"Trite as it may sound . . ."

"Nothing is impossible. Damn you," Linda said.

Galen's fixed smile widened, very slightly, and Linda flung herself out of her chair and began to pace. That was one of the reasons why she hated psychiatrists; she had the feeling that her every action was not only anticipated, but provoked.

"However," Galen went on calmly, "unless the evidence to the contrary is strong, I generally prefer the simplest hypothesis."

"A real dog," Michael said.

"A real dog," Galen agreed.

Linda turned, to find both of them watching her. For a moment, the open amusement in Galen's face almost provoked an outburst; then she saw the strained pallor of Michael's face, and she dropped into her chair.

"I'm sorry," she said.

"You asked me a question," Galen said. "About the letters. What did you make of them, Michael?"

"Not much. I was hoping you'd have more to say on the subject."

"I do. But I want your interpretation first."

"The thing that struck me was the Jonah effect," Michael said slowly. "The doom and destruction that hit the people closest to Randolph. That, and my father's inexplicable dislike of him. It was Linda who told me he must have been the head of the witchcraft cult, and thus directly responsible for the death of that boy—"

"Green. The author of *The Smoke of Her Burning.*" As they both sat speechless, Galen turned to Linda. "Didn't you suspect, Mrs. Randolph, that your husband never wrote that book?"

"I—I don't know. I never—" Linda rallied. "I guess I did. But not for a long time, and it was never more than a suspicion. I loved the author of that book before I ever met Gordon; I think it was one of the reasons why I loved him. The external brilliance, the polish—Gordon could have done that. What he lacked, what he never could have produced, was the soul of the book—the compassion, the tenderness."

Galen nodded. He turned back to Michael.

"That was what your father suspected, knowing both students as he did. That was what he told me, privately. Of course he could prove nothing. Green had told him he was working on a book, but had never showed him any of the manuscript. He said he wanted to have it complete before he submitted it for criticism."

"I should have known," Michael said,

flushed with self-contempt. "I call myself a writer. . . . But there were other things. The campaign speeches, even Kwame's songs . . . For a while I played with the idea that he had stolen them from Gordon."

"They were not written by the same man; but they were written by the same kind of man," Galen said. "Despite my reluctance to accept your theories of diabolic possession, I do believe in what you might call mental vampirism—a spiritual blood sucking, a leechlike drain of the intelligence and emotions of others. You've met people, I'm sure, who left you feeling drained and depressed after a few hours' conversation. Usually this is an unconscious demand, but Randolph is quite conscious of what he's doing. Make no mistake, he was never guilty of ordinary plagiarism. His victims gave him what he wanted, half convinced themselves that it was his work.

"Eventually, however, the vampire goes too far, and destroys the source from which it draws its vitality. It is symptomatic, not only of Randolph's effect on others, but of their personality weaknesses, that they should resort to suicide, or some other form of escape, rather than attacking Randolph. For it was not only intellectual brilliance he sought, it was brilliance coupled with a sense of insecurity. You might say, if you were mystically inclined—which I am not—that Randolph was drawn, by a kind of spiritual chemistry, to people of this sort, just as they were attracted to him. The stronger souls —pardon the expression—resisted him. As you did, Mrs. Randolph. He miscalculated with you, possibly because his instincts were confused by a more basic desire. But there lay the danger to you. Randolph literally could not let you go. What he fails to fascinate he must destroy, and eventually he destroys even that which he fascinates."

"Then everything he's done," Michael muttered, "all his success—a fraud. A gigantic fraud."

"Not at all. He had one undeniable talent. Charisma, we call it—the ability to charm and command affection, loyalty. All leaders have it, to some extent, and all of them depend on advisers, speech writers, hired experts, to supply any qualities they may lack. If Randolph had accepted that kind of help, he might have been a successful politician and a good teacher; he is not a stupid man. But he isn't content with mere competence. A healthy, strong body, and the finest of training, let him excel in the sports he selected—and don't underestimate the power of that confident personality on his opponents. But he knew that eventually he would lose, when he got into the big leagues, against opponents who were simply better than he was. So he quit."

"Well, I'll be damned," Michael said. "You're on our side after all, you old—"

"I am merely presenting what seems to me, at the moment, the most logical hypothesis. I've followed Randolph's career with some interest, since your father told me his suspicions. I respected his judgment, and I was intrigued by Randolph's behavior. If your father was correct, there were certain alarming tendencies. . . . Well. Candidly, I was relieved when he decided to give up his political career."

Michael opened his mouth to speak, but Linda forestalled him.

"So you believe in a perfectly materialist, rational explanation.

"Yes. Given your husband's personality, and motives, the rest is clear. The dog is a real dog, manipulated and concealed by Randolph in an attempt to play on your nerves. Your erratic behavior is a result of secretly administered drugs and a form of hypnotic control, intensified by your increasing suggestibility as doubts of your own sanity increased."

"But I thought no one could be hypnotized to do something he wouldn't consciously do."

"An error," Galen said succinctly. "Or, shall we say, a great oversimplification."

"My attack on Michael—"

"Posthypnotic suggestion, conditioning . . ." Galen paused. The gray eyes appraised her coldly. "I am not saying that your mental and emotional state is normal, at the present time."

"I know that," Linda said. "What I don't know is how abnormal it is."

"You mean, are you still a potential threat to Michael?" Galen pondered the problem with visible emotion. "I would guess that you may well be."

"God damn it!" Michael was on his feet, ignoring Linda's outstretched hand, and Galen's unperturbed smile. "Your theory stinks, Galen. Oh, I know, it all makes sense. It even explains why the dog attacked me, and left before it did any serious damage. The storm excited it, so that it broke away from its handlers, and they called it back before it could be killed or captured because they didn't want their supernatural effect ruined. I'll even admit to hearing a funny whistling sound that might have been Gordon, calling the dog. But your version doesn't explain Gordon's motive. Why the elaborate plot? Why all the hocus-pocus? And why me, for God's sake?"

"Your theory isn't strong on motive either," Galen pointed out. "The mechanism isn't that complicated, or obscure; Randolph's original reason for inviting you to his home had nothing to do with plots, supernatural or otherwise. He may have selected you, in preference to others, because of some amorphous idea of getting back at your father, who was one of the few people who never succumbed to the myth; after that, the development of the relationship between you and Mrs. Randolph would give even a balanced mind cause for dislike. What do you consider a motive, anyway? Four million dollars? You're talking about human behavior, which is difficult enough to comprehend even in so-called normal individuals. People have committed murder over a dirty plate, or a sum as small as three dollars."

"All right, all right," Michael said irritably. "Stop talking down to me. I'll accept any hypothesis you shove at me, if you'll just tell me what to do about it."

"You know better than to ask me for advice."

"Professional reticence?" Linda asked too politely.

"Professionally I'm full of advice. As a human being I'll be damned if I will take on the combined role of leaning post and punching bag. Make your own decisions and kick yourself if they turn out badly."

"There's something you may not know," Michael said. His voice was quiet, but he was furious; Linda knew him well enough now to recognize the signs. "If Randolph were just our personal Nemesis, you'd be justified in staying out of this. But he is planning to go back into politics. That's a fact; I've checked it out. By your own description he's a paranoidal maniac with enormous charm. Does that remind you of any other political figure in recent history? Gordon isn't a runty paperhanger with a funny moustache; he's got a lot more on the ball."

Galen's lips tightened. He showed no other reaction; but after a moment Michael flushed and turned away.

"I have not refused to concern myself," Galen said quietly. "What I'm trying to do is make this a joint project."

"I'm sorry," Michael muttered. "You're right; the long-range effects aren't important now. The main thing is to get Linda free of him. At the risk of sounding simpleminded, I suggest one of the quick divorce mills."

"What's happened to your brain?" Galen asked nastily. "You can't treat this as an ordinary case of mental cruelty. Randolph is not an ordinary man."

"He doesn't own the whole goddamned world."

"He owns her." Galen's head jerked in Linda's direction. Illogically, it was at that moment, with the impact of his brutal statement still aching, that Linda decided to trust him.

"He's right," she said to Michael. "Call it what you like—obsession, neurosis, whatever. He does own me." She turned to the psychiatrist. "You've been very persuasive, Doctor. But I don't believe any of it. Gordon isn't an ordinary man, you're right. He's not a man at all, not any longer."

Galen leaned back in his chair.

"At last," he said, with a sigh. "I thought I spotted something. . . . What do you think he is? Demon, disciple of Satan, werewolf . . . Ah. The dog."

In Michael's hurried, incoherent account, this theory had somehow escaped mention—probably because he rejected it himself. Linda knew there was no use trying to avoid it. Squaring her shoulders, she looked Galen straight in the eye.

"Yes," she said. "That's what I think he is."

"Hmph." Galen rocked back and forth. "Why?"

"If you don't stop saying that—" Michael began.

"Shut up. I'm investigating Linda's crazy ideas, not yours. Lycanthropy . . . You are not referring, I'm sure, to the mental aberration which involves cannibalism, necrophilia, sadism and a craving for raw meat, among other symptoms?"

"Is there such a thing?" Linda asked incredulously.

"As a form of psychotic paranoia, sometimes called zoanthropy, there certainly is such a thing. It is comparatively rare, but well documented; some of the famous mass murderers of history probably suffered from a form of this complaint—Gilles de Rais, Jack the Ripper. . . .

"But that's not what you mean. You are referring to the belief that some human beings can transform themselves into animal form, through the application of various magical techniques. The werewolf is the most famliar to us, because it is a product of European mythology and is described by the classical authors. In the East, however, one encounters were-tigers, and in Africa the supernatural beast may be a hyena or a leopard. The leopard societies of West Africa, which terrorized whole villages, are well known; there was a strong element of such a cult in the Mau Mau atrocities, in Kenya. The mutilations inflicted on the victims of these societies resemble those made by the claws of a predatory animal, and were done with artificial instruments designed to resemble claws.

"Of course it's impossible to separate the supernatural and pathological elements.

A culture with an implicit faith in lycanthropy produces men who are susceptible to the mania, and an individual who found it impossible to attain prestige by normal methods might well turn to lycanthropy as a means of intimidating those he cannot otherwise control."

"Good God," Michael muttered.

"There is, as well, a connection between lycanthropy and witchcraft," Galen went on calmly. "The tradition of supernatural animals is widespread and very ancient. The ability of a witch or warlock to assume animal form was one of the powers granted by Satan to his disciples. Often witches made their way to the Sabbath meeting in animal form. The great black goat was a manifestation of Lucifer. Black is, of course, the color of evil. And the black dog is not unknown as a supernatural animal, sometimes representing the warlock and sometimes Satan himself. The wild dog or wolflike beast is a symbol of the bestial qualities of the human mind, freed from the bonds of reason and conscience."

"A vile slander on animals," Michael said.

Galen went on, without appearing

to hear him.

"You see, I am sure, how the various traditions mingle—pre-Christian superstitions, perversions of Christian theology, and a variety of mental aberrations, ranging from paranoia to autohypnosis and hallucination. But the elements of the classic Western werewolf legend are explicit. Some werewolves, as in the popular films, are helpless victims of a curse, involuntary skin-turners. Most are innocent; they seek the change by diabolical means and use their animal form to satisfy bestial desires. According to these accounts, it is the soul, or astral body, of the man that takes the animal form. The real body lies in a cataleptic coma, barely breathing; but the astral form is actual, physical, in that it can inflict pain and death, and feel pain and death. Any wound inflicted on the animal is reproduced on the sleeping human body, and drawing the animal's blood forces it to resume human shape. In some traditions, the beast can only be killed by a silver bullet, or by a sword which has been blessed by a priest. When death occurs, the body of the beast disappears and the body of the lycanthrope is found with the same wounds that killed the animal. Intelligent observers have already suspected the werewolf's human identity because of such signs as hairy palms and eyebrows that meet in the middle. He is often strangely affected by the full moon. Has Gordon any of these traits, Mrs. Randolph?"

"Don't be ridiculous," Linda said disgustedly. "Those are old wives' tales."

Meeting Galen's gently ironic eye, she began to laugh, helplessly.

"Oh, dear . . . that's probably the craziest thing I've said yet. Maybe I'm not as far gone as I thought I was. No, I think Gordon belongs to your second category. How was it you phrased it? 'The ability of a warlock to assume animal form was one of the powers granted by Satan to his disciples.' "

"It makes sense," Galen said. "Given his past history, his dabbling in demonology as a young man, and his desire for control over others."

Linda's insane desire to laugh broke out again at the sight of Michael's stupefied expression.

"Wait a minute," he gasped. "First you said . . . And now you're saying . . ."

"You seem to be degenerating," Galen

snapped. "I'm not telling you what I believe. I am endeavoring to ascertain what Randolph himself believes."

"I think he believes it," Linda said stubbornly. "What I just said."

"I don't know," Michael said.

Galen rose. He seemed taller; from where Linda sat, on a low chair by the desk, he seemed to tower over her.

"Maybe we'd better ask him," he said.

For the last few minutes, Linda had been partially aware of background noises, but in the immediacy of the conversation she had paid little attention. Now the meaning of the muffled sounds came home to her—a doorbell ringing, footsteps down the stairs and along the hall, the rattle of locks, and the opening and closing of the door. She sprang to her feet. The footsteps were coming down the hall, toward the study. Footsteps she knew. Gordon's steps.

II

She was on her feet, halfway to the window in a mindless flight, when Galen's hand caught her arm. His grip was as hard as steel.

"I'm sorry, I meant to warn you," he said; the even voice contrasted alarmingly with the intensity of the hard hand on her wrist. "He came more promptly than I expected. Trust me, Linda. This has to be done."

Without waiting for an answer, he turned to Michael.

"Just keep quiet," he said rapidly. "Don't look surprised, at whatever I say, and don't contradict me or volunteer anything. If you weren't half-witted tonight, I wouldn't have to tell you—"

There was no time for further speech. The door of the study opened. Linda had a glimpse of the impassive manservant who had admitted them to the house; behind him was Gordon.

Without meaning to move, Linda managed to get behind Galen. He had released his grip on her arm. There was no need for further constraint, and he must have known it. She was as incapable of movement as she was of speech.

Gordon's fine dark eyes moved slowly over the three faces confronting him.

"My poor little errant wife," he said, "and—friend. I've never had the pleasure of meeting you, Dr. Rosenberg, but of course your reputation is well known. It was good of you to call me."

"Sit down, Mr. Randolph," Galen said equably. He did not, Linda noticed, offer the other man his hand.

Gordon took the chair indicated. He seemed perfectly at ease, except for the weariness in his face—normal in a man who has been trying to track down an insane wife.

Carefully, he did not look at Linda. He was acting again, and doing it well, simulating wary concern, pretending he didn't want to frighten her. . . . He looked at Michael instead, and a pathetic shadow of his old charming smile touched his mouth.

"Sorry, Mike. I've been a little off my head the last few days, or I wouldn't have thought—what I've been thinking. And all the time you were planning this. I'm eternally in your debt."

It was a little obvious, even for Gordon. Linda knew quite well what he was doing, but being able to analyze his methods did not make her immune. Huddled on the low hassock where Galen's ruthless arms had deposited her, she fought a doubt she had thought long conquered—doubt of

Michael, and of the doctor to whom he had brought her.

Michael said nothing. He was standing, as if he felt more secure on his feet. His wooden-faced silence did nothing to relieve Linda's doubts.

The silence deepened. Galen, who had seated himself behind his desk, picked up a pen and began scribbling with it. His eyes intent on the meaningless doodles with which he disfigured the pristine surface of the desk blotter, he was humming under his breath, and—Linda realized—flatting badly.

It was a crude trick, but Gordon succumbed. Linda didn't see the crack in the barrier at first, it was so small. Only later, when she recalled the interview, did she appreciate Galen's over-all strategy.

"I'm grateful to you, too, Doctor," Gordon said. "But I don't quite understand you . . . May I speak to you alone?"

"Why?"

Galen did not look up from his doodling. Critically he studied a scribble which looked like an arrow, and carefully added three oblique lines to represent the feather at the end of the shaft.

"To discuss what's to be done."

"That concerns all of us," Galen pointed out. "Your wife has told me a very disturbing story, Mr. Randolph."

He looked up; and Linda, who had felt the full effect of that passionless stare, was not surprised to see Gordon recoil slightly.

"Disturbing?" he repeated.

Galen, who had returned to his drawing, nodded vaguely.

"In what way?"

Galen shook his head and went on doddling. By now the precise movements of his pen had caught everyone's attention. Gordon was almost craning his neck to watch, and the distraction had shaken his concentration.

"I must insist, Doctor," he said; his voice was no longer pleasant.

"On what grounds?"

"Why—because she is my wife. I have the right—"

"You have no right." Galen's voice was remote. "Your wife has placed herself under my care. I called you in to ask you about certain statements she has made, not to report to you."

Gordon rose to his feet in a single

powerful surge, his face distorted by the expression few people other than Linda had seen. Disregarding his instructions, Michael took a step forward, but it was Galen who stopped Randolph, with a single small gesture of his right hand, so quickly done that Linda could not have described it.

The effect on Gordon was astounding. He fell back, his face losing its color. Then, as if compelled, he leaned forward and looked at the drawing Galen had made.

"The College," he said, in a choked voice. "You are one—"

"Oh, yes," Galen said cheerfully.

Because she was sitting by the desk, next to his right hand, Linda was the only one who saw that hand move. A long index finger flicked a switch; and all the lights went out.

With the curtains drawn and the door closed, the room was plunged into primeval blackness. Linda heard the long, shaken intake of breath that came from Gordon; it went on so long it seemed impossible that human lungs could hold so much air. Then it burst out, in a sound that shocked the brain and senses as it affronted the ears. She heard a heavy chair fall, and the rush of something through the dark, and she dropped to the floor, crouching, for fear his blind rush would bring him to her. He found the door, after an interval that seemed interminable; the light from the hall was yellow and comforting, silhouetting his tall body. Then he was gone. The front door slammed, waking echoes from the lovely crystal chandelier in the hall.

The lights came on again.

"Hmph," Galen said.

Crouching on the floor behind his chair, Linda was busy shaking. A pair of hands caught her by the shoulders and hauled her to her feet. She stared into Michael's face.

"You all right?"

He didn't wait for an answer, but dumped her unceremoniously on the hassock, and wheeled on the figure pensively posed behind the desk.

"What College, you congenital liar?"

"I haven't the faintest idea," Galen said placidly.

"Another lie . . . The drawing. What is it?"

Galen stirred and stretched.

"The drawing, like the gesture I made, is an invention. A meaningless hodgepodge of symbols and Hebrew letters. I regret to say that my years of Hebrew school are far behind me, and my knowledge of the Cabala is even vaguer. The effect on Mr. Randolph was interesting, though, wasn't it?"

Michael regarded him with no admiration whatever.

"Of the two of you, I almost think I prefer Randolph. The College, I suppose, is an equally imaginary group of—what? Adepts in magic, squatting on top of Mount Everest thinking about the universe? You deliberately let him think . . ."

"I let him think what he wanted to think. And I found out what I wanted to know." He turned a contemplative stare on Linda, huddled on the hassock. "You were right. I felt sure that you were, but I had to check. And implant a certain useful suggestion."

Michael picked up the chair Gordon had overturned in his flight, and sat down. Under its drawn pallor, his face held the first gleam of hope Linda had seen for hours.

"He thinks you're a powerful warlock

yourself. That isn't all you learned, is it?"

"I wondered if you'd notice."

"I was blind not to see it before."

"When you described his reaction to the power failure in your apartment, I wondered. Knowing that his concern for Mrs. Randolph was only problematical, I suspected another, more immediate cause for his panic."

"He's afraid of the dark," Michael said. Linda saw him shiver, and felt the same chill. She would never hear that word again without remembering.

"Yes. Significant, in view of the poetic words of your young friend at the college." Galen's voice changed. "Damn you for mentioning it, Michael; I should be immune to that kind of verbal magic, but when I think of what that poor devil sees, when the lights go out . . ."

"It isn't only the dark Gordon fears." For once Linda was immune to that kind of magic. "He's afraid of flying. He doesn't drive a car. He quit smoking."

"No contact sports," Michael muttered. "Even then . . . Swimming? Lots of other people around, spectators, competitors, just in case . . ."

"I believe that Elliott Jacques is correct

when he states that this particular anxiety comes to its peak during the crisis of middle life. Randolph is about forty, isn't he? I've seen a number of such cases, since the realization often produces symptoms which require psychotherapeutic treatment—psychosomatic illness, insomnia, claustrophobia, to mention only a few. Randolph's reactive symptoms are new to me; but they have a dreadful logic of their own. He fears, not only the dark, but the ultimate darkness. He is afraid of dying."

"And that's why he turned to Satanism," Michael muttered. "Those conversations we had about good and evil . . . He doesn't believe in God, but he can't accept the inevitability of death. There's only one other dispenser of immortality. 'Better to reign in Hell than serve in Heaven.' "

"Especially if you don't believe in Heaven," Galen said. "I hope you're enjoying your abstract intellectualizing, Michael. You may drown in it."

"What do you mean?"

"I took a calculated risk with Randolph. We've learned some interesting and useful things about him, but we've also stirred him up. He left here in a frenzy of rage and fear."

"You mean—he'll try something else?"
"Almost immediately, I should say."
Slowly, the two pairs of eyes turned to focus on Linda.

III

"No," she said. "No, he wouldn't dare. He was frightened. I've never seen him so upset."
"That's precisely the danger. A man of his temperament doesn't back down under a challenge. He'll be all the more eager to strike before, as he thinks, I have time to conjure up all my powers."
"God damn your arrogant soul," Michael said softly. "You deliberately, cold-bloodedly, stirred up that rattlesnake, knowing he can—"
"It had to be done." Galen's seldom-aroused temper showed in his flushed cheeks. "Oh, hell . . . I ought to know better. One of the basic rules of this trade is not to meddle with your friends' problems. . . . Tell him, Linda."
"Michael, he's right. How long could we go on, with this hanging over us? Watching each other out of the corners

of our eyes, afraid to sleep. . . . Twice I've tried to kill someone,'' she said, feeling Galen's silent commendation like a rock at her back. ''If I have to go on dreading that, I'd rather be dead. Gordon is off balance, for the first time since I've known him. We've got to keep him on the defensive.''

''How?'' Michael demanded.

''Don't look at me,'' Galen snapped.

''He's afraid of dying,'' Michael said. ''Why?''

''Give me five years of analysis and maybe I can tell you,'' Galen said. ''What the hell do you think I am, a mind reader?''

Linda wrapped both arms around her body, but their limited animal warmth did not touch the chill that froze her mind.

''You both know,'' she said, shaping the words with difficulty because her lips were stiff with that inner cold. ''You know what we have to do. Force the issue, keep him off balance. We'll have to follow him.''

''Where?'' Michael's voice sounded as stiff and difficult as hers.

''Back home, of course. Back to the house. Galen's absolutely right, he'll be wild with anger, he won't be able to wait; he'll try something tonight. And all his—his materials are back there."

"Doesn't he have a place here in town?" It was Galen who spoke; Michael was visibly struggling with conflicting emotions.

"A small apartment. He couldn't keep anything concealed there."

"Especially a large black dog," Galen murmured.

Michael, who had arranged a truce in his internal civil war, nodded thoughtfully. Having scaled one barrier, Linda faced the next.

"Doctor, I don't—I don't want to say this, but I must, I can't keep anything back now. Your theory appeals to me a great deal. If Gordon is a conscious villain, that makes me innocent, not only of intent to harm, but of serious mental instability. I'd like—oh, how I'd like!—to believe it. *But I don't.*"

Galen nodded. She knew that she had told him nothing he hadn't suspected, but that he was relieved by her candor. He turned to the other man.

"How about you, Michael?"

"I don't know. I just don't know."

"It doesn't matter." Galen got to his feet, rather heavily; for the first time Linda was conscious of his real age. "We'll go after Randolph. I have a few business matters to arrange before we leave, though. You two had better have some food. I ate on the plane."

Michael shook his head.

"I have some matters to arrange too. Can I borrow your car?"

"What for?"

"Never mind, then. I'll take a taxi."

"I'm incurably nosy," Galen said mildly. "Here, take the keys."

Michael caught the bright jingle out of the air with one hand. He looked at Linda with an expression that she was to remember, often, in the next hours. Then he turned on his heel and was gone.

Twelve

By the time Michael returned with the car, the other two were ready and waiting. The night had turned clear and chilly; Linda was wrapped in a huge cloak, which the doctor had mysteriously produced from some vast storehouse of improbable needs. Galen wore no coat, and his silvery head was bare. He carried a small flat case, like a briefcase.

As soon as the car stopped, Galen led Linda down the steps. He opened the back door of the car.

"You drive," he said to Michael, who was brooding over the wheel. "We'll sit in back where—For God's sake!"

Linda flexed her muscles just in time. From under her skirts came a wail of protest, and she reached down and lifted a dangling, muttering bundle of fur.

"Why the hell?" Galen demanded, slamming the car door.

His haste was unnecessary; Napoleon had no intention of going anywhere. He subsided onto Linda's lap and looked abused.

"He likes to ride in cars. Besides," Michael said, in a voice that ended Galen's objections, "I have a feeling he might be useful."

Fondling the scarred ears, Linda did not look up.

"The canary in the coal mine," she said. "Michael, I wish you hadn't."

"If he goes berserk, he can wreck the damned car," Galen said. "Haven't you got a carrying case for him?"

"On the floor," Michael said briefly, and put the car into gear.

They made good time; the streets were emptying. Staring out through the closed windows, Linda remembered that other, recent night drive. Night and darkness, the recurring motifs; there had been sunshine, once, but she could hardly remember that such a phenomenon existed. She was tired, so tired; not only in body but in every cell of brain and nerve. Desire for the endless sleep of death was comprehensible to her now; perhaps, she thought, it was not grief or despair that prompted suicide, but only sheer exhaustion.

Her eyes fixed unseeingly on the flashing, multicolored lights of the city, Linda knew that that was the solution none of them would admit. Sick or sane, right or wrong, she was not normal, and perhaps she never would be. While she lived, Michael would not abandon her—and neither would Gordon. Even if Gordon were defeated, Michael would be stuck with her and her inability to love; he was a stubborn man, he would keep on trying even though it was hopeless. But without her, Gordon would have no reason to attack Michael. He would be safe; and she could rest.

Dreamily and without interest, she wondered whether this black mood was Gordon's latest move. She didn't think so. It was far too pleasant a feeling to have emanated from Gordon's mind. And so reasonable . . .

In the warm, smothering shadow of the idea of death, two small, dissenting sparks burned. One was Michael—not desire, not even hope, just the thought of him. The other, absurdly, came from the scrubby patch of fur in which her fingers were entwined.

Napoleon stirred restlessly under her tightening hands, but she didn't let go. A mangy lifeline, that was what he was. A fighter. Battered and scarred and bloody, he had never thought pensively of the sweet sleep of death. Swaggering like Cyrano, his tail a scrawny panache, he took on all comers for the sheer glory of the fray: "Give me giants!"

The lights had disappeared now, except for isolated lighted windows. Linda recognized the terrain. Another hour . . . Even that thought could not rouse her from the drowsiness which numbed her limbs. Normal weariness—or the dangerous false sleep of Gordon's inducing? She could not tell, nor could she fight it. The solid, silent bulk of the man beside her gave her failing courage a slight lift, but even that faded out as the darkness closed in around her.

II

Absorbed in his driving and in the hag-ridden thoughts that made every effort doubly difficult, Michael had no warning. He didn't realize what was happening until he heard the sudden flurry of movement from the back seat, and the animal screams, and Galen's voice, sharp in command:

"Pull over! Quick!"

Michael jerked the car to a stop, half on and half off the road. He turned.

On the back seat, Galen's briefcase gaped open. Galen, kneeling on a heaving dark cylinder that sprawled half on the seat and half on the floor, held a hypodermic high, checking it. He must have had it ready and waiting, in that convenient case. . . .

Before Michael could move, Galen plunged the needle home in a reckless disregard of antisepsis. Hampered by the muffling folds of the cloak, Linda went limp as the drug took hold. Then Michael heard the sound that was coming from the floor of the front seat. Napoleon, inflated to twice his normal size, had removed himself as far as possible from what was happening in the back. Once before, Michael had heard him make a noise like that.

Galen looked up, his face a white

oval in the shadows.

"Get that cat," he said briefly, and reached down to tug at something on the floor, pinned by Linda's legs.

Napoleon erupted into hysteria when Michael tried to hand him into the back; and Galen, cursing in four languages, heaved the cat's carrying case into the front seat. Between them they got the frantic animal into the case and his cries stopped.

Nursing a bleeding hand, Galen spoke again.

"If a patrol car spots us, we're in trouble. Find a parking lot or a side street."

Michael obeyed. His own hands were scratched and painful. It seemed like hours before he found a place to park—a driveway leading to a private house, whose dark shape was hidden by trees. The muffled sounds from the back were driving him frantic. Almost as bad was the deadly silence from Napoleon's box.

He switched off lights and engine and made sure the doors were locked before he turned. Galen had propped Linda up in a corner of the seat. He was checking her pulse and respiration.

"How is—"

"She's okay. Physically. I was careful with the dosage."

"You expected this."

"For God's sake—didn't you? It was as predictable as sunrise."

"I'm sorry. I'm not thinking very clearly."

"*You* aren't?" Galen's voice was bitter. "For the last hours everything I've done has been in direct opposition to every medical ethic I've ever held. If I'm not caught in the act, and drummed out of the profession, I'll probably shoot myself in sheer self-loathing. . . . That reminds me. Hand it over."

"What?"

Galen snapped his fingers impatiently.

"You know what. The 'business matter' you had to arrange before we left. Give it to me, Michael . . . Thanks. Do you have a permit for this?"

"I do. If it matters."

"Probably not. What's a permit more or less?"

"Give it back to me, Galen. You've risked enough already."

"No, thank you. If any shooting needs to be done, I'll do it."

There was a moment of silence. Then Michael said, "I brought it for the dog."

"And that's not a bad idea," Galen admitted. "If the animal has been trained as an attack dog, it may take a bullet to stop it. No, Michael, I will keep the gun. I commend your intentions, but I cannot trust your judgment. Not in this case."

"Why?" Michael asked suddenly. "Why are you doing this? Risking your reputation, perhaps your freedom—"

"Arrogance. I think so highly of my own judgment, I even follow my hunches."

"You came," Michael said, "because you knew I'd do this anyhow, with you or without you. And because I—hit below the belt with a reference to your personal tragedies. What makes my remark so inexcusable is that I didn't give a damn about that aspect of Randolph; I just wanted to get you mad enough so you'd help us."

"Forget it," Galen said brusquely. "I don't know why I'm here myself; at the moment I couldn't analyze an arithmetic problem. Get on, Michael. Randolph must be home by now; we're over an hour behind him."

"What are we going to do when we get there?"

"I'll be looking up my horoscope for today while you drive."

"What about Linda?"

"She should be waking up by the time we arrive."

"I meant as a source of information."

Galen stared at him; Michael saw the faint glimmer of his eyes in the starlight.

"You have got a few brain cells working after all. It wasn't scopalamine I gave her, you know. However, she is in an extremely suggestible state, if Randolph has been working on her. . . . Oh, hell. Drive, will you? I'll see what I can do."

After twenty interminable minutes, while Michael drove like an automaton, Galen leaned forward to report.

"No dice. I'll try again when she starts to come out of it."

The night had sunk into its deadest hours by the time they arrived. Passing the now familiar landmarks, Michael recognized the entrance to the unpaved lane that led to Andrea's house. Darkness and silence, now, along its length . . . He wondered where, and how, the old woman had been buried, and who had come to mourn her. Poor old witch—another victim of Gordon's insane urge for human souls, or the victim of her own—what had Galen called it?—thanatomania. The ability to induce death by suggestion alone. Mental aberration, or genuine curse, it didn't matter. Linda had it too.

The ornate gates that marked the entrance to the Randolph estate stood open. Michael brought the car to a stop just inside, switching off the lights. The house was invisible from this spot, and he doubted that anyone could have heard the car. Unless someone had been watching for it . . .

Linda was awake. For several minutes now he had heard the mumble of voices from the back seat. With the engine no longer running, he was able to make out the words.

"What the hell are you doing?" he demanded.

"Shut up," Galen said. "All right, Linda, you believe me, don't you? Say you do."

"I believe you."

Her voice was slurred and drowsy.

"Tell me again."

"I can't hurt you," Linda said obediently. "I can't hurt Michael. I don't want to hurt anyone. No one is going to hurt me. . . ."

"And you aren't afraid."

"I'm not afraid," said the soft doll's voice. The hairs on Michael's neck lifted.

"You," said Galen, turning on him with a cold savagery that made him flinch, "are going to keep quiet. You will not speak unless I tell you to, or move unless I tell you to. Understand?"

"Yes, master. . . . What did you do, hypnotize her?"

"No," Galen said, in a peculiar voice. "I didn't. Just keep your mouth shut and come along. We must get into the house. Linda, you have a key?"

"Yes."

"Where is it?"

"In my pocket."

"Get it out."

The way she moved made Michael feel cold. Her gestures were competent, without fumbling or hesitation, but they lacked all her normal grace. He followed the stiff, mechanical figure up the driveway, and he let Galen take her arm; he had the feeling that it would have had the solidity and coldness of wood under his fingers.

After some probing—she only answered direct questions, and those absolutely literally—Galen had got her to produce a back-door key, and led them to that entrance.

The servants' rooms were on the upper floors, so there was no danger from them; but the kitchen entrance was the length of the house from their ultimate destination. That couldn't be helped; Linda had no key to the other doors, and to climb the twisting stairs around the tower would give those within warning of their approach.

Michael could see the light in the tower window; it shone like a sleepless eye on the topmost floor, the window of Briggs's study. His sleeping quarters were on the floor below; the secretary was the only inhabitant of this part of the house, which was out of bounds to the servants. Briggs did his own cleaning. Linda herself had not been in the tower since the man moved in.

Galen elicited this information while they stood shivering in the shadows outside the house. He had already made it plain that he wanted no conversation after they entered. A slim sliver of moon had risen, and its rays were enough to show Michael the tension of Galen's body and the waxlike calm of Linda's face. Her face, and her soft, docile voice, gripped him with a pain as sharp as an actual wound. How much more could she stand? He had read some of the literature of witchcraft, and he had seen Gordon's livid face; he had an excellent idea of what they might discover in the tower room. The sacrifice, the shrouded altar, drugs and incense . . . A sight like that might break her mind completely.

"It's not too late to turn back," he said, turning to Galen.

"It is too late."

"We're guilty of breaking and entering. . . ."

"Don't be melodramatic. Mrs. Randolph is the mistress of the house. She has every legal right to go where she chooses, and to invite her friends to accompany her."

The shrubbery rustled as they crossed the wide lawn, silver-washed by moonlight. On such a pale expanse an object would be clearly visible; but the absence of any seen threat did not calm Michael's nerves. He was half hoping that the dog would come. It was better to know where it was than to imagine it, lurking unseen.

Somewhere, back on a tree near the gate, a petrified cat squatted on a branch. It had been Galen's suggestion that they free Napoleon; he had not needed to give his reasons. Gordon's malice might extend to any creature Michael was fond of, and the cat had a better chance, free, against danger. As Michael extracted the limp, unprotesting body from the carrying case, he recognized the symptoms. Only one thing roused Napoleon to his former fury, and that was when Michael inadvertently brought him near Linda—one of the few people for whom he had displayed a tolerance verging on affection. Michael had to lift him up into the lower branches of the tree, and as he turned away he saw Napoleon squatting there, motionless, looking like the Cheshire cat, even to the twisted snarl of his teeth. There was a certain element of the gruesome in *Alice,* come to think of it. . . .

They made their way through the darkened kitchen, with its vagrant gleams of chrome, and down the hallways. Wide double doors admitted them to a part of the house Michael had never seen. At the end of a long corridor, flanked by closed doors on either side, the tower steps led up. One window gave a scant light—a narrow, mullioned window half obscured by tendrils of ivy through which the moonlight slid in surreptitious trickles, casting more shadows than it relieved.

Linda stopped. It was so dark Michael could not see her face. Not until he put a steadying hand on her shoulder did he realize that she was shaking from head to foot.

His hand was struck down.

"Don't touch her," Galen hissed in his ear. "Linda. Go on. Up the stairs."

Michael didn't need to touch her to feel her resistance. It was a painful thing to witness, for the struggle was mute and confined. Galen's command broke her will instead of calming it. She shivered violently, and went on.

They were almost at the top of the stairs before Michael heard the sound. Its faintness made it worse, for it seemed to come from the inner chambers of his brain instead of an outside source.

Michael half recognized it, and wondered why his mind should reject the attempt at identification so violently. A picture formed in his mind, to match the sound: a high-vaulted place, great expanses of marbled flooring, adorned with columns . . . the walls a blend of colors and shapes . . . and the high, pure, sexless voices filling the echoing heights of the . . .

"God!" he said, involuntarily, and heard Galen's hand thrust heavily against the panels of the door.

The entire picture came at him in a single vast blasphemy; it was much later before he could isolate the details, and by that time he was already trying to forget them. Lights all around the room, burning with the clear softness of wax. Lights on the black-draped, tablelike object at the far side of the circular chamber. Black candles. Black hangings, draping walls and ceiling. Briggs stood before the altar; and as Michael's mind had denied the parody of the ritual music, it rejected the obscene caricature of priestly vestments that adorned Briggs's fat body and set off the pallor of the pale, epicene face. The reek of incense he has expected was present; some of it came from the golden censer in Briggs's hand. It was mixed with another smell. Michael averted his eyes from the thing that lay, mercifully motionless now, on the table.

Even Galen was struck dumb and motionless; and while the two men stood frozen, Linda moved past them, out into the room. Michael made a futile grab at her. Before he could move again, Briggs spoke.

"Gentlemen," he said, "pray don't be hasty."

He had a gun. Michael repeated the words incredulously to himself. Proud Satan's aide, allied with the powers of Hell—Briggs had a gun. A pretty little pearl-handled job, which he held as demurely as a woman might fondle a flower. It seemed innocuous after the things Michael had imagined.

It was enough to stop him, though, even without the restraint of Galen's outflung arm.

"Linda," he said helplessly, knowing he could not reach her.

She had advanced into the center of the room. The hood of the cloak had fallen back over her shoulders, and her hair streamed down around her face. It had the pure pallor of a saint's image as she stopped, facing the man who stood in the middle of an elaborately figured, colored carpet. Behind him the black draperies billowed, and Michael realized there must be a window there, or a door, leading to the outside stairs.

Unlike his coactor, Gordon was not in costume. He had discarded coat and tie; his shirt was open at the throat and his sleeves were rolled up. Hands and bare forearms were splashed with drying stains. His handsome, tanned face was calm. Michael was struck with a realization of the man's power—physical strength and beauty, combined with enormous will, and with another quality that Michael had not recognized until he saw the slender, submissive figure of Gordon's wife facing him with bowed head. A surge of hate rose up and nearly choked him. He would have moved then, forgetting the gun, if Galen's arm had not barred his way.

"You better come in and close the door," Gordon said calmly. "There. That's far enough."

He lifted both hands in a convoluted, ritual gesture.

He believes it, Michael thought. He really believes he can stop us, like that. . . . Glancing at Briggs, he felt sure that the secretary had no such faith. His narrowed eyes were as cynical as his gun.

He was leaning back against the table; the plump pink feet and calves were bare.

"Briggs," Galen said. "Don't be a fool. So far you're guilty of nothing the law can touch you for. You can't possibly expect to get away with murder. Put down the gun."

"Gun?" Gordon seemed to see the weapon for the first time. His face twisted with annoyance. "Come now, Briggs, you know we don't need that. I can hold them."

Galen ignored him.

"I'm a doctor, Briggs. This man is psychotic, and very dangerous. If you cooperate with us, I'll see that you get away scot-free."

For a second Michael thought it was going to work. The fat man's eyes narrowed until they almost disappeared. Briggs was perfectly sane, in the usual sense of the word; his faith in his dark master was almost all sham. Michael could see him weighing the advantages: Gordon's money and influence, the satisfaction of the various lusts of the flesh to which Gordon's patronage gave him access, against—what? Freedom and immunity? Freedom to return to the cold, hostile outer world and abandon his nice soft nest.

"Briggs," Gordon said impatiently. "Put away that silly toy and go on with the ceremony. Our audience has arrived. I want them to see everything."

"Yes, master," Briggs said quickly. "But—can you keep your control of them, and give your mind and heart to the offering?"

"I have bound them in the web of darkness. There they will stand until they rot, unless my will releases them."

Michael was dangerously close to jumping the main actor. Briggs's ridiculous gun had destroyed the aura of superstitious terror that had hitherto shielded Gordon; he saw the man for what he was, half mad, wholly evil. He felt light-headed with relief at the removal of that greatest fear, and was inclined to dismiss the menace of the weapon. A little thing like that, in Briggs's pudgy, womanish hand—hell, he probably couldn't hit a barn door at ten paces. Two things kept him in his place. One was his promise to Galen, silent at his side. The other was the sight of Gordon's big-muscled hands, so close to Linda. He could snap her neck with one twist of those brown hands. And he was capable of doing it, if his fantasy world was destroyed.

Michael heard a controlled, barely audible intake of breath from the man beside him. Galen's first attempt had failed. Briggs's weapon enforced, and reinforced, Gordon's madness, and Briggs was now committed. In seeming obedience he had stepped back behind the makeshift altar, his hands outstretched over it; but the wide sleeves of his robe, and the spacing of the candles, left those hands in shadow, and Michael had no doubt of what they still held.

Galen knew the danger as well as he did, or better. But his friend's next move took Michael completely by surprise.

"I am bound in the web of darkness," Galen said suddenly. "But not forever. I call upon the Masters of the Great College to come to me."

Hands lifted, he spat out a string of strange syllables, rich in gutturals. Michael wondered what half-forgotten adolescent lesson he was using; but he forgot that when he saw the impact of the words on the other listeners. Linda's body jerked violently, as if something had struck her.

Gordon went pale. He fell back a step, and after a moment his voice rose up, clashing with the other voice in an equally unintelligible chant.

Galen, rock-still in his place, waved his hands and switched to Latin.

His attention fixed on the combatants, Michael did not see what, if anything, Briggs was doing; later, he had to admit that Briggs might have thrown some new chemical into the smoldering bowls on the altar. But he felt the change in the air; it smelled like the acrid stench of burning flesh, and it made his head spin.

Backing away, step by dragging step, Gordon resembled a fighter reeling under the blows of invisible fists. His face was no longer pale; it was dark with fury, and swollen out of recognizable shape. The words still poured from his distorted mouth; and Michael imagined, insanely, that he could see them take shape in the air and strike back, against the shapes of Galen's incantation.

Galen had gone back to Hebrew, having exhausted his stock of appropriate Latin and Greek. Alone in the center of the room, Linda swayed back and forth, eyes glassy. Michael had forgotten his desire to go to her; he was only half aware of a pudgy, dark form, creeping at them from the direction of the altar.

Gordon was back now within a few feet of the shrouded window, his hands writhing, his face unrecognizable. Then Galen's breath failed; and in the split-second lull, Gordon's voice rose to a howl. The curtains behind him bellied out as if in a sudden gust of wind; the nearby candles flickered and went out. The black draperies wrapped Gordon around like enormous sable wings. Within their shelter he swayed, staggered, and dropped to his hands and knees.

Galen's voice faltered and went on; Gordon's answered. The droning beat of the two voices, the evil stench in the air—untouched by the chill blast of wind—the effect of shadows and the movement of the shaken draperies . . . All these, and other, equally explicable factors, might have explained what Michael saw. The shape of Gordon Randolph—on hands and knees, four-footed like a beast, dark head lowered—blurred and shifted. When the outlines coalesced, they were no longer those of a man.

He was not the only one to see it.

Linda screamed and covered her face with both hands. Michael moved, without plan, his only motive the need to get between Linda and the thing that paced slowly down the length of the floor toward her.

What Briggs saw, or thought he saw, they would never know for certain. Michael heard the gun go off, at close range; the entire magazine let loose in one undirected, hysterical burst. The bullets had no visible effect on the dog. It came on, with the unnatural slowness of nightmare, its padded feet making no sound on the carpet. Michael saw something fat and black in his way; he removed it with one sweep of his hand and then caught Linda in his arms, turning, holding her head against his chest so that she could not see.

Another shot and another . . . or was it the blood pounding in his ears? The room had gone dark—or was it because his eyes were closed? There was only one sense left to him, but it was enough—the feel of the warm, living body in his arms, and its response.

Galen had to shake him, hard, before he opened his eyes. The older man's pallor was so pronounced that he looked bleached—hair, face, eyes.

"It's all right," Galen said. He laughed, shortly and humorlessly. "What a description . . ."

"You got it?" Michael asked.

"Got it? What?"

"The dog . . . Don't, I don't want her to see." He stiffened, trying to shield Linda as Galen's impersonal hand caught her chin and forced her face up.

"She's all right, too," Galen said. "I'm sorry, Linda; you're entitled to a nice long hour of hysterics, but not just yet and certainly not here. The servants must have been wakened by that cannonade. We must leave before someone comes."

"I don't want her to see . . ." Michael repeated, with idiot persistence.

"She had better see it." Galen turned them both, and Michael saw the sprawled body of Gordon Randolph. The white shirt was no longer white. The face was as blank as a wax dummy's.

"Dead," Galen said. "Like any other mortal creature."

Michael felt Linda shiver, and lifted her into his arms as he heard the first tentative rap on the door.

"It's locked," Galen said softly. "But we'd better get going. Down the outside staircase."

When they got to the car, Michael was somehow not surprised to see a familiar shape sitting on the roof. Galen grabbed Napoleon, who came without protest. They were back on the main highway before anyone spoke.

"Put about ten miles behind us and then find a place to stop," Galen ordered. "I'm going to put Linda to sleep. And you aren't fit to drive far."

Michael nodded. He knew, better than Galen possibly could, how unfit he was. When Galen told him to pull over, he was glad to change places with the other man. Linda was already half asleep. She looked so fragile that Michael was almost afraid to touch her. She opened her eyes and gave him a wavering smile.

". . . Love you. . . ." she whispered, and drifted off.

"I wonder," Galen said, after a time.

"Wonder what? Whether she loves me?"

"Oh, that. No, I think you'll make out all right there. You're her hero, aren't you? Fighting the powers of darkness for her soul . . . What are lions compared to that?"

The familiar sardonic tones woke

Michael completely. He leaned forward, arms folded on the back of the seat.

"What did you see, Galen?"

"At the end?" Galen slowed for a blinking stop light and then picked up speed. "The original delusion of lycanthropy was Randolph's, as I suspected. He reverted completely."

"I saw him change," Michael said quietly. "I saw the dog. How do you define a hallucination, Galen? If three people out of four see one thing, and the fourth sees something else—which of them is hallucinating?"

Galen's silence was eloquent—of what, Michael wasn't sure.

"How do you know Briggs saw a dog?" he asked finally.

"What was he shooting at, his beloved employer?"

"He flipped," Galen said shortly.

"I admire your technical vocabulary. Where did he go, by the way?"

"Out and down. I didn't think the little swine could move that fast. . . . It's possible that he was aiming at you. When the gun was empty, he made a dash for it, and I can tell you I didn't try to stop him."

"And then you walked out on a murder. In view of your haste to leave, I gather you don't intend to inform the police that we were there."

"No."

"Why not, Galen?"

"There is no purpose to be served by such an act. Briggs killed his employer during one of their insane rites. If the police wish to question Mrs. Randolph, she has been with me. No problems."

"What a nice bloody liar you are," Michael said admiringly. "It all spells Merry Christmas, doesn't it? Satisfies you completely?"

"I've explained everything."

"Yes, you have. Galen—what did you see? Honestly?"

There was a pause. Finally Galen said,

"Drop it, Michael."

"But if you—"

"Drop it, I said." Eyes steady on the road, Galen drove on. "I saw what I wanted to see. Collective hallucination is a catchword, but it satisfies me. I don't want any glimpses of the dark on the other side."

"Only one problem," Michael said.

"What's that?"

"They'll do an autopsy, of course. On Randolph's body."

"Naturally."

"Which gun fired the shot that killed him, Galen?"

Galen didn't answer immediately. When he did, it was not in words. Michael took the object that was passed to him. To his overheated imagination, the barrel still felt warm.

"Are you sure?"

"Not of which shot killed him, no. I fired at Briggs. He was spraying bullets around like a machine gun, and I thought he was aiming at you. But people were moving pretty fast."

"They'll be able to tell, if it was a bullet from this gun."

"They won't find either gun. Briggs took his with him, and if he has a grain of sense he'll destroy it."

"And this one?"

"I've got to go back to Europe next week."

"Some convenient lake in France, or a ditch in Holland . . . Nice."

"What do you suggest I do, hand it over to the police?"

"Don't lose your temper. I'll never be

able to thank you for what you've done tonight. . . . Maybe I shouldn't tell you."

"Tell me what?"

"It was a bullet from this gun that killed Randolph."

"That wouldn't keep me awake nights," Galen said icily. "But how do you know?"

"There was only one bullet in it."

"So?"

Michael put his head down on his arms. His bad arm ached and he was sick with exhaustion. But tonight he would sleep without fear, or remorse.

"It was a silver bullet."